What Love Looks Like

Praise for What Love Looks Like

In *What Love Looks Like*, contemporary issues such as grief, foster care, and opioid addiction are interlaced with doses of humor to keep the tone light and sweet. Cozy up with a cup of coffee and a box of tissues, as Stacy Boatman welcomes you to this charming lake community. Full of colorful characters with a vast range of quirks, she'll keep you turning pages through this heartwarming read.
—**Julie Cantrell**, New York Times and USA TODAY bestselling author of *Perennials*

I can't remember the last time I flew through a book this fast—there were no lulls in which to grow distracted enough to set it down! With *What Love Looks Like*, Stacy Boatman has masterfully woven together three beautiful and unique stories of growth, healing, and forgiveness. Her characters come alive, and readers will certainly both cheer and cringe their ways through this moving story, rooting for them with every turn of the page and fully investing themselves in the characters' complex spiritual journeys. Open this book now, and remember Boatman's name in the future—I know I will.
—**Jessie Mattis**, award-winning author of *Power Up*

What Love Looks Like

A Lake Diamond Romance

STACY BOATMAN

ELK LAKE PUBLISHING INC

PUBLISHING THE POSITIVE
Plymouth, Massachusetts

Copyright Notice

What Love Looks Like

Cover and Interior Design: Derinda Babcock
Editor(s): Marcie Bridges, Deb Haggerty
Author Represented By: Dunamis Words Literary Agency

PUBLISHED BY: Elk Lake Publishing, Inc., 35 Dogwood Drive, Plymouth, MA 02360, 2021

Library Cataloging Data

Names: Boatman, Stacy (Stacy Boatman)
What Love Looks Like / Stacy Boatman
286 p. 23cm × 15cm (9in × 6 in.)
ISBN-13: 978-1-64949-358-3 (paperback) | 978-1-64949-359-0 (trade paperback) | 978-1-64949-360-6 (e-book)
Key Words: Aging out of the foster care system; Falling in love with a widower; Moving on from past mistakes; Forgiveness and friendship; Cozy read; Sweet, clean, inspirational, tear-jerking romance; Midwestern small town romance

Library of Congress Control Number: 2021944735 Fiction

Dedication

To Mom and Dad
Under your care, I've always known what love looks like.

Acknowledgments

The solitary exercise of writing is exceedingly more fulfilling when shared with fabulous people.

Thanks to my agent, Cheryl Ricker at Dunamis Words, for supporting me every step of the way, believing in this story, and encouraging me. Your friendship and prayers mean a lot to me.

I'm grateful for Deb Haggerty at Elk Lake Publishing, Inc. for bringing this book to publication. C.S. Lakin, your editing helped make the characters and setting come to life. Thank you, Cristel Phelps and Marcie Bridges, for polishing the manuscript. Cristel, your emails make me laugh. Marcie, I love how your editorial suggestions are laced with kindness.

Mom and Dad, dedicating this book to you is a no-brainer. You've believed in my writing ability and encouraged me to pursue publication since my first, fantastically green story. I love that you read my books out loud to each other—multiple times—and share my books with everyone you know.

For my beta readers, I'm incredibly grateful. A special shout-out to Kristen, Laura, Ingrid, and Jaime the Great. I value your honest input. Many more family and friends have supported my writing endeavors in countless ways. I love and appreciate each one of you. Thank you, Morgan Godfrey and Tom Shiah for discussing legal matters of the story. Any mistakes are entirely mine.

Sarah Moen Runck, thank you for supplying Nikki Dropik Meyers's recipe for Adelia's Seven Layer Bars, which will bring joy to many people!

And thanks to you, reader, for spending precious hours of your life entering into this story which I hope and pray both entertains and inspires you. I would love to connect with you. Facebook: Stacy Boatman; Instagram: stacyboatmanbooks. Visit my website at stacyboatman. com. Hearing from my readers is always a treat!

"Forgetting what is behind and straining toward what is ahead, I press on toward the goal to win the prize for which God has called me heavenward in Christ Jesus."

—Philippians 3:13-14

Chapter One

Mica Stark's truck tires squealed as he sped into the parking lot of Diamond Elementary and came to an abrupt stop by the front doors. "Let's go, Hannah. Unbuckle your seat belt and get out. School is starting."

"I need help, Daddy." Mica turned in his seat to see his daughter merrily swinging her legs as if she had all the time in the world. At five years old, she was new to time restraints. From the instant he'd woken her with a smattering of kisses, he'd struggled to keep her moving, precisely so this very thing would *not* happen.

Mica jumped out, and with Hannah's pink kitty backpack bounding over his shoulder, he darted to the other side to throw open her door. "Hurry, you're late." Hannah fumbled with the seat belt buckle.

He checked his watch: 8:35. "Push the red button. You're a big girl now. You can unbuckle yourself." The words came out harsher than intended. But after a morning of prodding her along, patience had worn thin.

Hannah had been eagerly anticipating kindergarten, crossing off days on a calendar. But so far, their morning would go down under the "bit-of-a-disaster" category. First, she'd insisted on wearing her new sweater Grandma Stark had sent in the mail as a back-to-school present. Minnesota weather was still hot and humid during the first week of

September. Let her show up to school in a sweater and risk getting heatstroke? Fat chance! He finally talked her into wearing a T-shirt and shorts by bribing her with pancakes, but then she'd asked to have her hair braided like Mommy used to do. How could he say *no* to that? YouTube came to the rescue with a how-to video, and he managed a very lopsided, chaotic braid that satisfied Hannah enough. After the hair fiasco, there was hardly time for pancakes. But he'd promised. Now she was late, and he was losing patience with her on what was supposed to be a special day.

"Daddy, I can't unbuckle." Tears pooled in her eyes.

He took a deep, calming breath. "I'm sorry, baby." It wasn't her fault they were late. He released her seat belt and wiped her teary cheeks with his thumbs before cradling her in his arms. "Daddy's just excited for your first day of school. I don't want you to miss anything."

Hannah sniffled, trembling with each breath.

Mica cupped his little girl's face as he peered into her shimmering baby-blue eyes. With all his heart he wished Josie could be here to see their daughter off on her first day of school. Clearing his throat, he choked back his own tears. "Are you ready to go in and show them how smart you are?"

Hannah nodded, lighting up. "I can count to one hundred."

Mica chuckled. "I know you can. I've heard you many times." Too many times.

"Daddy?"

"Yes?" He swept stray, blonde hair from her eyes, tucking a strand behind her ear.

"I wish Mommy was here."

"Me too, honey." These conversations never got easier. Josie had passed away fifteen months ago, and he still hadn't figured out how to make sense of her sudden death. Let alone explain it to his daughter. "Maybe she's watching over you right now."

"In heaven?" Hannah leaned out of the truck, angling her face to the clear blue sky. A faint smile, tinged with sadness, lit her face. She waved to her mommy. His daughter's innocence broke his heart. But she proved resilient, always making the best of the situation. Mica smirked. He could learn from her.

She wrapped her arms around Mica's neck, and he lifted her from the truck. He walked Hannah into her classroom, prepared to get a rap on his hand with a ruler for tardiness. To his surprise and relief, a few other parents lingered with their kindergartners, giving their kiddos repeated hugs and kisses. Reminding them to wash their hands before lunch. Telling them to share with friends. There was hope Mica's tardiness might go unnoticed.

"I see my name!" Hannah dragged Mica by the hand to a locker marked with her name in perfect teacher-style printing. She hung up her backpack and skipped off to explore the classroom.

Mica stood back, watching his daughter acclimate. She appeared to be on cloud nine—checking out the art easel, the reading nook, and the pet hamster, seemingly unfazed by the hectic morning.

"Excuse me." A woman's voice snatched him from his thoughts.

He turned to see a petite brunette who didn't look a day over twenty. "Can I help you?" he asked.

The young woman laughed lightly. "I'm Simone Clare. I'll be teaching this class." She extended her hand, and he shook it.

"You're Miss Simone?" Apparently, he'd underestimated her age. "So, you're in charge of this crew?"

"I am." She looked like a little Southern belle, but she spoke with authority and shook his hand with the grip of a politician's. He didn't doubt she'd be able to handle this class of rambunctious five-year-olds. Overall, she seemed nice—and real pretty too—with sparkling brown eyes and a smattering of freckles across her nose. Hannah would like her. "And which of my charges belongs to you?"

Mica pointed to his pride and joy by the hamster cage. Hannah was cradling a furry critter in the crook of her arm. "That's my Hannah. She can already count to one hundred."

The teacher laughed at him a second time. "Is that so?"

Heat warmed Mica's cheeks. Maybe all kindergartners could count to one hundred. "I'm just a little proud of her."

"Of course you are. She's adorable."

He ran a hand through his hair—his un-showered hair. What a disheveled mess. Of course, the basketball shorts, old T-shirt, and bare feet in running shoes didn't help his look either. Taking a step back, he lengthened the space between them—just in case yesterday's deodorant wasn't holding up. "I'll be going now. It was nice meeting you, Miss Simone."

"Nice to meet you too, Mr. Stark." She cleared her throat. "Be sure to have Hannah here by eight thirty tomorrow. I'm flexible on the first day of school. I realize the parking lot can be crazy, but things should be settled down by tomorrow."

Had he just been scolded? Her statement felt condescending. This was only kindergarten, after all, not a military camp. "Sure thing." Feeling a tug on his shirt, Mica looked down to see Hannah.

"Bye, Daddy." She reached for a hug.

Mica knelt and hugged his little girl. She deserved the best, and he feared his parenting skills lately had been subpar. "Have a fun day." He kissed her rosy cheek.

Maybe the best idea would be to leave before Miss Simone could discover a second reason to patronize him. She had plenty of fodder to choose from. He waved goodbye to the teacher.

Miss Simone smiled politely and turned her attention to the gaggle of children. She did a weird clapping rhythm and caught the attention of the kids. "Students, sit on the circle rug."

Outside the classroom, Mica leaned against the cool, tiled wall, collecting his thoughts. Josie had died last summer when a horrific tornado leveled their house. He still missed her as if it had happened yesterday. He tried to forge ahead but struggled to balance letting her go with keeping her memory alive. The absence of Josie cut especially deep on milestone days like today. Josie would've made the morning run flawlessly. Hannah's outfit would've been planned out the night before, and the family of three would've enjoyed breakfast together instead of rushing through it to fulfill a last-minute bribe. *Lord, help me do better for Hannah.*

Mica pulled himself together and headed home to change into his work clothes. His building company, Stark Homes, could function smoothly in his absence only because he had excellent foremen on each work site. His hardworking crew had picked up his slack since the rug had been pulled out from under him. He'd paid them generously and thanked them profusely, so the guys didn't seem to mind the extra work. But it was time to step up and be the boss he was. Showing up hours after everyone else because he couldn't drag his weary self out of bed didn't inspire his crew to stay on schedule.

When he opened the door to the two-bedroom apartment, he was greeted by Hannah's cat rubbing her face on his shin. "Hi, Petunia." He scratched the gray-and-white tabby behind the ear. "I suppose *you* need breakfast."

The cat meowed, scuttling over to her dish and looking up at him with expectant green eyes. As he poured a scoop of kibble, his phone rang. "Stark Homes. Mica speaking."

"Hey, Mica. How's it going?"

His friend, Adam Calhoun, seemed to know when he was having a rough time. "I'm all right. Recovering from

Labor Day weekend." The holiday had almost been enough fun to snap him out of his funk.

"We had a good time, didn't we? I'm glad you and Hannah decided to join us at the cabin. The girls were sure excited to have Hannah to play with."

Mica smiled. "I'm glad Gigi and Sadie talked Hannah into tubing behind the boat."

"Next year, we'll get her up on water skis."

"I'm sure she'll love it."

"I bet she's a natural, just like her mom and dad." Mica's business partner's chronic cheerfulness—although annoying at times—had brought Mica through the roughest days since Josie died. "The highlight of the weekend had to be that wakeboard stunt you pulled."

"You mean when I spun a three-sixty? That little trick?"

"That's the one. That was incredible, especially at your age."

"Hey, watch it, buddy—you're only a few months behind. Soon you'll be meeting the big three-O head on."

"Yeah, yeah. And when that happens, I'm expecting you'll throw me a big party." He laughed. "Listen, about the lakeside house …"

Josie's and his dream home. Mica collapsed into a kitchen chair and planted his elbows on the table, wishing he could avoid this conversation.

"As I'm sure you're aware, the work permit expires in November. We need to finish up the project this fall."

Not a chance. Mica couldn't imagine stepping foot on the site yet, finishing Josie's customized kitchen cabinets, installing her closet systems, painting the walls of the bedroom she would never share with him. "Extend the permit. I need more time."

Adam paused. "Sorry. I couldn't get an extension. The homeowners' association is pressuring us to finish the project or sell. We can't just let it sit any longer."

Mica had been expecting this phone call. Even so, he felt as though he'd been sucker-punched. "I'll think about it and get back to you."

"They want an answer by the beginning of next week. Monday afternoon at the latest."

"That soon?" Mica sighed. Maybe this was the kick in the pants he needed to get his life back in order. The apartment had been a temporary living arrangement until the house was finished, and the one-year lease was almost up. It didn't make sense to continue paying rent when he could be putting that money toward a mortgage. He knew he'd been stalling, unwilling to face a lifetime without his soul mate. He worked the muscles in his jaw. "I'll let you know as soon as I've made my decision."

"Jeremiah 29:11."

Adam often reminded Mica of the Bible verse, reassuring him God had a plan for his life. Plans to give him hope and a future.

"Thanks, man. I'll talk to you soon." Mica hung up and paced to the balcony window and back to the kitchen table, at least three times, finally landing out on the balcony. *Lord, how can your plans not involve Josie? Why did you take her from us?* Such a useless question. No matter the answer, she was gone. He leaned against the building, facing the courtyard. The space was devoid of people, leaving him and God alone out there. "What am I supposed to do now?" The sound of his voice surprised even himself. He hadn't meant to speak out loud. But it felt good. He set his hands on his hips. "Hannah loves that house. It's all she and Josie talked about." He went to the railing and looked up toward heaven as Hannah had done earlier. "But how can I live in that house without Josie?" The morning sun beat down on his face; sweat trickled down his back. "You could've saved her, God. And you didn't." He shook his fists in frustration.

He could just imagine Josie's reaction to him yelling at God. She'd remind him of God's great love by quoting John

3:16—her favorite verse and the first one she'd taught Hannah. *Josie, I just don't understand why He took you from me.*

Inside the apartment, the air conditioning hit him like a refreshing spray of cold water. He sat on the edge of the couch, propping his elbows on his knees. "I don't get it, God. But I'm putting my faith in you. So, what are these big plans you have for me? Plans to prosper me, to give me hope and a future? What are your plans for Hannah? I need to know, Lord." He sat quietly for a moment, wishing God would answer audibly and explain how He'd work everything out according to a divine plan.

Then he changed his clothes and went to work.

Chapter Two

Simone circled around Lake Diamond and pulled her Volkswagen Beetle into a parallel parking spot on Lakeview Drive. The first day of teaching kindergarten had always been a whirlwind, and this year was no exception. A refreshing treat would help her unwind. Perhaps an iced mango black tea. She stepped into Lakeview Brew, welcomed by soft instrumental jazz music humming over the speakers and delicious aromas of coffee and pastries. Her friend, Jade, was behind the counter taking orders. As soon as she spotted Simone, she waved an employee over to take her place at the register.

"Hey, girl," Jade said, pulling Simone into an enthusiastic embrace. Jade Powers was the sweetest person Simone had ever met. Only Jade would abandon a line of customers to greet a friend with a hug. Her friendliness surely played a part in her business's success. "You look nice. Cute dress."

"Thanks. It's a splurge. I felt like dressing up a bit today. I've always loved the first day of school." Considering the building's lack of air conditioning, the flowy cotton dress, paired with comfy sandals, was also a practical choice of attire. She'd curled her dark brown cropped hair just enough to give it volume. Wavy tendrils fell slightly over the left side of her face, and she tucked a strand behind her right ear. A hint of pink colored her cheeks and lips. Her dark eyelashes and brows didn't require extra maintenance—at least, that's what her friends told her. For a low-maintenance girl like Simone, she'd outdone herself today.

"I always dreaded the first day of school. I guess that's why you went into teaching, and I did not." Having been adopted from Korea as a baby, Jade's hair was almost black. Today, she wore a frazzled-looking ponytail with wisps gone astray, a T-shirt sporting the Lakeview Brew logo, jeans, Nikes, and an apron tied around her waist. "I know what you're thinking. Don't even consider returning the compliment." Jade brushed rogue hairs out of her eyes. "I've been running my tail off all day. Business is bustling. I guess everyone needs a little pick-me-up after Labor Day weekend. Is MJ coming?"

Right on cue, the door swung open, and MJ Oliver walked in. Her wheat-colored hair stopped short just above her shoulders, framing her heart-shaped face. A handbag, which doubled as a diaper bag, dangled from her elbow. Simone and Jade watched her remove her sunglasses and place them neatly in their case. MJ's attention to detail made her an excellent music teacher at Diamond Elementary. The students learned to read music by the third grade. The fact she enjoyed teaching almost as much as she loved mothering her four little girls, resulted in music being a favorite class of many students.

There was an exchange of hugs, but the conversation was cut short by the burgeoning line of customers as the after-school crowd shuffled in, comprising mostly of backpack-clad teens.

"I better get back to work," Jade said, backing away. "Drinks are on the house for teachers today." She rushed to assist the baristas.

As Simone and MJ joined the queue to place their orders, MJ's phone rang. "Sorry, it's Branson. He's home with the girls today. I better take this."

Simone nodded. Biding time as the line inched forward, she scrolled through her Facebook feed. A notification signaled a friend request. A weight settled on her chest as she read the name. *Gale Wells.* Her foster sister.

Her carefree joy was sucked away in a tide of fear. Although Gale might be interested merely in catching up over social media, more likely she had ulterior motives. She always did. Simone closed the app and dropped the phone into her bag, unwilling to allow a ghost from her past to hijack this lovely day.

She ordered her drink to go and exchanged goodbyes with her friends, the lure of home beckoning her. Home—in the older part of town, while the coffee shop was in the newer end of town, along with a few other independent businesses. She loved how folks came here to start a new business—a new life—and most proved successful. Diamond was a perfect merger of the old with the new. The established part of town had roots supporting the newly developed part—each strengthening the other. Just the sort of town she needed.

She turned on her car radio and sang along as she headed into town. Veering onto Main Street, she passed a few of her favorite haunts: Adelia's Bakery, Diamond Diner, and Vintage Treasures. In summertime, vacationers strolled through the quaint downtown during their stay at Lake Diamond Campground or Willows B & B. Now, Labor Day had come and gone, the school year was resuming, and tourists were sparse. She enjoyed the serenity of the quaint lake town after growing up in urban Saint Paul.

Mature maple and oak trees adorned the lawns of her neighborhood, forming a canopy of leaves over the residential roads. She pulled her car into the driveway of her cozy rental home. The faded yellow rambler hadn't been anything to brag about when she'd moved in, but she'd fixed it up nicely over the past five years. The porch housed a matching wicker sofa and chair. She'd found the furniture at a yard sale and had freshened up the pieces with a coat of white paint. They'd come with seat cushions she'd redone in a shabby chic floral pattern. Once weathered and broken-down, the house was now on the mend—almost pretty.

Pulling into the detached garage, she remembered the day her landlord had handed her the key. The cool jagged metal had felt like precious gold in her hand. The key, along with her new job in Diamond, had given her a new lease on life. A fresh identity. She was no longer a foster care child, tossed around from house to house like a scrap of litter blowing in the wind. She'd become a woman with a respectable career and skills to contribute to society. And for the first time in her life, she had the home of her choosing, in the town of her choosing.

She flung her workbag over her shoulder, locked the garage, and crossed the driveway to the side door of the house. The afternoon sun drenched her dark hair in warmth, and the chrysanthemums she'd planted seemed to lift their colorful faces to her in greeting. Home sweet home.

Stepping under the maple tree in her front yard, she took a selfie in the dappled sunlight. She sent the pic to her Snapchat group—Jade and MJ.

A tapping sound at the neighboring house drew her attention. The sweet face of ninety-year-old Pearl Jones was peering out her kitchen window. She wore a lavender nightcap edged in lace, and a smile shone through her teddy-bear brown eyes. She cranked the window open. "I was praying for you today."

"Thanks, Pearl." Simone wasn't a believer in prayer, or in God, but she respected her friend's faith and the fact Pearl cared enough for her to send prayers up on her behalf. "I'll tell you all about it."

"Come on over." Pearl touched her head. "Oh, my." She lifted the cap off. "I just had myself a nice afternoon nap."

Simone giggled. She hadn't known nightcaps still existed. "I just need a minute to freshen up." Simone loved visiting with the older woman as much as she knew Pearl needed the company.

"Take your time. I'll wait for you on my front porch. It's a good time of day for people-watching."

People-watching in Diamond? Simone looked over her shoulder toward the quiet residential street. A gang of fourth-grade boys she recognized from school sped by on bikes, juggling Nerf guns on their laps. That was as exciting as it got in this town. Just the way she liked things. "I'll be out soon."

Sliding the key into the lock, Simone noticed a folded paper stuffed into the door. She was glad she'd missed the solicitor—most likely a door-to-door salesman. She crumpled the paper and threw it in the trash can under her kitchen sink.

In her bedroom, she slipped out of her work clothes and donned shorts and a T-shirt. She studied her reflection in the full-length mirror. Who would've thought she, a troubled foster-care kid, would become a professional? She had beaten the odds when she earned a college degree. Of course, the financial help her foster father provided made her success possible. But some of her success—okay, a lot of her success—was a result of hard work and determination. To this day, after five years of teaching kindergarten, she still struggled to commit that truth to heart.

She washed her face, then went to the kitchen and fixed Pearl a tall glass of lemonade and grabbed her tea she'd brought back from Lakeview Brew. A plate of sugar cookies caught her eye—she snatched the plate as well, then headed over.

"Looks like you're ready to relax," Pearl said, eyeing the treats. "Long day?" She accepted the glass of lemonade, taking a sip and smacking her lips in satisfaction. "I'm dying to hear every detail. Got any rascals in your class this year? Or are they all angels?"

Simone took a seat on the rocker separated from Pearl's by a circular metal table. She thought of sweet little Hannah Stark, so eager to learn. "It's a good class. I mean, they were all a little squirrely, but I expected such antics on the first day." Simone sipped her tea, holding the cold, sweet beverage on her tongue before swallowing. "Tommy kept swishing Kenzie's ponytail during calendar time. That was annoying. And Jillian whispered in her friend's ear during free time, and Lucy thought Jillian was talking about her and started crying. Oh, and—what's his name—Braden ate his napkin at snack time, so then all the boys tried it."

"Sounds like a bunch of rascals to me." Pearl shook her head. "Sure takes a lot of patience. I admire you teachers."

Simone smiled. "I have my moments, but I love my job overall."

"I'm glad. You deserve it." Pearl knew the obstacles Simone had overcome to get where she was. As a Black woman, Pearl also had faced an unfair share of obstacles in her life. Pearl had talked about a high school teacher who never called on her once throughout her entire high school career, murmured racial slurs as she walked by, and graded her schoolwork harshly. Simone's heart broke to think anyone would treat such a kind person so poorly. Pearl was resilient. She graduated high school with honors. "You're spoiling me with all this sugar." She took a bite. "Did you get the note from that young lady?"

"Note?"

"I was pulling weeds in my rose garden when a pretty girl came asking about you. What was her name?" Pearl squeezed her eyes shut, concentrating. "Grace? Gabby? Gwen?"

Simone held her breath, the muscles in her chest tightening. *Not Gale. Please don't say Gale.* "Was it Gale?"

"Yes. Gale. Is she a friend of yours?"

Simone swallowed, acid rising to the back of her throat. She shook her head, setting her cup on the table. "I can't believe she tracked me down ... after all these years."

"Honey, are you all right? You look like you've just seen a ghost." Pearl stretched her thin arm across the table, placing her warm, gentle hand on Simone's.

"You know I grew up in foster homes." Her voice was shaking.

Pearl nodded, squeezing Simone's fingers, urging her to continue.

"Gale lived at the last house I stayed at. She was their biological child. Same age as me." Simone chewed at the fingernails of her free hand, a habit she'd kicked since moving next door to Pearl. "That girl got herself into a whole lotta trouble. And, somehow, I always got the rap for it. With her looks and as a mastermind at manipulation, she could get away with murder if she tried."

Pearl gasped. "That's a bold statement. She's that nasty?"

"Who knows what she's capable of. She's psycho. Once, she threatened to accuse me of vandalizing her car if I didn't give her gas money to go on a spring break road trip with her snobby friends. She ran out to her car, knife in hand, ready to slash her own tires and rip up the leather interior. I caved and gave her money I'd saved from babysitting jobs." Pearl listened intently, shaking her head in dismay—hopefully at Gale's actions and not Simone's weakness. "Their house was one of the better ones. I didn't bother trying to rat her out. No one would've believed me. I wasn't willing to risk being dragged away by my caseworker. I haven't seen Gale since the day I turned eighteen and took off on my own."

"Why would she come looking for you now?"

Simone shrugged. "My fear is she's in some kind of trouble and wants me to bail her out again. But I don't want anything to do with her drama. She'd refer to me as her sister and act all buddy-buddy when she wanted something from me. The rest of the time, she'd treat me like trash. She used me ... time and time again."

A familiar feeling of helplessness she'd endured throughout her childhood resurfaced and crawled under her skin. "And when she got caught for her shenanigans, she blamed it all on me. Like the time she called me from the mall and asked me to bring her mom's Kate Spade handbag to her. She said her mom let her borrow it for a job interview, but she'd forgotten it at home. It was a lie. Gale pawned it. Then told her mom I'd stolen it. The maid saw me leave the house with it on my arm. I never stood a chance." Simone stuffed her hands under her legs so she wouldn't bite her nails to the quick. "People always believed her. She was a member of the beautiful, rich Wells family rescuing me from life on the streets. The foster kid was the good-for-nothing bad influence."

"Honey, I'm sorry."

"You've got nothing to feel sorry for, Pearl."

"But I do. I told Gale you work at Diamond Elementary. I shouldn't go telling people your business."

"I'm sure she already figured that out. It worries me more she drove out to Diamond to harass me in person." Maybe accepting the Facebook "friend request" would've prevented Gale from physically stalking her. Too late now. Simone moaned. "I have worked too hard building a life for myself to have Gale come through and make a mess of it."

If she were honest, she wasn't perfectly innocent. She'd done her fair share of mischief alongside Gale. Rebellious high school stuff, like partying. There was the time they TP'd the head cheerleader's house. And the night they broke into the high school and swam in the pool, along with about twenty of their closest friends. If only those were the worst things she'd done.

She shivered. Images of the night she wanted so desperately to forget flashed through her mind like scenes from a horror movie. Gale was the only person to bear witness. Neither girl ever spoke of that Friday night, the spring of their junior year. A mutual understanding formed between them. Gale wouldn't tell—if Simone honored her every request.

After high school graduation, Simone purposely distanced herself from Gale, weary of enslavement to her and the secret they shared. She needed to stay out of trouble, succeed in college, and build a new life for herself. Unlike Gale, she didn't have a rich family to fall back on.

"What's she been up to all these years?" Pearl asked.

"Last I heard, Gale dropped out of college, drank too much, and couldn't hold down a job. She is leading the kind of life I'm trying desperately to avoid." Simone feared her genetic makeup leaned to the same hapless lifestyle. She inhaled deeply, letting the fresh air fill her lungs. Then she exhaled, commanding herself to relax. "I'm a grown woman. She can't intimidate me anymore, and I'm secure enough to resist peer pressure."

If only she believed the words she had just spoken.

Chapter Three

Simone drained the last of her lemon tea just as the first bell rang, signaling the start of the school day. The second day of school had always been more enjoyable than the first. With first-day jitters behind them, the kids were more focused. They knew the rules yet were too obedient to break them.

As the children trickled into the classroom, Simone stood in the doorway to greet them. Parents had been prompted to say their goodbyes at the front door of the building today. Some of the kids, still unaccustomed to leaving Mom and Dad, had a sheen of tears in their eyes. But not Hannah Stark. She came bouncing down the hall checking out all the colorful paper decorations pinned on bulletin boards. Simone bent down to her student's eye level. "Good morning, Miss Stark."

Hannah giggled, covering her pearly white smile with cupped hands. "I'm not a grown-up." Hannah wrapped her arms around Simone's neck. "Nobody called me Miss Stark before."

Simone returned the hug, and then looked into her young student's blue eyes. "You don't have to be a grown-up, just someone important."

"Am I important?" Hannah's face twisted in confusion.

Simone laughed lightly. "Of course you are. Now, go hang up your bag and put your homework paper in the file."

Hannah looked down at her feet, almost instantly in tears. "What's wrong, Hannah?"

Her bottom lip turned out, and she sniffed. "My dad didn't help me. He said we'd do my homework after dinner, but then he fell asleep, and when I woke him up, he said it was too late, and we'd do it another time."

Simone remembered Hannah's dad clear as day. He'd dropped his daughter off late the first day of school, looking like he'd just rolled out of bed. He'd probably been up late partying the night before. She knew his type. Simone's stomach twisted. She knew why Hannah was an independent girl. She needed to be because Dad wouldn't give her the time of day.

The assignment was meant to be a fun activity to share with her family. It wouldn't have taken much time or effort to complete it. All Hannah had to do was write her name on the paper and draw a picture of her family. She had noticed Mr. Stark had a gold band on his ring finger. A little more parental responsibility, and this wouldn't have happened. Simone felt for Hannah. "You can take it home again and work on it tonight. I bet some of the other families will need more time too."

Hannah rubbed her eyes with balled fists and nodded. She entered the classroom, perking up as soon as she laid eyes on the class pet. Simone watched her greet the little critter with a cheerful "good morning" as if her woes had already been forgotten.

"There's always one in the bunch." The nearing-retirement-status teacher, Thelma Wilson, was in the common area, stacking boxes of tissues in a cupboard. "The deadbeat dad." She shook her head in dismay, apple-shaped dangly earrings waggling. "Sometimes, I think the parents are more work than the kids. I've got a meddling mom to deal with. I'd like to tell her to stay home and bake cookies. Let me do the teaching instead of trying to tell me how to run my classroom."

Simone smiled politely, although she would've preferred to tell Mrs. Wilson to mind her own business and learn some manners herself. Thankfully, the older woman related better to her students than to adults. Her class seemed to view her as a grandmother type.

Simone closed the classroom door as soon as the last student entered. As she was about to clap for attention, her cell phone chimed. Simone lifted the phone from her desk and read the text. Goose bumps tickled the back of her neck as she read the message.

GALE: Hey! It's your long-lost sis. Can't wait to see you!

How did she get my number? She stuffed the phone deep into her purse, wishing she could bury the memories as easily. She had no time for Gale and her drama. The past needed to stay in the past!

The day dragged on with Gale's text weighing heavily on her mind. Even more daunting than the text was the note Gale had tucked into Simone's door. After spending time with Pearl the evening before, she'd dug the note out from the garbage.

Hi, Simone,
I've missed you. I'll stop by another time.
Love, Gale

Simone's students' energy trumped her own, leaving her with a room of kiddos practically bouncing off the walls. Gale was already ruining a perfectly good day with just a simple text. Simone remained on pins and needles throughout the day, half-expecting Gale to show up in her classroom unannounced. At three o'clock, she dismissed the backpack-clad kids and watched them skip down the hallway.

Hannah, her favorite of the bunch, navigated her way through the throngs of older children, looking so small yet so confident. The sparkly kitty on her backpack peered out from under a veil of wavy blonde hair cascading down

Hannah's back. The girl looked as though she belonged in a Hallmark commercial.

Hopefully, Hannah's dad saw the potential in his precocious daughter. And hopefully, he'd make time to work on their family portrait tonight. Simone looked over at Hannah's cubby and saw the blank portrait paper sitting there. She grabbed the paper and raced out the classroom door. "Hannah," she called out, trying her best not to trample the children.

She caught up to Hannah just before she left the building. "Miss Stark, you forgot something."

Hannah's eyes lit up when she saw her teacher. "Hi, Miss Simone. You were running in the hallway."

"Oops. I forgot about the no-running rule." She looked over her shoulder dramatically. "Did Principal Finch see?"

Hannah shielded her eyes from the sun pouring in through the glass doors, searching for the principal, worry creasing her brow. Students were terrified of Principal Norma Finch. Frown lines were etched on the sides of the woman's mouth and between her eyes, creating the appearance of a permanent scowl. Lucky for the kids, she mostly stayed tucked away in her office.

"Looks like I'm safe." Simone bit her lip, stifling a giggle. "I brought your portrait paper. I wrote a note for your dad too." A little note stressing the importance of helping Hannah with her schoolwork and making sure she was prepared for school each morning. Punctuated with a smiley face, so there would be no hard feelings.

Hannah threw off her backpack and unzipped it. "Thanks. Me and Daddy can do it tonight."

"And your mommy?" Simone hoped she hadn't overstepped her boundaries. Maybe her mom wasn't in the picture. Perhaps her parents were in the middle of a messy divorce or something. In her defense, as Hannah's teacher, she did have a right to know the home situation.

A truck roared to a stop in front of the building. "Daddy's here!" Hannah ran off before answering Simone's question.

Anger burned inside Mica's gut. How dare Hannah's teacher imply he wasn't a good father. She hadn't written those words exactly, but she may as well have just come out and said it. He read the note again.

Mr. Stark,

Please work on Hannah's assignment with her tonight. As her father, you play an important role in her education. Each morning, she needs to be at school, prepared to learn at precisely 8:30.

Sincerely, Miss Simone

The smiley face at the end was the icing on the cake. Passive-aggressiveness had to be the most irritating quality in a person. He tossed the note on the front passenger seat and spun around to see Hannah. She had buckled her seat belt and was gazing out the window, watching kids file out of the school. "Wait here, honey. I need to have a quick chat with your teacher."

He rolled down her window and instructed her to stay in the truck. Then he ran into the school and found Miss Simone in the kindergarten pod talking to another teacher. He was ready to tell her off—until he looked straight into her face. She had an innocent look to her. Almost like a child. She reminded him of Snow White, the story he'd read countless times to his own little princess.

"Can I help you, Mr. Stark?" Her voice authoritative, not childlike.

"Yes." He cleared his throat. "I came to talk to you about the note you wrote me."

"Of course. Hannah was in tears over not having her family portrait finished, so I just wanted to make sure you helped her with it tonight."

Hannah had cried about it? He put a hand over his chest, soothing an almost physical ache. Maybe he deserved a tongue-lashing from Hannah's teacher.

The silver-haired teacher patted Miss Simone on the shoulder—a sort of "good luck" gesture—and cracked a sympathetic smile.

Mica's anger returned. "I don't appreciate that kind of behavior. Every time I step into this building, I'm treated like *I'm* a kindergartner. I am a father, doing my best. Is it too much to ask for a little respect?"

The pitter-patter of little feet echoed from down the hallway. "Daddy!"

Mica turned to see Hannah running toward him, her eyes wide and fearful.

"Daddy, a guy is stealing our truck."

"What? Someone is stealing my truck?" Mica picked his daughter up, snuggling her into the safety of his arms, and raced to the nearest exit, wondering how on earth someone could steal a truck from a school parking lot. Had he left the keys in the ignition? Hannah had been in there. Terror punched his gut. She could've been whisked away along with the truck. "Are you okay, honey?"

Hannah nodded. Her face was stuffed into the crook of Mica's neck as he ran out the door.

"Did the guy hurt you? Tell me what happened." Then he saw for himself. His truck was hooked to a tow truck. "You've got to be kidding me." Mica set Hannah down. Anger streaked through him, making comforting her difficult. He stood helplessly watching as his vehicle was hauled away by Toby's Towing.

"The man told me to get out because he had to tow." Hannah was bouncing on her toes in a jittery dance.

"I can guess what happened," Miss Simone said, stepping up beside him. "You were parked in the bus lane. It's a tow-away zone. Principal Finch has a zero-tolerance policy for parking in the bus lane."

Then he noticed the yellow diagonal lines painted across the pavement and the signs posted on either end of the area. He cringed. *Oops. My bad.* If the teacher hadn't written that irritating note, he probably would've noticed. "But I was only parked there for a couple of minutes."

Miss Simone placed a hand on Mica's shoulder. "Mr. Stark, for future reference, leaving your child unattended in your vehicle is dangerous. School staff is under obligation to notify the police if we witness this happen."

He shrugged her hand off his shoulder. "So now you're going to have me arrested?"

"Of course not." A corner of her mouth inched into a half smile. "I just wanted you to be aware of the school policy."

Having heard enough from the teacher, he turned to Hannah. "Sorry, honey. Daddy made a mistake."

"How will we get home?" Hannah's sweet little face scrunched with worry.

"I'll drive you to Toby's," Miss Simone said. "Wait here. I'll grab my keys. I have a booster seat in my classroom Hannah can use."

Great. Miss Simone to the rescue. Calling an Uber wasn't an option since Uber drivers were scarce in Diamond and likely wouldn't have a booster seat for Hannah anyway.

Mica folded his long legs into Miss Simone's Volkswagen Beetle. Hannah buckled herself into the booster seat a family had donated to the kindergarten class. The car had retained its new car smell, although the model hadn't been in production for years. As Miss Simone opened the door and scooted in, a hint of her perfume wafted by him—a flowery scent. Or was it her shampoo? He resisted the urge to close his eyes and breathe in the aroma.

Mica's phone rang, interrupting his wandering thoughts. Caller ID flashed Adam's name on the screen.

"Go ahead and take the call," Miss Simone said, steering the car out of the parking lot. "Judging by the look on your face, it must be important. I'll try not to eavesdrop." She winked.

"Thanks. It's business-related. I'll make it quick." He accepted the call. "Hey, Adam. What's up?"

"Mica, you need to come to the lakeside house right away."

"What's going on? I'm kinda tied up for a few minutes."

"The homeowners' association is threatening to sell the house. They're out here now taking pictures. You need to talk to them."

"You said we had until Monday afternoon." This was the last thing he needed to deal with right now.

"Regardless, they're here."

"I'll get there as soon as I can. Stall them." He ended the call.

"Daddy, who called you?"

Mica tried to keep his temper under control. "Adam. He wants us to meet him at the lakeside house."

"Mommy's house?"

A pain stabbed his heart every time Hannah spoke of her mommy. "That's right." He hoped Miss Simone wouldn't ask questions because he didn't feel like explaining to her.

"Daddy is building a house for Mommy."

Thanks, Hannah. Just tell the whole story while you're at it. Well, maybe if she told the story, then he wouldn't have to.

"That's nice of your dad." Simone looked pleasantly surprised by this information, looking at him as if seeing him for the first time.

Mica breathed a sigh of relief grateful she didn't probe.

"Do you need me to take you there? It sounds urgent. I don't mind."

Mica hated drawing Miss Simone into his personal business. Even more, he hated relying on her to bail him out again. But he did need this favor. "Actually, I'd really appreciate it if you'd drop us off at the work site. It's out on Lake Diamond. My buddy can give us a ride home from there."

"No problem."

Gravel crackled under the tires as Simone pulled into the driveway of a sprawling two-story craftsman-style house with a three-stall garage. Various shades of gray and white colored the exterior. A generous porch extended from the front of the house and wrapped around to the back. "Wow. You built this place?"

Mica didn't seem to hear her. He was staring at the house, deep in thought.

"Daddy and his friends built it. Do you want to see my new room?"

"I'd love to, but only if it's okay with your dad."

Hannah unbuckled her seat belt and threw her arms around her dad's neck, snapping him out of his reverie. "Daddy, can Miss Simone see my room? Please?"

He laughed, prying little fingers from his Adam's apple. "Sure. I mean, if she wants to. But Miss Simone probably needs to get home."

"Yay!" Hannah scrambled out of the car and ran up the porch steps to the front door. She turned to Simone and waved her to come. Simone followed, admiring the professional landscaping skirting the base of the home in a colorful array of flowers. She thought of taking pictures as inspiration for her personal garden. She stood on the porch looking around at the developing neighborhood. She drove in the area all the time on her way to Lakeview

Brew but never paid much attention to the houses. She'd simply noticed a few extravagant houses getting built on big acreage around Lake Diamond. Now she saw the *Stark Homes* signs stuck in the front lawns of these new mini-mansions.

Simone followed Hannah into the house while Mica met with some official-looking guys in the front yard. One man wore a suit and tie and was clicking a pen, although he held no papers. A second man, whose brown hair was salt-and-pepper by the ears, was dressed in khaki pants and a polo shirt and had a camera strapped around his neck. A third man, wearing carpenter pants and a neon T-shirt, looked stressed out and angry by the way he was making big hand motions and talking fast. Mica had stepped alongside this guy and had his hands on his hips, nodding in support of the hand-gesture guy.

Mr. Stark was not having a good day, indeed. Simone felt a little bad for the guy. She stepped into the house. The barebones of the home were complete, but it lacked the finishing touches.

"This is the kitchen," Hannah said. "My favorite part is the fridge. It's not here yet. It can make a glass of water just by pushing buttons on the door. Cool, huh?"

"Very cool." The roomy kitchen didn't have cabinets installed yet, but it was easy to picture a family of three eating at a breakfast bar, facing windows overlooking Lake Diamond. The kitchen flowed into a spacious room with a wall of windows that gave way to a gorgeous view of the water.

"My room is up here." Hannah skipped up the stairs, her shoes tapping the wooden steps. She turned to the right at the top of the banister and entered a room with slanted ceilings and a window seat. She stood at the closet, concentrating. "I think I'll put my bed over here, and I'll put Petunia's bed here. Petunia is my kitty."

The room was huge for a five-year-old, complete with a walk-in closet and her personal en suite bathroom. Simone inwardly groaned. She was learning more about this deadbeat dad by the minute. This guy was so obsessed with his job, making money, buying his family fancy things—including an oversized house—he obviously didn't bother to spend time with his daughter. Simone had learned quickly, living with the Wells family, money doesn't buy happiness. Where was Hannah's mother anyway? Did she work longer hours than her husband?

Hannah skipped out of the room and down the hall. Simone followed her and stopped when her eye caught sight of the most stunning room she'd seen so far. She stepped in, feeling small in the great room with its high-peaked ceiling supported by wooden beams, and windows large enough to supply nearly a full view of the lake. Built-in bookshelves lined the walls, the woodwork giving a cozy feel to the large space. A fireplace surrounded by stone anchored the room. "Beautiful," Simone whispered, taking it all in.

Hannah danced into the space and twirled. "This is Mommy's scrapbook room."

"A room just for scrapbooking?" Simone blurted, quite by accident.

Heavy footsteps sounded behind her. "I take it you're not a fan of scrapbooking?" Mica stepped in beside her, a scowl on his face.

"I'm sorry. I ... I didn't mean to be rude." Simone walked to the fireplace, running her fingertips over the mantle. "This room is beautiful. I just pictured a different use of the space. Maybe a rug rolled out in front of the fireplace that you could lie on while reading your favorite books to each other." Simone walked to the center of the room where Hannah had twirled. "I'd set up a table under the window with a puzzle for everyone to work on at their leisure." Simone set her hands on her hips, thinking maybe she should've been an interior designer. "You know, a room that brings the family together."

Mica narrowed his eyes. "Nobody asked your opinion."

He was angry. She needed to explain. How ridiculous for a mom to be tucked away in her very own room, scrapbooking pictures of her family, when she could be spending valuable time with them and making memories from day-to-day life. Simone watched the Wells family go on vacations to magically make the family bond. Then, they returned home to their separate lives and busy schedules. Simone imagined that's what was happening here. The mom scrapbooked their fancy trips and went AWOL the rest of the time—working, shopping, or whatever it was she did. Simone wanted Hannah to have a truly close family. Every day. She'd do her best to make that happen for Hannah. "Sorry, I just—"

He left the room.

Hannah watched her dad leave, looking like she was debating whether to follow him or stay with her guest.

Regret filled Simone's heart. What was she even doing here? And why was she giving her opinion? She didn't know anything about family. Maybe it was only in books and sappy movies where families spent quality time together. She knelt in front of Hannah. "I didn't mean to upset you or your dad. I'm sorry."

Hannah looked up at Simone with her big blue eyes and nodded. "It's okay."

"I think I'd better head home now. Thanks for giving me a tour. Your new house is lovely. Walk me out?"

Hannah held Simone's hand as they descended the staircase and walked outside. Mica was standing on the porch talking with the guy in the neon-yellow shirt. The words *Stark Homes* were printed across the back, and *Adam* was printed in small letters above the breast pocket. The man nodded hello as Simone passed by.

She descended the porch steps feeling foolish about the comments she'd made to Mica about the scrapbook room. She'd insulted his beautiful home and his wife. "Hannah, I need to talk with your dad. I'll see you in school tomorrow." Hannah released Simone's hand and knelt by the garden, smelling the flowers and touching their soft petals.

Simone turned to the men and cleared her throat, interrupting their discussion. "May I have a word with you, Mica?"

Mica let Adam know he'd be a minute, then stepped in stride with Simone. "Sure, Miss Simone. You can talk as I walk you to your car."

Clearly, she was no longer welcome here. They walked to the car in silence as Simone gathered her thoughts. She'd called the guy out on his lack of parental skills one too many times and had overstepped her boundaries as Hannah's teacher. She leaned a hip against the driver side door and fished her keys from her purse.

Mica folded his arms across his chest, probably guarding himself against her next criticism. "Did you have something to say to me? Because I really need to get back to my meeting."

Standing at eye level with his tanned, muscular arms, she felt even smaller than when he'd reprimanded her up in the room. "I ... I'm sorry."

"For what? For making me feel like the worst father in the universe?"

Heat filled Simone's face and neck. "No. You are not the worst father in the universe. Hannah is lovely. I never meant to make you feel that way." She thought about the times she'd chastised him the last couple of days—after he'd arrived late on the first day of school, when he failed to complete homework, when he left Hannah in his truck in the tow-away zone. She'd meant for this to be an apology, but instead she was getting angry all over again. "Okay, well maybe a little bit. I mean, I want to apologize for what I said in that fabulous room. It's none of my business what you do with your house."

His anger appeared to wane only slightly. "I appreciate that. Apology accepted." He uncrossed his arms and stuffed his hands into the front pockets of his jeans, looking down at his work boots. "As I told you before, I'm doing my best with Hannah."

His best? Really? His statement didn't sit well, but she figured she should just get in her car and leave while she was on good terms with this father. She opened her car door, glanced over at Hannah counting the flowers, and couldn't make herself get in the car. Hannah deserved a father who *really* did his best for her. A pep talk was in order. She faced Mica. "You can do better."

He stumbled back a couple steps as if she had slapped him. "Excuse me?" He was angry, as expected. But she wasn't intimidated by this big strong man. As a foster kid, she'd dealt with plenty of angry dads in her life. But this dad's eyes held an element of hurt mingling with the anger. She considered this to be a sign that she was getting through to him.

"You heard me. You can do better. You can get up earlier in the morning so you have enough time to get your daughter ready for school, and you can spend quality time with her in the evenings. You obviously work hard at your job and are successful. I just don't want you to look back some day and wish you'd spent more time together as a family."

Mica continued to back away. He shook a finger at her. "You have no idea what you're talking about." He was struggling to keep his voice low and controlled. Both Hannah and Adam had taken notice and were watching them.

Simone closed the gap with Mica so Hannah wouldn't overhear. "This house is amazing. The nicest house I've ever seen in my entire life with this amazing view. But a big house doesn't buy happiness."

"Are you kidding me?" Mica choked out a sarcastic laugh.

Simone needed to make her point and get out of here before Mica exploded. She'd pushed his buttons enough. "All I'm saying is, you have a precious, smart little girl over there who needs you to love her, nurture her, and cherish her. You have everything. Don't take it for granted. I mean, look at you. You have it all. A beautiful daughter, a gorgeous house you built yourself, you're handsome—I mean healthy ... and strong." That came out wrong. Simone fidgeted with her purse strap.

Mica smirked, although still notably mad. He planted his feet on the ground and set his hands on his hips. "Are you finished?"

Simone maintained eye contact despite feeling more foolish than ever. "Yes. Have a good evening."

Simone drove away, kicking herself for giving a pathetic apology. She glanced in the rearview mirror and saw Mica still standing there with his hands on his hips, watching her drive away.

Chapter Four

Hannah placed her portrait in the file on Simone's desk. She wore an ear-to-ear grin. "I did my homework, Miss Simone. And guess what?" Her hair was held off her forehead with a bright yellow headband decorated with a plaid yellow and pink bow on the side.

Simone swiveled her chair to face her eager student with her full attention. "What?"

"Daddy says we're gonna do more family time. He said it was your idea."

"Oh really?" Simone's eyebrows rose in surprise. "I don't know if I said that exactly."

Hannah shrugged and then skipped off to the hamster cage.

So, she was getting through to Mica Stark after all. She felt bad about the spectacle she'd made of herself in that amazing room and calling him out on a couple of things yesterday. She worried she had overstepped, but maybe it was a needed wake-up call for Mica.

The Stark family's progress put Simone in a good mood, along with her students being on their best behavior. She rewarded them with extra free time out on the playground in the afternoon, and she couldn't help but enjoy the few extra minutes of sunshine herself.

She roamed around the playground, ensuring kids were safe and being kind. She spotted MJ, bag on her arm and car keys in hand, exiting the building. Simone jogged over to her. "Hey, girl. On your way home already?"

"Yep. Well, I'm going out to Lakeview Brew to look over lesson plans. Wanna meet me out there after school?"

"Sure thing." She checked her watch. "See you there in about thirty minutes."

"Perfect. I need to run a couple errands first."

Simone looked in the direction of boisterous cheering to see Tommy and Kenzie racing across monkey bars. She'd need to keep an eye on Tommy. He was always either pestering Kenzie or eyeing her dreamily. From Simone's experience observing kindergartners, Tommy's actions indicated he was crushing on Kenzie. He seemed the type to lay a kiss on a girl. There was always one kid to pull such a stunt each year. The recipient, and often the parents, weren't too keen on displays of affection, innocent though they may be.

"Is that the Stark girl?" MJ asked, pointing to Hannah.

"Yeah. She's in my class. I adore that little girl. At first, I thought her dad was a total loser. I pegged him as that stereotypical egotistical guy who thinks his money and good looks give him immunity to rules. For example, he sauntered in late with his daughter on the first day of school. I mean, isn't the first day of kindergarten, or any grade, a highly anticipated day in a child's life? He flew in the door at 8:40 with Hannah. Her hair looked like ... you know when someone sleeps on their French braid for a few days?"

MJ nodded.

"He couldn't even brush her hair the first day of school. That sent my post-foster-kid, neglect radar up."

"Simone—"

"It's not just that. He didn't do Hannah's easy little homework assignment with her. It broke my heart when she told me her dad didn't participate in the simple project. And—"

"He's a good guy. I've been praying for that family."

"Why? How do you know them?"

"The Starks go to my church." MJ watched Hannah claim a swing and dig her toe into the wood chips to push off but making little leeway. MJ smiled as she looked on, in a melancholy sort of way. "We'll talk at the café." Ominous. But MJ was always praying for people. Her praying didn't necessarily mean something bad had happened.

"Okay. I'll bring my students' family portraits to look over."

"See you there."

After the final bell rang and Simone had doled out goodbye hugs, she gathered up the homework papers from her file and put them in her bag. The portraits would give her a glimpse of each student's family while also indicating each child's drawing and writing abilities.

Waving to Mrs. Wilson on her way out, Simone drove to Lakeview Brew happy with the way the first week of school was shaping up. She had great kids, and she'd already positively influenced one family. While she was happy about the Starks' progress, the look on MJ's face told her there was more to the story. She hoped, for Hannah's sake, the story wasn't tragic. Simone's imagination, fueled by her personal history, tended to get the best of her when she suspected a child might be in harm's way.

The other quandary hanging over her head was the anticipation of Gale showing up on her doorstep. But she wouldn't let the impending encounter dampen her mood. She would not allow Gale to occupy thought space. She rolled down the windows, turned on the radio, and sang along to the music as if she hadn't a care in the world.

Turning onto Lakeview Drive, Simone couldn't help but be in a good mood. A fragrant intermingling of fresh lake water and pine trees blew through her open window. Something about being by the lake softened her hard edges, soothed her worries, and made her feel at peace. She'd grown up near the Mississippi River and had loved watching the water skirt along the shore as it moved with the current. She and her friends would toss sticks in the water, watching them until they were out of sight. It was fascinating to think the very water she was viewing was traveling to the ocean. But the stillness of the lake water was different. Calm. Serene.

Jade's café occupied prime realty, separated from Lake Diamond only by the street. Outdoor seating in front of the shop was nearly always in use on nice weather days like today. Jade was fortunate enough to live in the loft above the shop, making Jade's residence the obvious choice for meet-ups.

MJ's minivan was already parked near the coffee shop, and MJ was seated outside at a bistro table, waiting for Simone. As they stepped into the café, Simone breathed in the aroma of roasting beans. A heavenly scent, even to a tea-drinker. Jade was sweeping up beans littering the floor in front of the coffee roaster. "Hi, ladies. Are you getting drinks to go, or can you stay a while?"

"We're staying," Simone answered. "Gonna catch up on some paperwork. Can you join us for a bit?"

"Absolutely. I need to order supplies. Wanna go up to my place? It's quieter up there, and you still get the great view."

As the café was bustling with high schoolers drinking frappes, the quiet of Jade's loft was appealing. Simone nodded.

"Sounds good to me," MJ said.

"Place your orders, and I'll bring them up. I'll put them on your tabs." Jade winked. There was no tab.

"Thanks, Jade. Although, you know that's not a great way to do business," Simone said.

"It keeps you coming back, doesn't it?" Jade unfastened her apron and said something to the employee behind the counter, pointing to Simone and MJ. The barista nodded. She disappeared through the swinging door into the kitchen, calling over her shoulder, "It's unlocked. I'll see you up there."

Simone and MJ placed their orders, leaving a generous tip, and went upstairs. Jade's loft modeled the same interior design as the coffee shop. A brick exterior wall encased generous windows. Hardwood flooring was covered with an eclectic variety of rugs. High ceilings, both upstairs and downstairs, were supported by wooden beams. Exposed ductwork ran along the ceiling, giving an industrial feel. The spaces were cozied up by plush seating, watercolor artwork supplied by local artists, and warm, calming shades of turquoise and butter yellow. A notable difference between the two spaces was the coffee shop was always tidy while Jade's loft—well, maybe she didn't have time to keep it clean with the long hours she put into being a business owner.

Simone removed a sweater draped over a chair at the dining table, folded it, and set it on Jade's dresser. She and MJ cleared the table of mail and odds and ends to prepare a workspace. "I wonder if Jade could use an assistant at Lakeview Brew. The poor girl hardly has time for herself," MJ said as she rinsed out a mug and loaded it into the dishwasher.

"I've wondered that myself," Simone said. "But she loves her work so much. I don't think she'd have it any other way."

Footsteps sounded on the wooden steps, and Jade appeared with a tray in hand. MJ and Simone claimed seats at the table. "An iced lavender Earl Grey for the lovely Simone. A Café Americano for the working mama. And a decaf Pumpkin Spice Latte for the café owner who has had more than her fill of caffeine for one day," Jade said, handing out the beverages. She looked around the loft, a smirk playing at her lips. "This is why I don't charge you two for drinks. You tidy my loft in exchange. Sorry it was such a mess in here. I've been so busy."

"Don't worry about it." Simone tried her iced tea. *Delicious.* "This is my new favorite. Do not take it off the menu. Ever."

Jade giggled. "That's another thing. You ladies try my new concoctions and give me your honest opinions. I can't put a price on that. Oh, I have to tell you about my latest business venture." Jade sat at the head of the table and opened her laptop. "So, we usually close at seven, but I thought it would be fun to stay open late one night a month to host a community event. I decided to test it out the Saturday between Christmas and New Year's, when a lot of people have guests in town, and, let's be honest, there's not a lot of entertainment to be found in Diamond."

"I love that idea," MJ said. "What's the event?"

"Karaoke night."

"Yes! Count me in," MJ said. Of course, the music teacher would love karaoke.

Simone, on the other hand, was less than thrilled. "I do not sing in front of people."

Jade scowled. "Oh, come on. You'll love it. Back in college, my friends and I had so much fun at karaoke bars. My event will be alcohol-free, of course. Family friendly. And you don't have to sing."

"Yes, you do." MJ clapped her hands in excitement. "We can sing Spice Girls. I'm Baby Spice."

Jade cocked an eyebrow at the out-of-character statement from MJ. Simone held back a chuckle. One would assume MJ would aspire more to maybe Barbara Streisand than Baby Spice. "I was thinking we'd do The Supremes," Jade said.

"Yes. Let's do it." MJ and Jade high-fived.

Simone hated to be a stick in the mud. She used to sing for an audience. As a middle-schooler, she had been selected to perform *The Star-Spangled Banner* before the homecoming high school football game. Senator Wells was there, and he was congratulated publicly for his election as a Minnesota state senator. She was proud, walking onto the field with him by her side. He'd hugged her right there on the field. She'd felt this strong sense of connection, both to the Wells family and to the community. The feeling was as unfamiliar as it was wonderful.

But that was the only time the senator or his wife had shown up to hear her sing. She had to find her own ride to the school Christmas choir concert the same year, and they didn't even buy tickets for her performance in the school musical, *Fiddler on the Roof.* She'd perfected her lines, eager to please the Wellses—to make the senator proud like she had out on the football field.

She finally realized everything was just for show—the hug, the look of pride in his eyes. It was meaningless. She even wondered if she was a good singer at all. Maybe she'd only been selected to sing *The Star-Spangled Banner* because of her connection to Wesley Wells. She didn't join choir the following year or try out for any more musicals. She still loved singing, but she was done singing for others. These days she reserved singing for the car and the shower. She hadn't sung in front of an audience, other than a class of kindergartners, since the seventh grade.

"You two can sing a duet. Salt-N-Pepa. Or Heart," Simone said.

"We'll change your mind."

Simone knew MJ didn't want her to miss out on the fun. MJ didn't understand, but Simone didn't want to be a Debbie Downer. Time for a change of subject.

"So, you know the Stark family from church?"

MJ looked caught off guard. "Yep. Jade goes there too." MJ turned to Jade. "Hannah Stark is in Simone's class."

Jade suspended her cup halfway to her mouth, setting the cup back down without taking a drink. The laughter from moments ago had been replaced by an eerie silence. "I haven't seen them much since the tornado."

"Tornado? What am I missing?" Simone's heart rate tripled.

Jade crossed her arms and propped her elbows on the table. "You don't know?"

43

MJ cleared her throat. "Josie Stark, Mica's wife, was killed in a tornado the summer before last."

Simone gasped.

MJ adjusted her glasses. "She was the only one home. Their entire house was leveled."

Simone struggled to process the horrible news. "What tornado? I don't remember a tornado. How did I not know about this?" She cringed thinking how hard she'd been on Mica.

Jade stared blankly at her laptop while MJ continued. She obviously cared for the Stark family. She must have known Josie. "They lived in a rural part of the next county. There aren't many churches out that way, so they drove over here."

"That sounds familiar. I remember hearing there was a fatality in a tornado somewhere, but I didn't recognize the name of the town." Simone shrank back into her chair. "She died?" It was a statement more than a question. Simone felt as if she'd been stabbed in the chest as the truth sank in. Her heart ached at the notion of Hannah losing her mommy. Tears filled her eyes. Mica *was* trying his best. Alone. While grieving the loss of his wife. "You guys, I messed up."

"What do you mean?" Jade asked. "What happened?"

"I chewed Mica out for being a terrible father and gave him a lecture on how to parent. I even insulted his late wife." Simone stood, rethinking all the awful things she'd said to Mica, wishing she could get away from herself. "What kind of person does that?"

MJ came to her. "A concerned teacher who was looking out for the best interest of her student. You care about each kid that comes through your classroom, and you would do anything to protect them."

Jade handed Simone a box of tissues. "Don't be so hard on yourself. You didn't know about Josie."

MJ and Jade spoke the truth. Still, remorse consumed Simone when she recalled the judgmental words she'd hurled at Mica. She felt herself spiraling down into a dark place she didn't want to go. A place she'd spent too many years of her life already.

"Who do I think I am—meddling in people's lives? I'm not equipped to hand out advice. I can't go around fixing people when I'm so … broken." She blotted her face with the tissue.

MJ put her arm around Simone. "That's not true. You are so strong. You've overcome so much in your life, and now you want to pay it forward. Hannah is blessed to have you for a teacher."

Simone begged to differ. She just hoped not to do more damage. Simone smiled at MJ and moved out from her embrace, needing space to process. She plopped into a comfy chair and hugged a velvety pillow to her chest.

Jade sat on the loveseat. She untied her hair from the messy bun propped on her head and began fiddling with the elastic. "I'm sure Mica will understand. He hasn't seemed himself since Josie died. Naturally. I mean, when I see him around town, he looks kinda homeless sometimes. Messy hair—like he's overdue for a haircut. Sloppy clothes—like he just rolled out of bed. When Josie was alive, he always looked put together. I thought he was super handsome. And he was always helping church people out with projects and stuff. Now he keeps to himself a lot. I can't blame you for thinking he was some kind of loser. He's really not though."

MJ rummaged through her purse and pulled out her phone. "I have his number. You can text him right now."

Simone decided this time she would think before she spoke. "I need to think about it. Let's get some work done." Simone heaved herself out of the chair and took out her papers, ready to move on. Her friends joined her at the table, and they worked fastidiously for some time.

Simone's phone chimed— she had been jumpy every time it chimed since Gale's last text. Sure enough, Gale was contacting her again. *Groan.*

GALE: Planning to stop by tomorrow night. Will you be home?

Simone wanted to lie and text back she wouldn't be home tomorrow night. In fact, she'd moved out of the country so, regrettably, she wouldn't be available at any time in the foreseeable future. But realistically, avoidance would only prolong the inevitable. Maybe she should just meet with Gale and see what she wanted this time. Better to get it over with. Simone texted back.

SIMONE: I'll be home.

"Everything okay?" MJ asked, peering over her laptop. "If looks could kill, I wouldn't want to be the person on the other end of your phone."

Simone didn't feel like talking about it. "It's nothing." Ignoring MJ's curious gaze, she returned to her work. She hovered over the papers, taking her time to study the portraits before turning each page. She'd have the kids repeat the exercise again the last week of school. Comparing each child's two drawings was always a fun way to see the kids' progress. The artwork would get tucked into a folder, along with other special kindergarten keepsakes, for each child to take home at the end of the year.

"You've got your work cut out for you with that one," Jade said, eyeing Braden's picture of indiscernible scribbles.

"Hey. Keep your eyes on your own work," Simone said, flipping the paper over while agreeing wholeheartedly. She wondered what Hannah's picture would be, but she tried not to flip ahead. Her other students deserved her attention too.

Turning to the next page, her eyes swept over a picture of a little blonde-haired, blue-eyed stick figure girl, with a wide grin, holding the hand of a giant-sized stick figure version of her dad. The father's mouth was turned down in a frown. Above the father and daughter, a ribbon of blue sky was dotted with puffy clouds. As Simone's eyes traveled to the top of the page, her breath caught in her throat. Perched on a cloud, was a blonde-haired, blue-eyed lady. Hannah's name was printed in the middle of the paper in a rainbow of colors. The picture tore at Simone's heart. "Check this out." She showed the picture to MJ and Jade.

MJ touched the frown on Mica's face. "Even Hannah notices Mica is sad."

"How could she not?" Jade said.

Simone decided she needed to make things right with Mica. He needed to know he was a good father, and she was there to support him and Hannah. "I'm gonna talk to him." She put the papers in her bag. "I'll see if he's over at his new house. I had to give him and Hannah a ride there once when his truck got towed."

"I have his temporary address too," Jade said. "They're living in an apartment in town."

"Or you could email him or text him. Even just to give him a heads up that you're coming over." MJ was so considerate, whereas Simone just wanted to get things done.

"I think a face-to-face apology is best. Humiliating as seeing him may be. I'll text him first. MJ, can you give me his number?"

"Sure." MJ checked her phone, then rattled off the number. "Speaking of texts, Branson is asking when I'll be home. I better get going. Sounds like the girls are getting *hangry*. I tried a new chicken and rice crockpot recipe I found on Pinterest. I'll let you know how it turns out."

"Living on the edge, are we?" Jade winked. The ladies often teased MJ that she was a regular Martha Stewart.

MJ ignored the comment. "Thanks for the coffee, Jade."

"Yeah, thanks, Jade." Simone put the empty glassware back on the tray to take downstairs.

As she drove to Mica's place, she rehearsed her apology. His truck wasn't outside the lake house. She texted but got no response. He was either busy or was ignoring her—which she couldn't blame him for. She drove out to the apartment address Jade had supplied. She hoped to deliver an actual apology this time, and she hoped he'd understand.

Chapter Five

"Cannonball!" Mica took a running start before jumping, hugging his knees to his chest, and making a big splash. He may have failed in several areas of parenting, at least by Hannah's teacher's standards, but he'd always succeeded in making his daughter laugh. When he came up for air, her giggles were music to his ears.

"Do it again, Daddy."

Mica swam to the shallow end of the pool to join Hannah, the cool water soothing his aching muscles as his body glided through the water. He'd always preferred a wide-open lake to a chlorine-saturated pool, but he'd have to get used to the apartment pool since he was being forced to sell the lakeside house. Until he found a different house that didn't remind him of Josie every day. Hannah loved the house, but Mica couldn't go through with the sale just because his five-year-old wanted it. Could he? "That's enough cannonballs for one day. Let's work on your back float."

Although it pained him to admit, Hannah's nosy teacher was right. He needed to make more time for his daughter. It had been too long since he'd spent quality time with her like this, just the two of them, laughing and playing and talking. Adam's wife often stepped in for him—taking Hannah with their two little girls to the zoo and the Mall of America and inviting her over for slumber parties—on the countless days when Mica made a weak attempt at running a business and even on the days when he struggled to drag himself out of bed. Days when he missed Josie so much, the ache in his heart made breathing almost impossible.

Hannah doggy-paddled over to him. She attempted to float on her back, her arms flailing. "Relax, honey. I've got you." He supported her back with his hands. "There you go. You're doing it." Mica's heart filled with pride as he gazed down at his little girl. She was smiling, squinting against the evening sunlight, looking like a child without a care in the world.

The hum of a car pulling into the parking lot caught his attention. He looked up to see a Volkswagen Beetle circling the lot at an unusually slow speed. Someone driving that slowly could only be one of two things: a stalker or— more likely—a sassy kindergarten teacher. His peace and contentment dissolved like sugar in boiling water. What was Miss Simone going to yell at him about now? Ducking down, he crossed his fingers and hoped she didn't spot them in the pool.

"Miss Simone!" Hannah waded through the water to the concrete steps and dashed out of the pool. "We're over here." Hannah jumped up and down by the fence, waving her arms above her head. So much for his idea of flying under the radar.

Soon, Simone was climbing the steps to the pool deck. She wore a summery dress, and her dark hair was braided down one side. She looked different than she had at school. More carefree. Sweet. He knew better though. Under her charming exterior, the lady was a bear with claws. She walked to the side of the pool and accepted Hannah's soggy embrace. She listened with apparent rapt interest as Hannah told her about floating and her daddy's amazing cannonballs.

Mica begrudgingly exited the pool, believing Simone wouldn't be so kind to him. He walked to a lounge chair to retrieve his towel, aware of the teacher's watchful eyes.

She was still listening to Hannah, nodding at all the right times, but now she was far more focused on him. She was probably resisting the urge to punch him, or maybe she was silently rehearsing a speech about how he was the world's worst father. Sighing, he picked up his towel and headed to the bear's den. Better to get this over with.

"Hannah, it's time to towel off. We'll go in for dinner when I'm finished talking to Miss Simone." She did as she was told, wrapping her towel around her shoulders and curling up on a lounge chair.

Mica turned his attention to Simone, waiting to get berated. She stood at the edge of the pool looking at him almost sheepishly—completely out of character. Then it dawned on him. She must be working up the nerve to apologize again. *This should be interesting.*

He toweled off his hair, arms, back, and chest. She just stood there, staring at him with her mouth agape. Wait ... was she squirming? The way she was tucking hair behind her ear, fidgeting with her earring, biting her lower lip. *Ha!* She was attracted to him. His lips inched into a smile. He wrapped the towel around his waist, thoroughly enjoying her discomfort. It was about time she was the one squirming. He'd have to be the one to start off this conversation. "Nice of you to stop by."

"Thanks." Her voice was low and raspy. She cleared her throat. "I mean, I have something to say to you."

Mica nodded. "I had a hunch. We could go inside—"

"No. This will only take a minute." She closed her eyes momentarily and took a deep breath. "It's really hot out here. Mind if we sit?" She kicked off her sandals and sat on the edge of the pool, dangling her feet in the water. Mica followed suit, sitting next to her.

"I saw Hannah's family portrait."

"Ah, yes. The drawing of Josie in heaven, smiling down at us." Mica felt the familiar tug at his heart that accompanied thoughts of Josie.

"I'm so sorry, Mica. I had no idea." She dabbed trembling fingertips at the corners of her eyes.

"I figured you didn't know I was widowed." With such a heartfelt apology, Mica couldn't help but feel sorry for her. She had apparently beat herself up enough over the misunderstanding. Seeing her cry, he was consumed by an urge to comfort her like he did whenever Hannah cried. Or whenever Josie had cried. He resisted the urge to put an arm around her or rub her back. "I accept your apology. In your defense, I admit I pretty much suck at the single dad thing."

"No." Simone placed a hand on his shoulder. "You don't *completely* suck."

Mica was torn between laughing at the humor in her statement or sighing in pleasure at the feel of her soft hand on his bare shoulder. He decided laughing was the more appropriate choice and went with that. "Well, I'm not a workaholic as I feel you've implied. But you were right about one thing. I don't spend enough quality time with Hannah. Since losing Josie, I've struggled to find energy for day-to-day responsibilities. Scheduling in fun father-daughter activities hardly made it on my radar. But I'm working on it. For example, I took her for a swim today." He motioned to the pool with a sweep of his arm.

Simone removed her hand from his shoulder. "I see that." She smiled at him. He noticed flecks of gold in her brown eyes, highlighted by the setting sun. Her eyes were pretty—when they weren't glaring at him. "I imagine it must be difficult to make new memories without Josie."

She'd hit the nail on the head. Why would he want to take a family vacation without Josie? And whenever Hannah did something new or adorable—like learning to float on her back—he wished he could share the excitement with her mother. Already, she had missed out on so much of Hannah's firsts. "It was a year ago in June." He observed Hannah from across the pool. She had ditched the towel and was lying on her back, singing an indistinguishable song, her bent legs swaying to the tune. Joy filled his heart every time he saw Hannah doing happy, normal-kid stuff.

"We were living in a rental home while the lakeside house was under construction. A rambler with no basement." He shook his head, wishing he could turn back time and move them into a safer home. "It was on a ten-acre plot of rolling hills. Breathtaking." He paused, then cleared his throat. "A tornado ..." He heard a soft gasp from Simone. He couldn't bring himself to finish the sentence.

"You don't have to talk about it."

"It's okay." He didn't mind telling the story to someone who genuinely cared. He swirled his feet in the water—a slight distraction from the pain squeezing his heart. Survivor's guilt threatened to plague him, but he shooed it away. He couldn't be fully present for Hannah if he was wallowing in guilt. "It was a sweltering hot summer day. The house didn't have central air. Just a window unit in each of the two bedrooms. I took Hannah to the beach for a couple of hours while Josie went out and bought groceries. I was going to grill sweet corn and chicken for supper. We were at the lake when a wall of clouds started moving in. They came so fast. We packed up and headed home." He swallowed around the lump in his throat. "I was hoping Josie was still at the store." Talking about the moment his family was ripped apart was never easy, but at least this time he got through it without getting too choked up to speak. He shook his head to rid his mind of that fateful day.

They sat in silence for a while. He appreciated her not filling the void with senseless words. When she did speak, her words were thoughtful. "Thank you for sharing that with me." For the first time since he'd met her, the schoolteacher's presence was a comfort.

"Daddy, I'm hungry," Hannah whined not so softly from her lounge chair. "Can we go in?"

"Sure, honey." Mica regretted ending his conversation with Simone so soon. He was finally connecting with her. They pulled their legs from the water and walked to the gate to exit the pool area. "Thanks for stopping by. I appreciate it."

"You're welcome. I'm really sorry from the bottom of my heart." She peered up at him, her long, dark eyelashes wet from the tears she shed. His story was the sad one, yet the tears were in her eyes.

Mica hated to see this vulnerable version of Simone, which baffled him since the confident version was incredibly irritating. Somehow, when she looked at him with those doe eyes, he wanted to hold her and console her. He'd only known this woman for a brief time, yet he sensed a depth of empathy was sheltered under a hardened exterior. As if she was protecting her vulnerability. She'd allowed him a glimpse of her heart today through a narrow, guarded opening. He was grateful. Instinct took over, and he pulled her into an embrace.

Realizing he was hugging his daughter's teacher while wearing only a towel and swim trunks, he pulled back and lengthened the space between them. Why hadn't he just shaken her hand? Patted her on the back? He tried to act natural. "It's all good."

Hannah ran over and hugged her teacher too. "Bye, Miss Simone."

For the remainder of the evening, the memory of Simone in his arms—awkward as it was—stayed with Mica. She'd felt soft and gentle. He would've liked to linger in her embrace and touch her silky dark hair. Her shampoo had left a delectable scent on his shoulder and continued to fill his senses. She'd reciprocated the hug, as he recalled. She hadn't pushed him away at least. Had he pushed her away? He hoped not.

His lingering thoughts about Miss Simone confused him. Was it weird to have intimate feelings toward his daughter's teacher? Was he breaking another school rule? Plus, Miss Simone could be downright rude and condescending. Those were not flattering attributes.

Mica pondered these enigmas as he tucked Hannah into bed and sat outside on the apartment balcony in the quiet of the night. Most confusing of all—he hadn't experienced romantic feelings for any woman since Josie. He and Josie had discussed the possibility of remarrying if either of them passed away at a young age. He argued she was the one and only love of his life. How could he love another woman the way he loved her? She'd kissed his cheek and told him she never ever wanted to leave him. But if she did, she wanted him to be happy. The only stipulation was the woman he remarried would need to love Hannah.

Mica swallowed a lump in his throat. The memory was so vivid he could feel the gentle caress of her kiss. Oh, how he missed her. Josie had wanted him to be happy, but he could hardly remember what *happy* felt like.

Perhaps it was time to rediscover happiness. He would always love Josie, and he would certainly always miss her. But to honor her wish, he would allow himself to fall in love again if the right woman ever came along. Who knows? Maybe such a woman was Simone Clare.

The next morning while standing in his kitchen, pouring freshly brewed coffee into his travel mug, Mica phoned Adam. "I've made my decision about the lakeside house. I've decided to finish the project so Hannah and I can move in as soon as possible." Relief washed over him as the words spilled out. After a year of standstill, he was ready to get his life back in order. He had decided to honor all of Josie's wishes to the best of his ability.

"That's so great." Adam roared a celebratory yell. "I've been waiting to hear those words from you. I've been praying for this, and it's good to hear how God is answering my prayers."

"You've been praying I'd move into the lakeside house?"

"Not exactly." Adam's voice cracked. He was getting emotional. "I've been praying you'd get back in the game. You've been … sidelined for too long."

"Well, I'm back." Mica sipped his coffee. Even his coffee tasted fresher this morning, which was a good thing since he would need lots of caffeine to keep him going today after his late night out on the balcony, mulling things over.

"How did you make the decision? I mean, will it be hard to move into the house … you know … without Josie?"

Mica sighed. "You bet it will. I'll miss her every day." Going on with life in her absence would be brutal, but it was better to move on with life than to just give up on it. "I want to honor Josie's wishes. We had made plans together for our future with Hannah. I can't just throw away those plans and come up with a new plan. It wouldn't be fair to Josie or to Hannah. That home will be perfect for us. Hannah is so excited about it. I don't want to let her down."

Adam was quiet, allowing Mica to talk through his feelings.

"Completing the house will give me closure. Living in the house will help me move on with life. Am I making any sense?"

"Sure." Adam's voice was calmer than before—pensive. "I'm happy for you, Mica. This is a big step. I'll keep praying for you." Mica appreciated Adam's prayers.

"Thanks, Adam." He hung up the phone, ready to start the day. It was time to finish Josie's house. No, it was time to finish *his and Hannah's* house.

Chapter Six

Saturday morning, as Simone and Pearl worked in their neighboring gardens, Simone filled Pearl in on the saga with Mica. She started at the beginning with her judging him the first day of school, learning he was a widower, and ending with her big apology, complete with details about the half-naked hug at the pool. "Sounds like you are more than forgiven." Pearl winked.

Simone felt her face redden and not from the sun. Pearl's implication that Mica had been flirting or even slightly attracted to her was absurd. She'd been nothing but cruel to the man. "Don't get the wrong idea. He regretted the hug immediately. He backed so far away from me, I thought he might fall into the pool."

"Sounds to me like he could've used some cooling off." Pearl grinned.

Simone contemplated Pearl's words all day and into the evening hours as she cooked her meal of macaroni and cheese and ate it while sitting on the living room couch, not hearing a word of whatever was airing on the television. She found him extremely attractive. Could Mica develop feelings for her? He obviously still mourned his wife. His heartbreaking history coupled with her childhood baggage would make for one complicated relationship.

The doorbell rang. Simone's heart jumped into her throat as an image of Mica standing on her doorstep with a bouquet of flowers and an invitation to the movies sprang to her mind. She leapt from the couch and tossed her dirty dishes into the sink. She controlled her breathing as she sauntered to the door, straightened her posture, turned the knob, and opened the door.

"Hey, Sis!" Gale jumped into Simone's arms, hugging her dramatically. *Ugh.* Her little fantasy of Mica popping in smashed to smithereens. "I've missed you all these years."

Simone didn't believe her for a second, but she played along, pretending this was a welcome reunion. "Gale. You look exactly the same." Which was mostly true. She was still tall, thin, and beautiful, except now she looked more mature and distinguished. More like her politician mother. "How did you find me?" Simone eyed a suitcase perched on the step. Oh no. Gale would not be staying the night.

Gale waved her phone in Simone's face. "The internet."

A taxi pulled up in front of Pearl's house, expelling two plump gray-haired ladies. They ambled up the walkway to Pearl's front door carrying their baskets of homemade goodies. Simone had witnessed the same scenario every Saturday night since moving in.

"They're so cute," Gale said. "That will be us in sixty years."

Simone bit her tongue. She hoped it wouldn't take sixty years to fend off Gale's antics. "Good evening, ladies," Simone called out, waving.

The older women stopped in their tracks and simultaneously turned their faces to Simone like a couple of sunflowers. "Well, hello there, Miss Simone. Care to join us tonight?" Hazel asked. "Bring your friend. I made sugar-and-spice cookies."

"We're studying Job tonight," Hazel's sister, Ethel, added. "Nothing will make your life look peachier than reading the story of Job."

As much as Simone would like an excuse to get away from Gale, she didn't see a Bible study offering any more appeal.

"Sorry, ladies. Maybe some other time." Simone declined with those same words each weekend. When would they get the hint? She wasn't a Bible-study type of girl.

Gale picked up her suitcase. "Since we're not going to Bible study, how about if we relax at your place? We have a lot to catch up on. I can't believe we're not Facebook friends. I sent you a request."

Well, they couldn't just stand out on the porch all night, so Simone invited her in.

Gale unzipped her suitcase and pulled out a bottle of wine. She went to the kitchen and rifled through drawers. "Can I help you find something?" The woman didn't need to be told to make herself at home.

Gale held up a corkscrew. "Found it." She poured two glasses of white wine while chatting about her parents' political careers. She handed a glass to Simone before sinking into the couch. Simone had eschewed alcohol since overindulging in high school. She considered refusing the glass from Gale but reminded herself she was of age now, and mature enough to drink responsibly. Plus, a little alcohol would help her tolerate Gale.

"It feels good to relax," Gale said, unfastening the top button of her dress shirt. "I've been running around all day." She released her hair from the bun at the base of her neck. "I love your place, by the way. It's so ... quaint."

Simone bit her tongue once again, aware Gale's use of the word *quaint* wasn't meant to be a compliment. She ignored the comment and sat on the overstuffed chair, curling her legs under her. Might as well get comfortable since Gale didn't appear to be leaving anytime soon. "Is there something on your mind? I mean, I haven't seen you since we were eighteen-year-olds, and suddenly, you show up on my doorstep." Surely there was a reason Gale was here. Better to get it out in the open.

"Listen," Gale said, tapping manicured nails against her wine glass. "I know we didn't always get along, but we've both matured. Let's make amends. After all, we are sisters." Gale punctuated her statement with a syrupy smile.

Gale had never acted like a sister to Simone. She'd always made clear Simone was a foster child, privileged to live with the Wellses. She had never been allowed to take her time with them for granted. "I'm all for making amends."

Gale lifted her glass. "Allow me to make a toast. To leaving the past behind and beginning a new journey. Sisters for life. Friends forever."

Simone resisted the urge to roll her eyes. Gale had certainly inherited the gift of political drivel. "Cheers." Simone clinked her glass with Gale's. "Remember when you ran for class president?"

Gale laughed. "I made you stay up all night with me making posters by hand. 'Vote for Gale. She'll pave a new trail.'"

Simone was also laughing. "That was so bad. It's not surprising you didn't win."

"I guess some degree of the political gene skipped a generation."

Simone cleared her throat. Time to cut to the chase. "What are you doing here? In Diamond? It's a little out of the way, isn't it? I mean, do you still live in St. Paul?"

Gale shrugged. "I missed you, Sis. Seriously, I haven't seen you in years. It's not that far of a drive. It's not as if I had to catch a flight here or anything." Gale set down her glass and removed her earrings. She was getting awfully comfy. "We made some good memories. I was looking through my Google Photos the other day, and I saw the pics from when we went cliff jumping at Taylor Falls."

Simone smiled. "That actually was fun."

"A bunch of us were working up the nerve to jump off the lower ledge, when all of a sudden we see petite little Simone flying off the one-hundred-foot cliff." Gale laughed. "I wish I could've gotten a recording of that."

"But I wouldn't do it again. No matter how you begged. It hurt!"

"You should've worn shoes to take the brunt of the impact."

"Now you tell me."

Simone couldn't help but laugh at some of the high school memories surfacing. She'd repressed all positive feelings toward Gale, guarding against further hurt by her. It was time to acknowledge the good times and leave those negative memories in the past. Maybe Gale had matured. In an effort to move on, she decided to relax and enjoy the evening.

A while later, Simone was topping off the wine glasses with red wine, the white having been emptied, when there was a knock on the door. "Come in," she called out.

The door creaked open. Pearl stepped in and surveyed the scene. Gale was lounging on the sofa with a cigarette propped between her fingers. Simone didn't normally allow smoking in her home, but she picked her battles with Gale. Simone sat cradling a glass of wine in her hand when, clearly, she'd already had enough. She struggled to act composed. She'd never drunk alcohol in front of Pearl before, let alone been buzzed in front of her. In fact, she hadn't had a sip of alcohol since moving in. Until tonight. She paused the music they'd been listening to. Simone held her breath awaiting Pearl's response. She felt like a high school kid caught in underage drinking.

The elderly woman gazed into Simone's eyes, penetrating the barrier of small talk. "I came to invite you to my house for Bible study tonight. Your friend is welcome too."

Hmm. Interesting approach.

Gale snickered. "Ma'am, you sure are thoughtful, but I'll pass. You can say a prayer for me though. I need a job. Oh, and pray for my dad's campaign. Don't forget to vote this November." Gale took a puff of her cigarette and blew out in Pearl's direction.

Simone cringed. First, because Gale admitted to needing a job. Simone hoped she wasn't looking in Diamond.

Secondly, she loved Pearl and hated how Gale was mocking her. Pearl, however, handled it with grace. "I most certainly will pray for you Miss ... Gale, is it?"

"Thank you for the invitation," Simone said, setting her glass of wine on a coaster. She stood—a bit wobbly. "But I must decline also." She leaned in, whispering so only Pearl could hear. "Don't worry about me. I'm having a good time." She smiled in case Pearl needed reassurance.

Pearl nodded but didn't look convinced. "All right then. In any case, would you mind keeping the music down? We're singing praise songs, but it's awfully distracting with that bass rattling my windows."

Gale broke into a fit of laughter. "And what do you know about bass? Do your hymns have bass?"

"Shut up, Gale." Now Simone sounded like a teenager, but she wouldn't allow Gale to treat Pearl with disrespect.

Pearl strode over to Gale and sized her up with a stern glare. "What do I know about bass?" Pearl shook her head. "Listen, child. I could school you when it comes to musical jargon. My daughter played cello in the Minnesota Orchestra for ten years." Pearl walked back to the door. "Not to mention I danced at Juilliard. I best be getting back to my friends. Have a good night." Apparently, Pearl could stand up for herself.

Gale took a drag on her cigarette, staring down at her lap, looking like a puppy who had just been shamed for peeing on the carpet. Simone struggled between kicking Gale out or trying to regain the positive energy that had suddenly been sucked out of the room. "She really is a sweet lady," Simone said. "She's a good friend of mine."

Gale rolled her eyes. "She's a tough old bird."

Simone couldn't help but smile. Gale had just been intimidated by little old Pearl. "Yes, she's a tough lady."

After two wine bottles had been emptied, Simone couldn't recall why she'd despised Gale so much. Nostalgic stories of high school flowed as richly and easily as the wine. All disputes were forgotten.

Gale nudged Simone's shoulder. "You gonna answer the door or what? Your friendly neighbor must be back. I'll try to be nice this time."

Simone stumbled to the door, wine glass in hand. "Turn down the music, Gale." She swung the door open. "Sorry, Pearl!" She froze. Music from inside the house rolled over her, spilling onto the doorstep. Wine danced through her body, muddling her mind. She grabbed the door frame to steady herself. "Mica? You're at my house?" His handsome face sent a rush of warmth from the top of her head to the tips of her toes. She reached out to caress his clean-shaven cheek. "How do you know where I live?" He looked more delicious every time she saw him.

Mica stepped back, out of reach. The rejection hit Simone like a slap across the face. Her legs wobbled as alcohol swam through her veins. In Mica's presence, she was suddenly aware she'd consumed one drink too many. "Sorry. I—"

"Hi, Miss Simone! We found your address on the postcard I got in the mail." Right. The postcard she sent in August introducing herself as Hannah's teacher. Hannah beamed, holding out a bedazzled envelope. The little girl stood, hand in hand, with her father, oblivious to the tension between the adults.

Simone straightened her posture and cleared her throat. "Hello, Hannah." She made a valiant effort at faking sobriety. Simone looked over her shoulder to check the state of her house, hoping it didn't look like a frat party with empty wine bottles strewn about. The wine bottles turned out to be the least of her worries. Gale was lighting a joint. Seriously? Pot was absolutely not allowed in her home. This couldn't be happening. Simone flew out of the house, nearly plowing little Hannah over, and slammed the door closed behind her. "Let's have a seat." She motioned to the wicker porch furniture.

Mica pulled his daughter close to his side, his blue eyes emanating dismay. "We shouldn't have just shown up like this. We were out picking up a late-night snack—"

"Ice cream!" Hannah said.

"I should've called first. Excuse us." Mica turned to his daughter. "Miss Simone is busy. C'mon, honey." The smell of weed floated out the open window. She couldn't blame him for leaving.

"But, Daddy," Hannah protested. "We need to give Miss Simone our invitation."

"Another time." Mica marched to his truck, Hannah reluctantly following.

The truck roared to life, and the father-daughter pair was gone as quickly as they had appeared. Simone sank into a heap on the doorstep. As much as she wanted to chase after them and scream for them to come back, she knew it was better for them to leave than to join her drunken party.

The clicking of heels approached from behind. Gale sat down next to her. "Who was the hunk?"

Simone ignored her.

"Too bad he has a kid." Gale flicked the remains of her joint into the chrysanthemums. "You have enough baggage of your own."

Rage roiled inside Simone's gut. In the few hours Gale had been welcomed back into Simone's life, she'd already insulted two people she cared about. "Get out," Simone murmured.

"What did you just say?"

"You heard me." Simone couldn't take one more minute of Gale's narcissism. "I can't believe you were smoking pot in my house."

Gale crossed her arms. "Stop acting like a goody-goody. You're a criminal hiding out in a small town."

Simone stood and jutted her index finger to the street. "Leave! Stay out of my life!"

"You don't mean that. Sisters for life, remember?" Simone glared at her, making her intentions clear she wasn't backing down. "Where am I supposed to go? I can't drive like this. Unlike some people, I don't drive drunk."

Nausea rolled through Simone's body. She wasn't sure if it was from the wine or the cheap shot. Gale was trying to play on Simone's guilty conscience. *I am a grown woman. I will no longer be manipulated by Gale.* She chose to ignore the comment about driving drunk and considered the current situation.

Gale had consumed just as much wine as Simone had, if not more. Plus, she was high on marijuana. Gale was right. She couldn't drive. How did Gale's problems always become Simone's?

She marched into the house and grabbed Gale's suitcase, Gale following behind. "You can walk to Willows B & B. Go two blocks north, take a right at the Stop sign, then take a left at the next Stop sign. That's Main Street. Head north another block or two. It will be on your left."

"How do you expect me to remember that? What is your problem anyway? I can't believe you're just throwing me out on the street. I'll call a cab."

Simone rolled the suitcase to Gale. When Gale didn't reach for it, Simone pushed it out the door. "I'm sure you can find Main Street. You'll sober up on your walk." Simone needed to stand her ground. She didn't care how Gale got to Willows. She just wanted her to go away.

Gale stomped out, flinging expletives at Simone as she dragged her suitcase behind her.

Simone wanted to feel proud of herself for standing up to Gale, but she felt more like a hypocrite. They'd been having a fun time. Both of them had been drinking. She'd probably overreacted.

Simone leaned over the porch railing sucking in fresh air. MJ and Jade would never find themselves in this position.

They were genuinely good people. Her stomach lurched, emptying its contents onto her pretty flower garden. She stared into the mess, waiting for her stomach to settle, recognizing irony in the situation. The picture before her was the story of her life. She had worked so hard to create something beautiful, but in the end, she destroyed it all with the ugliness inside her. How poetic.

She was giving way to self-pity again. But her life really was loathsome. Maybe she was just hiding out in this small town, as Gale had said. She clung to dignity by a thread that frayed under the slightest pressure—because she wasn't inherently good like her friends.

"Everything okay over there?" Pearl called out from the neighboring porch. Simone cowered under Pearl's sympathetic gaze. How foolish she must appear. Pearl scurried over, her slippers swishing across the wooden porch floor. Wiry arms wrapped around Simone's waist, pulling her to an upright position. "Let's get you cleaned up."

Simone tucked her face away from Pearl's, sparing her the wretched smell of alcohol and vomit as much as possible. "What about your friends? Is your Bible study over?"

"My friends can manage just fine without me. We were wrapping things up anyway."

Pearl helped Simone to the kitchen and poured a glass of water. "Drink this."

Simone's stomach turned. She pushed the glass away. "I'm not thirsty."

"You *will* drink this. I know you know how to drink."

Simone cocked an eyebrow at her elderly friend. She sipped the water. "That was a low blow, Miss Pearl."

"Let's get you to bed."

Simone sat obediently on the edge of her bed as Pearl scrubbed her face and pulled a clean shirt over her head. The image of Mica's look of disdain haunted her memory. Simone licked her lips, tasting salty tears that had slipped down her face. "I've really made a mess of things."

"Shh. We can talk in the morning. For now, you just sleep." Pearl pulled back the covers and ordered Simone to lie down. Pearl sat on a chair next to the bed, her presence like a ray of sunshine after a storm. Pearl bent down and kissed Simone's forehead tenderly. She smelled of apple cinnamon tea. "Now I lay me down to sleep," Pearl whispered. "I pray, dear Lord, my soul you'll keep. The angels watch me through the night and wake me with the morning light. In Jesus's name, amen."

Simone nestled under the covers, basking in the tenderness of Pearl's presence. The prayer settled over her like a warm blanket. She closed her eyes, floating toward unconsciousness with an unfamiliar notion everything would be okay.

Early the next morning, the aroma of toast wafted into Simone's bedroom. Had Pearl stayed the whole night? Simone dragged her ragged self out of bed, pulled on some clothes, and ambled into the kitchen. Pearl, all dressed up in her Sunday best, was at the table drinking a cup of tea and nibbling on toast. The smell made her queasy.

"Good morning, sunshine."

How did this elderly lady always manage to be so chipper?

Simone slid onto a chair next to her friend. "Sorry about last night." She felt shame color her cheeks.

"I forgive you. Not another word about it."

"Did you stay here all night?"

"I went home after you zonked out. Figured I'd come back this morning to check on you." Pearl scooted her chair back and began fixing Simone's breakfast.

"You don't have to wait on me. I don't deserve it. Especially after the way I let Gale treat you."

Pearl didn't say anything. She heated water for tea and buttered a slice of toast.

"I knew Gale was trouble. I shouldn't have let her into my life again."

"You share a history. There's comfort in that."

"Not a good history. I just wanted to let go and have fun for a night. Sometimes I crave a break from being strong and independent. I'm sick of trying to be perfect all the time. It's exhausting … and lonely. I don't identify with the Wellses, and I don't want to be like them anyway. But I don't quite fit the mold with MJ and Jade either."

"You don't have to be perfect."

"But I do. Look what happened when I let loose for just one night. I made a mess of my whole life. Sometimes I just don't feel cut out for this have-it-all-together kind of life."

"That's a heavy burden you carry on your shoulders. Giving the impression you lead a picture-perfect life."

"Tell me about it." Simone closed her eyes, wishing she could erase last night's fiasco.

Pearl set Simone's breakfast on the table. "Come to church with me this morning."

Simone laughed at the prospect. "Either I've fooled you into believing I belong in this picture-perfect life, or you think I'm so bad off I'm in need of a savior."

Pearl shook her head. "I just want you to meet a friend of mine."

"Are you trying to set me up again? If that's the case, then, no thank you. I went on a date with that dude, Walter, you set me up with. Did you know he lives with his mother? And he's forty?"

Pearl cringed a bit. "Sorry about that. This *dude* is a good one. I promise. You did say you're lonely."

"I did say that, didn't I? You've always been a good listener." Simone sipped her tea. The warm liquid was both comforting and delicious. "Maybe another time. I'm sure no guy would find a hangover attractive."

"Oh, he'd see straight through that hangover to the beauty that's in here." Pearl tapped an arthritic finger over Simone's heart.

"Now that was sweet." Simone's eyes welled with tears. More than anything, she wanted to find someone who saw her for who she really was and loved her despite her past. Someone who cared for her when the façade of perfection crumbled away, revealing the vulnerable little girl lying hidden beneath. A tear slid down Simone's cheek. She wiped it with the back of her hand. "I'll think about it, Pearl. But not today." She propped her elbows on the table and rested her chin on her hands. "Tell Ethel and Hazel I'm sorry about last night."

"I'll tell them." Pearl grabbed a napkin from the basket on the middle of the table and blotted the wetness from Simone's cheeks and nose. "You're a hot mess, indeed."

Simone laughed—a hiccup kind of sound. "A hot mess? You're the hippest ninety-year-old I know."

Pearl winked. "I have satellite TV." She covered Simone's hand with her own. "I'll tell my friend you'll see him in church next week. Now eat your toast."

"Thanks Pearl. Wait … what? Not next week."

Pearl got up and left the house, ignoring Simone's protests.

Chapter Seven

As Gale feasted on decadent homemade scones, fresh fruit, and almost-as-good-as-Starbucks coffee at Willows B & B, she contemplated her tactic to convince Simone to lend her money and/or a place to stay. Helping a sister out was the least Simone could do after freeloading off her family for years. She wouldn't have a cutesy little hole-in-the-wall in this Podunk town without her family's assistance. Gale planned to corner her this morning at school where she wouldn't dare cause a scene.

"Miss Wells?" The owner of Willows topped off Gale's coffee.

"Yes?" She had a bad feeling about the way the middle-aged lady said her name.

"I'd like you to … settle up before you go out this morning. You're welcome to stay longer, but I do need a credit card number. We ask that of all our guests."

Gale wasn't sure her card had sufficient funds. "Sure. Of course. Right after breakfast."

The woman smiled and returned to the kitchen.

Gale got lucky the first night she'd arrived when the teenage girl with the purple hair opened the door. The girl only let her stay after Gale handed her a couple joints. Bribes had never worked well for Simone. Simone responded better to intimidation.

Unfortunately, Simone was more recalcitrant this time around. No worries. Gale was up for the challenge. Simone was the one person Gale could think of to cough up ten thousand dollars, plus an extra two grand to cover interest, for Gale to buy back her father's collectible coin from Mr. Conners. Gale had stolen—borrowed—the coin from her father's study sixty-four days ago and sold it to Mr. Conners under agreement she'd buy it back. With interest doubling every thirty days, she didn't have time to try buddying up to Simone.

Gale hated stealing from her father, but it wasn't like she'd had many options. Her credit history was destroyed, and her parents had pretty much disowned her for stealing from them on multiple occasions, which meant an under-the-table loan had been the only way to go. She'd needed to pay Slayer the ten thousand dollars before he—

She didn't want to consider how he would've punished her for not paying up. Her hands shook just thinking about Slayer. The teardrop tattoo under his left eye was enough to scare her into submission. She set her coffee mug on a saucer, spilling a bit of its contents. She'd never mess with a big-time dealer again. Way too risky.

Lately, she'd resorted to doctor visits where she made up stories about car accident injuries and begged for Oxycodone prescriptions. She couldn't keep up this gig much longer. Her tolerance had notably increased, and the cravings were brutal. Plus, the drug was expensive. She'd tried to quit several times, but withdrawal was unbearable.

Ideally, she'd buy back her dad's coin and return it, get clean, land an honest job, and begin rebuilding her credit score. A girl could dream.

The teenybopper began clearing the dining table. "You made me a celebrity at school," she whispered.

"Don't go around telling people where you got it." The last thing she needed was a bunch of punk kids following her around.

"I won't. Are you done with the scones?"

Gale nodded. "Are you Willow?"

"No. I'm Frankie. Short for Francine."

Gale pointed toward the kitchen. "Is she Willow?"

"That's Alice. To answer your next question, I'm not related to her. Everyone asks me that." She took a bite of a scone. "There is no Willow."

"Well, there aren't any willow trees around, so—"

Frankie rolled her eyes. "Don't ask me. I just work here. I think Alice likes willow trees. Why do you care anyway?"

Gale shrugged. "Just curious." Of course, a business owner way out in the boonies wouldn't know anything about branding. The sign out front had a floral bouquet on it. Nothing to do with willow trees or a bed and breakfast. An imaginary lightbulb turned on over Gale's head. "Hey, do you know if Alice is hiring?"

Frankie looked Gale up and down. "Who wants to know?"

Alice came back out in the dining room. "Did I hear my name?"

Gale stood. "I'm wondering if you're hiring. I can help you with branding—your website, that sign out front—"

"What's wrong with my sign? Did those hooligans vandalize it again?" Alice opened the front door to check on her sign.

"No." Although a little vandalism wouldn't make it any worse. "I have suggestions for improvements."

Alice crossed her arms and furrowed her brow.

"It would help me pay for my stay. I could use the work." The woman didn't look too keen on the idea. "Your establishment is beautiful. I've never slept so well. I would be honored to work at such a fine ..." Gale searched for an appropriate word to describe the place.

Alice chuckled. "You can stop. It's not a royal palace. My mission is to create a homey feel while keeping it

73

affordable. I cater to friends and family of the community more than to honeymooners or high-end business folks." She squinted at Gale. "Do I know you?"

Perhaps she recognized Gale's face from a news story that was better not to recall. "I don't believe we've met. I'm Gale Wells."

"Alice Flores." They shook hands. "Okay, Gale. You're hired."

"Oh, thank you, thank you." That was surprisingly easy.

"How long do you plan to be in town?"

"I'm not sure." Indefinitely. She didn't have anywhere to go. She'd been fired from her lame job at the bank for missed shifts. Without steady income, she couldn't pay rent and lost her apartment. Her BMW could be repossessed any day. Her heart started palpitating. "Can we play it by ear? I'll earn my keep as long as I stay."

"I'd prefer a tentative timeline, but ... it's been a little slow lately. As long as I have a vacant room, you can stay. Deal?"

A weight lifted off Gale's chest. "Deal."

"You can start today."

"Ooh. I'm busy today. I'll start tomorrow." She moved toward the front door, ready to make a hasty exit. "Thank you so much. This means the world to me. Bye, now."

Gale had seen online the school day began at eight thirty. She had fifteen minutes to find the kindergarten rooms. She walked purposefully down the corridor, the tapping of her high heels echoing through the hallways. She nodded greetings to the teachers and staff, who cast questioning glances her way. Schools were so strict with their visitor policies these days. It seemed everybody recognized she didn't belong, but she looked too polished and professional to be suspect.

The kindergarten pod was easy to locate. Their rooms were the most colorful and had the most amateur artwork pinned to the walls. She found the door with the name "Miss Simone" inscribed on a paper apple. Simone was kneeling, tying the shoe of a little girl with blonde hair. By the smile on her face, Simone looked like she enjoyed working with these rug rats. The girl thanked Simone with a hug.

Something was familiar about the kid. Gale propped a hand on her hip. Oh yeah, she was the little girl who stopped by the house Saturday night with her hunky dad. How interesting and scandalous.

"Hello, there," Gale crooned. "If it isn't your little friend from the other night." Simone's face changed from rosy to chalk white. "Miss Simone, you're looking a little pale." She leaned in and whispered—loud enough for the little punkin' to hear, "Do you think you might be pregnant?" Gale winked at the kid.

Simone's eyes narrowed. "No. I surely am not."

It was too easy to get under Simone's skin. "Why so upset? Don't you like children?"

Simone told her student to hang up her backpack, then led Gale into the hallway, just outside the classroom door. "What do you want, Gale?"

Gale dropped the act. "I need some help. Just like you needed help a few years back. Remember how my family helped you so generously? You owe me."

Simone was speechless. Anger blazed from her eyes.

"See? You can't deny it."

"I don't owe you anything. Get out of here. Before I kick you out." Simone smiled at students as they entered her classroom.

Gale cleared her throat, checking to make sure nobody over three feet tall was in earshot. "Can you lend me some money? Please? We are sisters after all. I promise I'll pay you back."

"No. I told you to stay out of my life." She turned to go back in the room.

Gale grabbed Simone's wrist. "I always had your back. You can do this one favor for me. I need twelve thousand dollars." She let go of Simone's wrist, realizing she was losing her cool. "Please."

Simone laughed sarcastically. "You had my back? Is that how you remember it?" She shook her head. "You never wanted to be my sister. You didn't come here to make amends. You just want to use me, and I refuse to play any part in your escapades anymore. You're on your own. Now, if you'll excuse me, I have a class to attend to." She stomped into the classroom.

Gale marched down the hallway and out of the building. *The ungrateful street rat. She thinks she's grown a backbone now that she has a college degree. It's time to put her back in her place.* Gale cursed the blinding sun and stopped to dig her sunglasses out of her purse. It's not like she'd expected Simone to agree to handing over money, but neither had she expected Simone to be so obstinate. Back in the day, when Gale told Simone to jump, Simone would ask, "How high?" She donned her sunglasses and propped a cigarette between her lips.

"No smoking on school grounds, ma'am." A man approached her, wagging a finger at her. He was dressed in jeans, a T-shirt, and a baseball cap. He hardly looked authoritative.

"Look, I'm having a really bad day. So, if you'll just mind your own business and allow me to enjoy this little hit of nicotine, I'd appreciate it." She lit the cigarette and inhaled, feeling her nerves calm.

"That's not good."

"What? Are you going to lecture me on the consequences of smoking? Save your breath. I've heard it all."

The man chuckled. "You look like an intelligent woman. I assume you've been educated on the risks of smoking.

What I meant was, it's not good you're already having a bad day at only eight thirty in the morning. That's quite unfortunate." He sighed. "I would know. I've been there."

This guy wasn't so bad. "Sorry to hear that." She stepped in stride with him as they walked to the parking lot. "I'm Gale Wells."

His eyes widened in recognition. She loved having that effect on people. "Wells, as in Senator Wesley Wells's daughter?"

Gale held up her hands. "Guilty." She had a bit of a reputation as the Minnesota senator's daughter. Some called her *infamous*, while she preferred the term *socialite*.

The man took off his hat and ran his hand through his sandy-blond hair, as if the action would improve his appearance. If he was thinking of hitting on her, the guy didn't stand a chance. Although he was good-looking, she didn't date blue-collar men. "Actually"—she paused, studying his face— "I feel like I recognize you too."

"Oh, I'm no politician. Just a regular guy. A dad dropping off his daughter at school."

She snapped her fingers. "That's it. You're the guy who showed up on Simone's doorstep. I was hanging out at her place when you stopped by Saturday night. She hadn't mentioned she was dating anyone."

The man fidgeted with his hat. "Oh. I'm not dating her. She's Hannah's teacher."

Gale dramatically clapped a hand to her chest. "Well, that makes more sense. I mean, Simone isn't really the maternal type. I was surprised she'd date someone with a kid."

The guy wrinkled his brow. "She's really great with her students."

Gale touched his arm. "Yes, she's a fabulous teacher. Such a shame she isn't interested in having kids of her own." Gale leaned in and whispered, "You know, having grown up in foster care and everything. She wouldn't be the best influence since she didn't always have the greatest role models."

The hunky dad shook his head in bewilderment, exactly the reaction Gale had been going for. "I didn't know her personal history. That's none of my business."

Gale covered her mouth with her hand. "Maybe I shouldn't have said anything."

The guy put his hat on and fished keys out of his pocket. "I need to get to work. It was nice meeting you, Miss Wells."

Gale flashed her brightest smile. "You can call me Gale. It was nice meeting you too. I didn't catch your name."

He was distracted—probably thinking about the chick with a troubled past teaching his precious daughter. "Um, it's Mica." He walked away and climbed into a truck with the words "Stark Homes" printed across the side.

Pleased with herself, Gale settled behind the wheel of her BMW. That exchange couldn't have gone any better if she had planned it. Once Simone realized Mica had been informed about her precarious past, she would know Gale meant business. Simone would be putty in her hands. Just like the good old days.

Chapter Eight

The week flew by with Mica working late into the evening hours on the lakeside house. After school, Hannah kept busy playing in her future bedroom. He had set up a temporary table and chairs using turned-over five-gallon paint buckets and a sheet of leftover sheetrock in her room. She drew pictures, looked at books, and hosted imaginary tea parties. Sometimes she joined Mica in whatever room he was working on and talked his ear off.

On Friday, Mica decided to call it a night earlier than usual. He and Hannah had made it a tradition to grill on Friday nights, weather permitting. Adam and his family usually joined them. Adam had given him the idea to start the tradition in the first place. He'd told Mica traditions were especially important to children who had lost a parent because they provided a sense of stability. Adam and his wife, Brooke, had read a couple books about loss after Josie died hoping to help Mica out of his depression. Mica didn't know how he would've survived the last year without their friendship.

Mica packed up his toolbox. "Ready to go, Hannah?"

She zipped her backpack and skipped to the front door. "Can we have steak tonight?"

Mica laughed. "Steak? Since when do you like steak?"

Hannah shrugged. "I never tried it."

"I'll be grilling the usual hot dogs and brats tonight."

"Steak is fancier."

"True." Mica and Hannah stepped onto the front porch, and Mica locked the door.

Mica helped Hannah into the truck. As she worked on getting buckled, he placed his toolbox under her feet to serve as a footrest. Once she was settled, he kissed her on the cheek and admired her sweet little face. "You are growing up so fast." He shook his head, wondering where she got the idea she was too mature for hot dogs.

She gave him a toothy grin, beaming with pride.

He ruffled her hair. "Okay, young lady. Let's go buy some juicy steaks to put on the grill."

"Yay!" Hannah raised her arms in the air in a touchdown cheer.

Simone parked her car in the apartment lot and drew in a shaky breath. She turned the invitation over in her hands, carefully inspecting the kindergarten handwriting—for the hundredth time—to be sure she'd read the details correctly.

Come to our BBQ Friday night.

She exhaled. Yes, this was Friday night. Mica had signed his own name.

Simone had been surprised by the invitation when Hannah had handed it to her Monday morning. Mica was inviting her to hang out after the disaster she'd been the last time he'd seen her? She thought he would never want to lay eyes on her again. She worried he might even transfer Hannah to another class. Surely Simone wasn't a proper role model for Hannah.

After much contemplation, she considered the gesture to be a token of forgiveness for her despicable behavior. It was sweet. He must've realized it had been inappropriate for him and his daughter to drop in on her unannounced on a weekend.

She hadn't planned to go to the barbeque. Rather, she'd intended to keep as much distance from this precious family as possible before she had another chance to offend or hurt them. But as the week went on and she witnessed Hannah's burgeoning excitement as the barbeque approached, she just couldn't let the child down.

Simone craned her neck to look in the rearview mirror to touch up her lipstick. She smoothed back a wisp of windblown hair that had escaped the clip fastened at the side of her head. She skimmed over the invitation again knowing full well she was at the right place at the right time. *Enough stalling.* From the backseat, she grabbed the soft-sided cooler containing a pan of brownies and a pitcher of lemonade, and she exited the comfort of her car.

The setting sun splashed peach-colored light across a sky dappled with clouds. Yellow-tipped leaves rustled in a cool, gentle breeze. Simone pulled her cardigan sweater closed and was glad she'd decided to wear the sweater and jeans instead of the knee-length dress she'd initially donned. Not only was she warmer in this ensemble, but she also appeared more casual, as if she were just stopping by. Less like she'd been planning her outfit, anticipating Mica's reaction to her arrival, and rehearsing her greeting all week. She'd come to respect Mica since learning of his widowerhood. Being thrust into single parenthood couldn't be easy, but he'd been rising to the challenge. His love for Hannah was obvious. When she'd seen them swimming at the pool, Mica had been laughing and playing as boisterously as the five-year-old. Simone had been so wrong about him in the beginning. Mica was a loving family man. The kind of man she hoped to fall in love with someday.

She walked through the parking lot and past the pool area to a grassy courtyard encircled by the apartment buildings. Kids played on playground equipment and dog owners walked their pets on a pathway winding around the property. Simone felt more like she was at a park than an apartment complex. A picnic table was situated under the shade of an oak tree with people laying out a tablecloth. A man attended the nearby grill. Taking a deep breath, she stepped in the direction of the picnic area.

Her knees weakened as she crossed the grassy open space, doubts gathering in her mind. Maybe she should have declined the invitation. Was it too late to turn around? Had she even RSVP'd? She had told Hannah she would come, but she hadn't confirmed with Mica.

She slowed her pace. Maybe they hadn't seen her yet. She could sneak back to her car. On Monday, she could tell Hannah she'd misplaced the invitation. But Hannah would be disappointed if she didn't show up, and that little girl didn't deserve any more heartbreaks in her life. Not showing up wasn't an option.

She took a deep breath and continued walking. What should her opening line to Mica be? *Thanks for inviting me? Sorry I made a fool of myself Saturday night?*

"Miss Simone!" Hannah had spotted her and was running to her from the picnic area. Her blonde hair was pulled back into a neat French braid. She wore a denim jacket over a pink T-shirt, jeans, and pink cowgirl boots. She wrapped her arms around Simone's waist. "You came! I'm so happy you came!"

Too late to turn around now, Simone hugged Hannah back as best she could with one free arm. "Thank you for inviting me. I love picnics. And I adore your outfit."

Delighted, Hannah twirled, showing off her ensemble. "Brooke gave it to me." Hannah held Simone's hand, leading her over to the picnic area while chattering on about friends named Adam and Brooke and Sadie and Gigi. The tangy aroma of grilled meat filled her senses as they approached the grill. Simone's mouth watered in response.

"Daddy, look who came!"

Mica stood next to the grill, a pair of tongs in his right hand and a can of Mountain Dew in his left hand. His face held the look of pure, utter shock. He didn't smile or offer a greeting of any kind. He appeared to be frozen—like a wax figure in a museum.

Oh ... Mica hadn't intended for her to receive the invitation. Simone looked for a rock to crawl under. "Sorry," she mumbled. "I thought ... I mean ... Hannah gave me an invitation—"

"I'm Brooke Calhoun." A woman paused from setting the table and shook Simone's hand. "This is my husband, Adam, and our daughters Gigi and Sadie are somewhere around here." She shielded her eyes from the sun with her hand, looking out toward the playground. "There they are." Two little girls around Hannah's age took turns crossing the monkey bars. "Sit down. Join us." She took the cooler from Simone and gestured for her to be seated.

Adam, whom Simone had briefly met out at the house being built, looked about as puzzled and skeptical as Mica did, which was unsettling at best.

"Maybe I should be going." Simone looked over at her car wistfully.

"What did you bring, Miss Simone? Can I see?" Hannah was kneeling on the picnic bench, hunched over Simone's cooler.

Simone looked at Mica. His ocean-blue eyes sparkled in the sunlight. He shrugged. "You're welcome to stay." He turned his attention back to the grill.

Not the most heartfelt invitation she'd ever received, but at least she no longer felt like a party crasher. She sat down next to Hannah at the picnic table. "You can unzip the cooler. I brought a pitcher of lemonade and caramel brownies for dessert."

Hannah's eyes widened, and she licked her lips. "Yummy! Can I have one now?"

Simone looked to Mica to answer that question. He had his back turned to Simone and the others, all attention on flipping the sizzling meat. "You don't want to ruin your appetite. We'll save the brownies for dessert."

Hannah pouted. "I'm gonna play with Gigi and Sadie." She ran off to the playground, leaving Simone alone with the adults.

"So how do you know Mica and Hannah?" Brooke asked before popping a chip into her mouth.

"I'm Hannah's teacher."

Brooke raised her eyebrows. "Oh, yes. Miss Simone."

Uh-oh. Brooke must have heard stories about her. All good she hoped ... yet sincerely doubted. "That's me." She forced a smile.

"Hannah talks about you all the time." Brooke's friendly smile appeared genuine. Simone relaxed a bit. "She adores you, and she was just telling me she wants to be a teacher when she grows up."

Simone's heart filled with happiness—and relief—Hannah had been telling the stories, not Mica. The two ladies watched Hannah and Brooke's girls playing over at the playground. They were climbing up the steps to the slide, their fists full of pebbles they'd scooped up from the playground. "That was sweet of Hannah to say. The feelings are mutual. I admit Hannah is my favorite student this year. She gives me a hug first thing every morning." Simone beamed inside. "It's a great way to start my day."

The girls gathered at the top of the slide and—on the count of three—pitched their handfuls of pebbles down the slide, watching them cascade down in a rumbling deluge. At the finish, they clapped with glee. Brooke laughed, delicate lines creasing at the corners of her eyes. "Why do kids always do that?"

"The meat is done," Mica announced gruffly. Simone jumped at the sound of his voice.

Clearly, Simone wasn't welcome here. Mica had hardly acknowledged her presence except by turning his back to her. She stood, avoiding eye contact with everyone. "I'd better be going." How foolish of her to come. She should have known the invitation was only from Hannah. Mica despised her after seeing her sloppy drunk. He probably thought she spent every weekend drinking and smoking. If only Gale hadn't stormed back into her life.

She set the pan on the table. "I'll leave the brownies." Her voice was shaky, humiliation causing her to tear up.

Hannah came running up. "Miss Simone, Daddy made you a fancy steak. Brooke likes steak." She smiled proudly up at Simone, shielding her eyes from the sun.

An incredulous laugh escaped Mica. "So that's what this is about? Hannah, I thought the steak was for you."

Hannah scrunched up her nose. "I don't eat steak. I'm a kid!"

Tension drained from the air as laughter broke out from all present, including Mica. He shook his head and pointed the spatula at his daughter. "You're a clever little girl."

Hannah did a twirl, glowing under the attention. "Miss Simone says I'm important."

"Aw." Brooke sighed. "That's so sweet."

Mica rolled his eyes, chuckling. "Simone, please stay and have dinner with us." It seemed almost painful for him to look at her. She knew he'd invited her only to please Hannah.

Although she still wanted to bolt, she accepted the invitation for Hannah's sake. She would eat and then run. "Thank you, Mica," she said, looking directly into his eyes, wanting him to see she knew she hadn't earned his trust, and she was deeply sorry about the other night.

He held her gaze for a beat. So many emotions seemed buried behind those eyes. Hurt. Sympathy. Caution. She looked away. She had the impression he wanted to hate her but was struggling to follow through. "I hope you like steak," he said, transferring a slab of meat from the grill to a plastic plate.

"You're not vegetarian, are you?" Adam piped in. "I mean, it's fine if you are. Brooke made pasta salad, and we brought some apples and chips." He pointed at the items on the table as he rattled them off.

Simone waved her hand in a dismissive motion as she reclaimed her seat at the table. "I'm not vegetarian. I love steak. Can't remember the last time I had it. I don't cook much. I'm more of a Kraft Macaroni and Cheese girl, although I do enjoy baking."

Brooke began scooping pasta salad onto everyone's plate. "So, tell us more about yourself. Are you from around here?"

Simone nodded. "I grew up in St. Paul. Moved out here when I found the job in Diamond. I didn't have an ideal childhood. I grew up in foster care. My parents lost their rights ... or gave up their rights ... when I was young. I never knew my father, and I last saw my mother when I was four." Simone didn't hide her past. She was an open book to anyone who asked.

The usual moment of silence ensued as her audience digested the news and figured out how to proceed. Simone acted nonchalant about it to put them at ease. "It's okay. I survived the system, and here I am." Simone peeked at Mica out of the corner of her eye to gauge his reaction. He was squirting steak sauce onto his plate and sprinkling salt and pepper onto the meat. Not too shocked.

Brooke and Adam appeared to struggle with the news a bit more, while the children chattered and giggled among themselves. Brooke squeezed Simone's hand. "You not only survived. You went on to earn a college degree. As a social worker, I know the odds were against you. Takes resilience and determination."

Simone was the one at a loss for words now. She'd never received so much kindness from someone she'd just met, aside from Pearl. "Thank you," she managed to say, her voice thick with emotion.

Adam planted his elbows on the wooden table and held out his hands to Gigi on one side of him and Brooke across the table. "Let's pray." Everyone joined hands around the table. Simone followed suit, holding hands with Brooke and Mica and closing her eyes.

As Adam prayed, thanking God for the food, beautiful weather, and friends and family, all she could concentrate on was the sensation of Mica's strong hand gripping hers. His large fingers were calloused, no doubt from the hard work of building homes, yet his hand was gentle as it cradled hers. Quite possibly this man hated her, yet she swore there was a mutual attraction between them. She felt it on her end. She hoped Adam's prayer would go on forever so she could continue to feel the touch of Mica's masculine skin against hers. Unfortunately, Adam wasn't long-winded at all, and as he said "amen," she felt Mica lightly squeeze her hand and stroke his thumb over hers before releasing it. She looked at him, her heart fluttering in her chest, but he gave no indication he'd felt anything romantic for her. He dove into his food as if it were his last meal.

She nibbled at her food, scrutinizing the hand-squeezing, thumb-stroking thing in her mind. Maybe that's just what people did after they held hands and prayed. Maybe they squeezed each other's hands as a gesture of agreement or something. Maybe he hadn't stroked her thumb. Maybe he'd just brushed her thumb as he let go of her hand. She was acting childish. She poured herself some lemonade and gulped it down. The outdoor temperature was suddenly feeling hot.

The ladies packed up the picnic while Mica and Adam pushed the kids on swings. Mica watched Simone interact effortlessly with Brooke. They acted like old friends, not women who had just met an hour earlier. Simone remained a puzzle to him. Sometimes he couldn't stand her. Other times, he wanted to take her in his arms and—

"She's nice," Adam said.

"What?" Mica turned to Adam. "Who's nice?"

Adam chuckled. "You know who I'm talking about." He nodded his head in Simone's direction.

Mica shook his head. "Don't be fooled. She's got claws."

Adam dismissed the comment with a wave of his hand. "She's as harmless as a kitten."

"This is the first time she hasn't yelled at me for being a screw-up. Just wait. It'll happen sooner or later. She can't keep up this nice act for long."

Adam shrugged. "You are kind of a screw-up." His smile told Mica he was at least partially kidding. "Before tonight, you had me believing she was evil, but I think she's good for you."

"Higher, Daddy!" Hannah squealed from her swing. "High like Gigi and Sadie."

"You want to go high?"

"Yes!" Hannah yelled, giggling.

"Really high?" Mica pulled the swing back as far as it would go, holding it over his head. Hannah's feet dangled in the air just above his face. "Hold on tight!" He ran forward, under the swing, calling, "Underdog!" Hannah expelled an ear-piercing squeal of delight.

Mica came around to the back of the swings again. He jabbed Adam in the ribs. "By the way, what was that hand-holding about? We never hold hands when we pray."

Adam broke out in guilty laughter. "I couldn't pass up the opportunity. You sitting right next to Simone. Tension between you two thick enough to cut with a knife." He was laughing so hard he could barely speak. "The look on your face when we all joined hands—that was priceless."

Mica jumped on his friend's back and proceeded to give him a good old-fashioned noogie, rubbing his knuckles on the top of Adam's head.

Adam tried to fend him off. "C'mon, man. You should be thanking me for it."

Mica shoved Adam away playfully. "You need to mind your own business."

"Not a chance. I wouldn't be a good friend if I did. You need to ask that girl on a proper date."

Mica looked over at Simone. She sat cross-legged on the bench, her sweater blowing open in the breeze, revealing a fitted shirt hugging perfect curves. She was deep in conversation with Brooke, yet she must have sensed his gaze because she looked over at him. Her lips curved into a sweet smile, and she winked at him. He waved, feeling a surge of passion course through him.

Adam clapped him on the back. "You're welcome, bro."

Simone hugged Brooke and began to gather her belongings. Mica steadied Hannah's swing. "Looks like Miss Simone is heading out. Let's tell her good-bye."

Hannah ran to Simone, who in turn crouched and met her with open arms. Then Hannah rejoined her friends at the swings. Mica walked Simone to her car, their pace slow. He had hardly said a word to her all evening, and he needed to let her know he was glad she came.

"I had fun tonight," she said. "Even though you didn't want me here." She nudged him with her elbow and grinned.

"I'm really sorry about that. I did want you here. I mean—"

"You mean before last Saturday night."

Mica sighed. No use denying it. "Yes, but I shouldn't have judged you. I don't even know why I got angry. You can do whatever you want on Saturday nights. That's none of my business." They reached Simone's car, but Mica wasn't ready to end the conversation. He wanted to make things right.

"Were you angry because you thought you could trust me?" She displayed a vulnerable expression. "But then I looked like somebody you couldn't trust after all?"

Mica nodded. "That about sums it up."

Simone's eyes glimmered in the fading light. "I'm not gonna lie, Mica. I've got baggage. As hard as I try to leave it in the past, it … it's still a part of what makes me who I am. Sure, I've overcome a lot, met some really great people, have some really great memories. But the ugly stuff … I mean, you don't even want to know." She sniffed and looked away.

Oh no. She was crying again. A weight settled on his heart. He could relate to hurt and sadness. He prayed she hadn't suffered neglect or abuse. He was beginning to understand why she was so protective of Hannah. She probably had a hyper-sensitivity to signs of neglect. "I'm sorry, Simone." He wrapped his arms around her, hugging her to his chest. He was doing it again. He was hugging his daughter's teacher again. What was wrong with him? But before he could pull away, she dropped her cooler on the concrete, circled her arms around him, and hugged him back.

With her head resting against his chest and her delicate hands linked at the small of his back, he could hardly form a coherent thought. But he fought through the fog of desire to finish what he had to say. He lowered his head so that his lips were less than an inch from her ear. "I trust you, Simone."

Her body stiffened. She stepped back, wiping tears from her face and drying her hands on her jeans. She cleared her throat. "Thanks again for inviting me." Her face was devoid of the vulnerability she'd displayed mere seconds earlier. She held out her hand as if he were supposed to shake it.

"What?" They had just shared an intimate moment, and now he was supposed to shake her hand? Not that he had expected a kiss. But shaking hands seemed a bit impersonal at this point. "Did I say something wrong?"

"I just need to get going. Thanks again." She opened her car door and slid behind the wheel without saying another word. She drove off leaving Mica more confused than ever. Just when he thought he was connecting with her, she turned cold.

Simone stopped at the grocery store on her way home from the picnic and practically cleared out the entire baking aisle. It took her two trips to lug all the brown bags into her house. Baking would help her relax and keep her mind off Mica. At least she hoped so. Around midnight, she sat down on her couch with a plate piled with monster cookies. Unfortunately, she didn't have an appetite, and she was still thinking about Mica.

She had felt so good in his arms. Good in a way she'd never experienced with anyone before. There was a feeling of security and protection from him, which eased her sadness, as if he cared for her. Thing was, he didn't really know her. He didn't know about the ugliness that shaped her past. Sure, he knew she'd been a foster kid, but he didn't know she'd stolen money as a child or lied to get out of trouble. He didn't know how weak she was, being manipulated by Gale.

In the past, she'd claimed innocence when she'd been caught stealing or lying. She stole food from the store because she was hungry. She lied to the school secretary about being late because admitting her foster parents wouldn't give her a ride to school would have resulted in a beating by the foster parents. Despite being true, were those just poor excuses for bad behavior? When she really examined herself, she realized she hadn't known right from wrong. She didn't know if she'd been a good kid or a bad kid. She hadn't known what normal looked like. The more she saw normal, as she did tonight with Mica and his friends, the further she felt from it. Those people were happy and honest, with nothing to hide. They spent their Friday nights talking and playing games and sharing food. Whereas Simone, when she let her hair down, drank wine by the bottle and ended up regretful and barfing in the chrysanthemums.

And she harbored a secret that could land her in jail.

Simone stretched out on the couch and laid her head on a throw pillow. The living room was dark except for a glow of light coming from the kitchen. She wished she could be like Mica and Brooke and Adam. She longed to live in their lovely world of picnics and carefree laughter. But as long as her past followed her like a dark shadow, she couldn't survive in their world. She didn't know when she might sink back into the shadow, when it would envelop her and pull her into the dismal life she'd tried desperately to leave behind. But she was becoming weary running from the darkness. She feared she might slip back into it.

Which is exactly why Mica shouldn't trust her.

Simone woke to sirens blaring outside her window. She sat up, rubbing a kink in her neck, a consequence of falling asleep on the couch. Squinting against the sunlight pouring through the curtains, she made her way to the window.

An ambulance was outside Pearl's house. An icy fear ran down her spine. She shivered. Pearl's petite body was lying on a stretcher, being wheeled into the back of the ambulance. A man in uniform was pumping his hands on Pearl's chest while a second man in uniform held an oxygen bag over her mouth and nose.

"Pearl!" Simone yelled, running down the front steps and across the lawn. The dewy grass was cold and wet under the soles of her feet. "Wait! I need to see Pearl."

A medic waved Simone away. "There's no time. We need to get her to Diamond Hospital. Stay back." He slammed shut the ambulance doors, raced to the driver's seat, and drove off with Pearl in the back.

Frantic, Simone looked at the crowd of onlookers. "What happened? Someone tell me what happened!"

A lady wearing a tank top and spandex tights stepped forward. "I was running by and saw her lying on the ground. She must've been working in her garden." She pointed to a trowel lying on the dirt. "I called out to her and shook her shoulder. She was unconscious so I dialed 9-1-1." The woman hugged her arms to her waist.

"I gotta go." Simone dashed into her house, stepped into shoes, and grabbed her purse. She should notify Pearl's family.

She ran over and let herself into Pearl's house. The lingering aroma of toast and cinnamon tea hung in the air. Simone stood in the middle of the living room, panicked, trying to think of where a ninety-year-old woman without a cell phone would keep a list of contacts. A rolodex? An address book? Simone went into the kitchen, scanning every surface. She spotted Pearl's list of emergency contacts written on stationery, hanging on her fridge. Simone located the number for Pearl's daughter Rose and dialed it from Pearl's push-button phone. A woman answered immediately, and Simone told her the bad news. Rose said she could be at the hospital in half an hour.

Simone scanned the phone list again, spotting Ethel's and Hazel's numbers. She called them as well. They promised to get on their knees immediately, which Simone assumed to mean they would pray for Pearl. God—if He existed—surely would honor the prayers of those dear ladies. They were as faithful to God as Pearl was, with their weekly Bible studies and loyal church attendance.

With prayers in the making and Pearl's family en route, she got in her car and raced to the hospital.

The emergency room was eerily quiet. She'd never had reason to visit an ER before but had imagined them to be bustling with bloodied and moaning patients like on TV and in movies. Of course, a Sunday morning in the ER might be quiet. Nevertheless, Simone struggled to get news of Pearl's condition.

"No, I'm not family, but I'm her next-door neighbor," Simone explained to the man in scrubs behind the desk. "We're super close. She's *like* family to me."

The guy shook his head. "I'm sorry. I can only give information to a legit relative."

Frustrated, Simone paced to the bank of windows overlooking the parking lot, waiting for Rose to arrive. She had no idea what Rose looked like but imagined her to be an older, thin black woman. Simone had become extremely close to Pearl yet had never met her daughter or even seen a photograph of her. Pearl spoke fondly of her daughter, yet Rose rarely visited her mother. There was a history there Pearl wasn't forthcoming about.

Simone gnawed at her fingernails. *Hang in there, Pearl. You've got to make it through this.* She stared out the window at the nearly desolate parking lot. She checked her watch. Rose should arrive soon. Finally, a car pulled up, dispensing a neatly dressed elderly woman with white hair and fair skin—couldn't be Pearl's daughter.

The woman from the parking lot walked to the check-in desk. "I'm here to see Pearl Jones."

Simone's ears perked up.

"Are you family?" he asked.

The lady cleared her throat and straightened her shoulders. "I'm her daughter."

Simone stood.

The guy cocked his head, considering her answer. He leaned close to the lady and whispered something. The guy and lady simultaneously looked at Simone.

"Simone?" the lady asked.

She nodded. "Are you Rose?"

"Yes." Rose closed the distance between herself and Simone, pulling her into a warm embrace. When she pulled back, her eyes were red and spilling over with tears. "I've heard so much about you. I wish we'd met under better circumstances. How is she?"

Simone shook her head. "I don't know. This guy won't tell me anything because I'm not family." She shot the guy a dirty look.

"That's nonsense. You are family to Pearl." She grabbed Simone's hand and dragged her to the desk. "Take us back to see our mother."

"There are privacy laws, you know. I need to check her privacy status."

"I can vouch for her," Simone said. "She really is her daughter." At least she thought so. Pearl referred to Rose as her daughter.

The man checked something on his computer. "Your name, please?"

"Rose Bennett."

He gestured to the waiting area. "Have a seat. I'll see what I can do." He disappeared behind the double doors.

Relief washed over Simone. She kept a tight grip on Rose's hand, glad she no longer had to go through this alone. The two women stood in silence, staring at the doors, waiting for someone to walk through.

After entirely too much time had passed, the guy returned. "Follow me." He led them down a hallway and into a small room with a round table and a couple of chairs. The only inviting vibe stemmed from an arrangement of artificial flowers situated in the middle of the table. "Dr. Carson will be with you soon."

Simone unclasped Rose's hand to pull out a chair and sit down. Her legs had turned to Jell-O. She had a bad feeling Pearl wasn't doing so well. Why else would they usher them into this stuffy room to talk with the doctor instead of taking them to Pearl? Rose must have been thinking the same thing. She paced the room, clutching a tissue in her fist.

A doctor entered the room, offering a gentle handshake. Simone searched his light-brown eyes for answers, unable to wait for the words to come from his mouth. His eyes held wisdom, strength, kindness, and sympathy. Simone held her breath.

"Ladies, your mother is in a fragile state."

Simone breathed a sigh of relief. *Pearl was alive.*

"She suffered a severe heart attack."

Rose gasped, the color draining from her face. "Will she … be okay?"

Dr. Carson rubbed his stubbly chin. "It's too early to say. We're running some tests that will tell us the extent of damage to her heart."

"Can we see her?" Simone's voice was shaking. She wanted nothing more than to see Pearl.

"She's in the cath lab now." Dr. Carson proceeded to explain the medical procedures Pearl would undergo. As hard as Simone tried to listen, all she could think about was how happy she was Pearl had made it this far, dampened by an icy fear this woman she felt so close to might leave her. Simone commanded herself to concentrate on the doctor. "A nurse will take you to a different waiting room."

The next waiting area was slightly cheerier, with a vase of fresh flowers as opposed to the artificial ones in the cramped waiting room. This room was spacious enough to allow for a kitchenette, which ran the length of the back wall, while the rest of the room resembled more of a family room. Simone sat on a couch next to Rose, biting her nails. "Rose, I'm glad you're here. I was so scared sitting out in that waiting area alone with my thoughts. Pearl will be even happier to see you."

"I'm scared too. And I'm glad you're here," Rose said. "We have to do something." She turned sideways on the couch, her knees touching Simone's. She held out her hands. "Let's pray."

The gesture reminded Simone of the picnic at Mica's place when his friends had held hands and prayed over the meal. Simone placed her hands in Rose's. She would set aside her doubts about God to pray for Pearl. After all, Pearl believed in God. Simone would pray on her behalf.

Chapter Nine

Monday morning, Mica worked on the lakeside house while his crews tended to other projects. The house was nearly move-in ready. While installing the final touches, he recited the verse Adam frequently quoted. "For I know the plans I have for you," declares the Lord, "plans to prosper you and not to harm you, plans to give you hope and a future." When he and Josie had drawn up the design for this home, they'd believed their future would be lived out together inside these walls. God apparently had different plans, and Mica needed frequent reminders to trust in those plans.

Later in the afternoon, Mica walked through the house, taking it all in. Everything was exactly the way she had wanted it, down to the shelving in the closets and the light fixtures in the bathrooms. He had believed completion of the home would bring him closure. Instead, it brought him profound sadness. Josie would never see the finished home. She would never walk the halls, arrange her clothes in the closets, or hang her framed photos on the walls. She would never cook in the spacious kitchen or scrapbook in the room with the amazing view. She would never share the bedroom with him.

As he drove to Diamond Elementary to pick up Hannah, he questioned whether closing on the house was the best idea after all. But what choice did he have? Hannah loved the home and would feel her mom's presence there. He parked his truck and walked up to the entrance of the school, his mind burdened.

"Hey, stranger," he heard a female say.

Looking up, he saw the senator's daughter. "Hi, Miss Wells." He wasn't in the mood for conversation.

"Why so glum?" She gave a sympathetic frown.

"Am I that easy to read?"

"Like a book." She linked a slender arm through his. "And I love to read. Especially cozied up with a cup of coffee. I bet a trip to Starbucks would cheer you up. My treat."

He pulled his arm away, creating distance between them. "Coffee sounds great. However, the nearest Starbucks is at least twenty miles away." Her assertiveness was a bit brash. He looked around for Hannah. No sign of her yet.

"You can tell me about small-town life. My parents are always looking for ways to bring that small-town feel to the city, specifically by supporting small businesses and encouraging entrepreneurship."

He supposed boldness was inherent for a politician's offspring. She was a friend of Simone's, and he didn't want to be rude. He'd been trying not to be such a hermit. He supposed this was an opportunity to socialize. Wouldn't be like a date or anything since Hannah would be there. "Okay. Just for a few minutes. We could go to Lakeview Brew, a little coffee shop here in town."

Gale winked. "Fabulous. We can take my beamer."

Hannah rushed out of the school in a stampede of children, eager to enjoy the sunny afternoon. Seeing Gale, she stopped short. She wrinkled her nose and gave Gale the stink eye. "Let's go, Daddy." She grabbed hold of his hand, pulling him toward the parking lot.

"Hannah, Miss Wells is going to take us out for a treat. You can have hot chocolate or apple cider." He licked his lips dramatically.

Hannah glared at Gale, tugging at Mica's hand. "I don't like her, and I don't want a treat. I want to go home."

Embarrassed, Mica apologized for his daughter's behavior. "Just give me one minute with my daughter, please."

Gale nodded.

Mica knelt in front of Hannah. "You know better than to talk that way. Apologize to Miss Wells, and be polite when she takes us for a treat. She's Miss Simone's friend."

Hannah crossed her arms in defiance.

"Now." Mica warned her with a stern glare.

"Sorry, Miss Wells," Hannah sputtered.

Mica stood. "I'm afraid that's as good as it's going to get for now."

Gale hunched over, face-to-face with Hannah. "Apology accepted, sweetie pie." She patted Hannah's head.

Mica situated Hannah's booster seat in Gale's BMW. He buckled her into the backseat, then sat in the front. Her car, although impressive on the outside, was cluttered inside and smelled of stale cigarette smoke. Apparently, Hannah also noticed the odor, as she was pinching her nose.

"Sorry for the mess," Gale said, clearing the cup holders of lipstick-stained tissues and a pack of gum. She held the gum up. "Would you like a piece, Hannah? It's cinnamon-flavored."

Hannah declined with a shake of her head, her fingers still holding her nose. Mica pointed a threatening finger at his daughter. She folded her hands in her lap.

Gale popped a stick of gum in her mouth as she backed out of the parking space, joining a line of cars waiting to exit the lot. She tapped jeweled fingers impatiently on the steering wheel. Soon, she patted Mica's knee. "So, why the long face? Are you having another bad day?"

He was uncomfortable about the intimate knee-patting gesture, having recently met the woman. Not to mention his daughter was in the backseat. He shifted in his seat, and her fingers fell to the console. Unclear of her intentions, he'd need to be clear this wasn't any type of date and keep the coffee meeting brief. Maybe this wasn't such a good idea. Maybe he'd given her the wrong impression. "I had a good day, actually. I finished our new home today. We're ready to close on it."

"Yay!" Hannah shouted. "I can't wait to sleep in my new room."

Gale smiled. "That's exciting. Your wife must be happy about that." She winked. "I noticed your wedding ring."

Mica looked down at the gold band, the familiar pang of sadness jabbing his heart. The ring was a sad reminder of all he'd lost, yet taking it off seemed too final. His head knew the marriage was over, but his heart wasn't ready to let it go. He twisted the ring around his finger. "She passed away. I'm not ready to take off the ring yet." He wondered why Gale had invited him to coffee believing he was married.

"I'm sorry." Gale frowned again.

Mica directed Gale to the coffee shop. When they walked in, they gave their orders, and Mica paid despite Gale's insistence on covering it. Hannah chose a table and propped her apple cider on the windowsill, staring out at a veranda where a squirrel was skittering atop the fence. Mica sipped his black coffee while Gale nursed a cappuccino. Gale's diamond-clad rings glimmered in the light as she lifted the mug to her lips, a reminder of the Wells family's reputation for having money. Mica had never been friends with someone of Gale's status. Nor was he intimidated by or even impressed with affluence. He had built many houses for people with money and learned they were all just as human as he was.

"How did you become friends with Simone?" he asked.

Gale smiled, revealing beautiful white teeth. She set her mug on the table and traced the outline of a circular coffee stain on the tabletop with her slender finger. "Simone is like a sister to me. We took her in when she was a kid."

"Your parents fostered her?"

"Yes. She was a disaster. Poor girl." Gale sighed. "We enjoyed having her in our home. She was just … unpredictable, you know? Unreliable. A drinking problem will do that to a person." She sipped her cappuccino. "She wasn't at school today. Probably called in *sick*, if you know what I mean."

Mica's stomach turned. This information explained a lot about Simone. He had to agree she was unpredictable. For the most part, she seemed dependable, but he hadn't liked the side of her he'd witnessed Saturday night.

"That's why she doesn't want to have kids. Wise decision if you ask me. It's not fair for a kid to have to deal with an alcoholic mom."

Mica was suddenly disinterested in his coffee. He had been falling for Simone, but he couldn't allow himself to fall for a woman with an alcohol problem. Not when he had a young daughter to protect. "I didn't know." Gale had just saved him from making a huge mistake. At the same time, he cared about Simone. Those feelings weren't going to just go away.

Gale reached across the table and placed her hand on his shoulder. "Oh, you like her."

Mica nodded, feeling like a high school nerd guilty of crushing on the prom queen.

"Sorry to disappoint you. She's getting better though. She doesn't drive under the influence anymore. You know, ever since the time she hit that guy."

Bile sloshed to the back of Mica's throat. "That's horrible." Mica struggled to believe the news.

"She doesn't talk about it. But don't worry. The man recovered." Gale ran her fingers down his arm, and they came to rest on the back of his hand. His skin crawled under her touch. "It's such a shame, isn't it? She's such a nice girl."

Hannah stood up. "I want to go home." She threw her paper cup in the trash and marched to the door, standing with her hands on her hips.

Mica had almost forgotten she was there. "I apologize for her lack of manners today. We really should be going." He wanted to end this disturbing conversation and get home too. He slid his hand out from under Gale's and gathered the cups. He held the door open for Hannah and Gale as they exited the café.

"It's too bad we're leaving on a bad note," Gale said. "I invited you out for coffee to cheer you up." She unlocked her car with the click of a button.

Mica considered his response as he buckled Hannah in and eased into the front seat. "Don't be sorry. I'm glad you explained a few things." He hoped, for Simone's sake, her drinking problem really was a thing of the past. But he couldn't dismiss the fact she'd been drinking the other night. Unwise behavior for an alcoholic.

Gale winked at him. "Anytime."

Mica tucked Hannah into bed, then he read to her and prayed with her. Lately, he had been making a conscious effort to create a homey environment for his daughter with plenty of family time and a predictable routine. He completed this routine with a kiss on her soft pink cheek. "Goodnight, sweetie." He walked to the doorway and switched off the light.

"Daddy, don't call me sweetie. You call me honey."

Mica chuckled. "You are my sweetie *and* my honey."

Hannah wrinkled her nose. "Miss Wells calls me sweetie pie, and I don't like her. She's mean."

Mica's smile faded. Crossing his arms, he sagged against the door frame. "That's not nice, Hannah. You need to use manners with Miss Wells." Admittedly, Gale rubbed him the wrong way too.

Petunia sauntered past Mica and leapt onto the bed, snuggling her face under Hannah's chin. Hannah ran her hand down the length of the cat's back in gentle strokes. "She says bad things about Miss Simone. That makes me mad."

"I see." Mica sat on the edge of the bed. This wasn't going to be easy to explain. "Sometimes grown-ups have difficult things they need to figure out. Miss Wells told me some of the things Miss Simone is working on."

"She said Miss Simone doesn't like kids. That's a lie." Hannah furrowed her brow.

"Of course Miss Simone likes kids. That's why she's a teacher."

Hannah appeared pensive for a minute. "I still don't want you to call me sweetie."

"Okay, honey. I promise."

"Daddy?"

"Yes?"

"We should pray for Miss Simone. That God fixes her difficult things."

"You're absolutely right." Mica knelt at the side of Hannah's bed and folded his hands. "Dear Lord, thank you for this fun day. Thank you that we got to have a treat with our new friend, Miss Wells. Thank you for giving Hannah such a nice teacher. Please help Miss Simone. Most importantly, if she doesn't know you, please help her to find you. We love you. In Jesus's name, amen."

"Amen," Hannah said, wrapping her arms around his neck. "Goodnight, Daddy." She planted a wet kiss on his cheek. "I love you."

He kissed her forehead, breathing in the scent of her blueberry shampoo. "Good night, honey. I love you too."

Mica went to the kitchen and poured himself a glass of water from the tap. He took it onto the balcony and relaxed in a lawn chair, propping his feet up on the railing. The chilly mid-September breeze swept over him, sending chills down his spine. He pulled the hood of his sweatshirt over his head and tucked his hands into his pockets. Now comfortable, he reveled in the peaceful night.

His balcony faced the courtyard. The walking path was vacant except for an occasional dog-walker. The playground equipment sat devoid of children—as if resting up for the next day's playtime. Mica took a long swallow of water. His mind wandered back to the barbeque with Simone. She had blended in so effortlessly with his friends. Mica could imagine her as a part of his future, sharing life with her. He pictured bringing her out on his boat, teaching her to wakeboard or snacking on fresh fruit and sandwiches while Hannah doggy-paddled around the boat in her bright-pink life jacket. It was a nice little fantasy.

But then there was this ominous side of Simone. The hardened exterior. She would catch herself with her guard down and immediately put up a wall—probably some kind of coping mechanism from her past. Mica couldn't imagine the challenges and hurts she possibly endured as a foster child or in a struggle with alcoholism, as Gale had implied. When he was with her, he wanted to hold her and soothe all the hurt. Realistically, he knew his lame hugs couldn't solve her problems. He wasn't equipped to coach her through dealing with her past.

He stood and paced the balcony a couple of times, finally leaning his elbows on the railing as he stared out into the dark sky. As much as he didn't want to believe Simone had an alcohol problem, he couldn't ignore the fact he'd witnessed her intoxication. The night on her porch step, he was fairly sure he smelled marijuana too. As Gale said, Simone was unpredictable.

Why did he even care so much? What was it about this woman who captured his heart and his mind? Somehow—without Mica's permission—Simone was burrowing her way into his heart. She'd already nestled into Hannah's heart.

God would need to see him through this. He bowed his head to pray. As he folded his hands, his fingers brushed against the cool metal band of his wedding ring—a reminder of his beautiful Josie. His precious bride. His soul mate. No one could replace her.

"Josie," he whispered, longing to hear her voice in return. A lump formed in his throat. "Dear God, I miss her." He knelt in front of the railing, leaning his forehead on his folded hands. Tears rolled down his cheeks. No words sufficed to voice the pain of his loss, yet he knew God comprehended his unspoken prayer. Mica wept, feeling the comfort of Jesus as if crying on his shoulder.

Chapter Ten

Simone checked the clock hanging above her classroom door. Pearl was slated to be in the operating room in five minutes to undergo triple bypass surgery. Rose had offered to sit vigil at the hospital, allowing Simone to be present at school. Physically present, that is. However, she was struggling to keep her mind off Pearl.

At lunch, Simone checked her phone—no messages. She chalked it up to *no news is good news*. Simone, along with the other kindergarten teachers, suffered the unfortunate task of recess duty this week. She enjoyed recess on warm, sunny days. But today was overcast and downright dreary. Even the kids didn't have much energy to play. Most of them were whining and arguing with one another. *Let the other teachers settle disputes*. Simone lacked the energy. She sat on an aluminum bench, pulling her infinity scarf up over her ears as much to fend off the breeze as to mute the sound of screaming children.

Little Hannah Stark wandered over and plunked herself down on the bench next to Simone. "Brr!" She popped right back up. "This bench is cold." She rubbed the back of her thighs.

Simone giggled. "Yes, it is cold. Especially if you're wearing thin tights." Simone moved over. "This spot should be warmer." Simone motioned to the place she had occupied.

Hannah sat gingerly. "Ahhh. Much better." She swung her legs jauntily, her feet dangling inches above the ground.

"Oh, Miss Stark. You just made me smile."

Hannah scooted closer and looped her arm around Simone's. "I like you, Miss Simone."

A ray of sunshine filled Simone's heart. "I like you too, Miss Stark."

Hannah wiggled her small hand into Simone's and relaxed into Simone's side. Simone felt her body relax in return. They remained hand in hand throughout the duration of recess and as the pair led the students back into the classroom. "Thanks for making me smile," Simone said, releasing Hannah's now sweaty hand.

Hannah's expression turned serious. "Do you have difficult things?"

"Um …" Her students were running wild around the classroom. "Tommy and Braden, no wrestling." She rubbed her forehead. She wished she could push a fast-forward button on this day, skip to the time she'd hear news Pearl's surgery was successful. She focused her attention back on Hannah. "What, honey? Difficult things?" Hannah must have picked up on Simone's worry over Pearl.

Hannah nodded. "Me and Daddy prayed that God will fix your difficult things."

"What? When?" How had Mica found out about Pearl?

"At bedtime. Miss Wells told Daddy about your difficult things." Hannah twisted her face into a pout. "I don't like Miss Wells." Hannah crossed her arms and made a *hmph* sound.

The room began to sway. "Hannah, go to your desk." Simone slogged to the class restroom. Thank goodness kindergarten rooms each contained a restroom. Her legs felt heavy as if she were wading through mud. She closed the door and leaned against it with her hands on her knees, struggling to calm her ragged breaths.

Gale had talked to Mica.

The vile woman had set out to destroy her for refusing to hand over her hard-earned money. Watching Gale waylay the sweet Stark family sickened her with fury. What exactly were the difficult things Gale had told Mica about? She could only hope they were all lies. The truth was surely more devastating. Gale wouldn't have told Mica about the drunk driving accident. Exposing the truth would result in Gale losing her ability to blackmail her.

An image of the regrettable night flashed through her mind. The white-haired man, face down on the side of the road. His crumpled glasses a few feet away. She shook her head, refusing the memories, but they came of their own accord. Gale's voice insisting Simone get back in the car. Simone fighting an inner battle to drive away and pretend it didn't happen versus calling 9-1-1, risking charges of drunk driving and attempted homicide—at the age of sixteen.

She pulled in a long breath. Then exhaled slowly.

Arthur Briggs. She'd read his name in the news. A sixty-one-year-old. Out walking his dog. Was hit from behind. Never saw the car coming.

Inhale.

Exhale.

With her students running wild on the other side of the door, she needed to pull herself together.

Splashing cool water on her face, she gathered strength to simply survive the rest of the school day. A hefty knock on the bathroom door startled her. "Simone, are you okay?"

Shoot! It was Mrs. Wilson.

"I'm fine. Just felt sick for a minute." She blotted her wet face with a scratchy paper towel and opened the door.

Mrs. Wilson's brow was knit so tight the wrinkles on her forehead appeared impossibly deep. "Don't go leaving your class unattended. Your rowdy kids woke my nappers. I live for naptime."

Simone blinked. She'd expected the lady to show concern. Not berate her. "*Your* nap or your *students'* naps?"

"Very funny." Mrs. Wilson waddled out the classroom door, her ample hips bumping against the rows of chairs along the way.

The kids stared at Simone in wide-eyed wonder. Think fast. "All better." Simone faked a smile and strode to the front of the room. Her fake cheerfulness was admittedly over the top, but she needed to fool the kids into believing all was well. To survive the next couple hours, she needed to fool herself as well.

After school, Simone drove straight to the hospital. She was beginning to lose faith in the *no news is good news* theory. Simone speed-walked to the surgical wing of the hospital. Rose was pacing the waiting room. "How is she?" Simone asked, coming up to her.

"I don't know." Rose continued her path across the room. "I haven't heard anything in hours." They reached the far wall, and Rose turned around and walked in the opposite direction.

Not having the energy to pace, Simone placed a hand on Rose's shoulder. "Have you left this room today?"

Rose finally stood still and shook her head.

"Go grab a bite to eat at the café. Get some fresh air. I'll text you if I hear anything." Simone wanted to be alone for a minute anyway to contact Gale and ask what difficult things she'd told Mica about.

The door to the waiting room opened with a whoosh of air, and a sweaty Dr. Carson emerged. He wore blue scrubs with matching shoe covers. Simone sat down in the nearest chair, fear weakening her knees. Rose crossed the room to meet the surgeon. Dr. Carson spoke with Rose for only a minute or two, then left the room.

"It's good news," Rose said, practically dancing over to Simone. "She did well, and she's in recovery."

"She's okay? She's going to be okay?" Nearly bursting with joy, she hopped to her feet. "Can we see her?"

Rose sagged into a chair, releasing a drawn-out breath. "Not until she's out of the recovery room. It will be at least an hour." Rose yawned. "I'm exhausted. Wake me up when she's ready for us."

"Will do." Rose was snoring within minutes. The good news had the opposite effect on Simone. She was invigorated, wishing she could rush to see Pearl and give her a hug. She channeled her energy into the less joyful task of calling Gale.

"Hello?" Gale answered with a snobby tone.

"What did you tell Mica about me?"

"That you are my foster sister." Of course Gale was going to drag this out.

"And?" Simone tapped her foot, hating that Gale was undoubtedly loving the build-up of suspense.

"Oh yeah. I mentioned your drinking problem."

Simone balled her fist, fighting the urge to scream. How dare she paint such a picture of Simone? She never had a drinking problem, per se. She'd overindulged occasionally back in high school, as did many kids. Including Gale.

Simone needed the full story. "Did you tell him about the accident?" Her chest constricted. They rarely broached the subject.

There was too long of a pause for Simone's comfort. "I'll tell you for a price."

This woman was infuriating. "I'm a schoolteacher. I don't have loads of money."

"I'll do you a favor this time and tell you for free."

Simone was sure there would be a price of one kind or another. "So ..."

"Yes."

Simone grew dizzy. She hung up the phone. Gale may have finally achieved her goal of destroying Simone's life. Mica could easily divulge the information to the school principal or superintendent or the cops. What responsible parent would allow a criminal to teach their young child?

She plopped onto a chair across the room from Rose, not wanting to wake her. She needed to collect her thoughts and develop a plan. Gale could be lying—a plausible assumption. Maybe she hadn't told Mica about Arthur because Gale was guilty of being an accomplice.

Simone decided it was best to go on as if nothing had happened. She would address the matter should Mica bring it up. For now, she would continue living with the regret as she'd been doing the past ten years. Which was punishment enough.

Mica lifted the last cardboard box from his truck with *Hannah's room* printed on the side of the box. A horn honked from the road. He turned to see Gale Wells pulling into his driveway.

She rolled down the window. "Hi, stranger. I was just driving by when I saw you out here. Looks like you could use some help."

"Last box," he said, adjusting the weight in his arms. He really needed to keep moving, and he felt he could get the job done faster alone.

"Are you moving into this beauty?" She shaded her eyes from the sun, looking around the property.

"Sure am. Hannah and me. As much as I'd like to visit, I've got work to do. I wanna have the place ready for Hannah after school."

"So, you *could* use an extra set of hands." She turned off the engine and hopped out of her car. She was hardly dressed for labor, wearing high heels and a fancy suit. This woman was annoyingly forward. He had a feeling she planned to help whether he wanted her to or not.

"Actually, you have good timing. Mind opening the front door for me?" His forearms were beginning to burn from the weight of the box.

She opened the door, and then followed him through the house, commenting on the craftsmanship. "What a lovely home. Mind if I peek in the other rooms?"

"Be my guest." He set down the box in Hannah's closet and sifted through the contents for the baggie of hardware to the bed frame. Then he set to work while Gale commenced on a self-tour. He wondered what a city girl like Gale was doing hanging around Diamond.

Mica was tightening the last bolt of his daughter's newly assembled bed when Gale returned. "Are you sure she'd rather have the bed along that wall instead of under the window?" Gale stood back, assessing the configuration.

Mica nodded, tossing the wrench into his toolbox. "Yep. Hannah told me a million times this is where she wants her bed. Besides, she doesn't want to be sleeping under a window in case of storms. She's been a little afraid of tornadoes ever since ... you know. Her mom ..."

Gale stared at him with a clueless look in her eyes.

Mica combed his fingers through his hair. "Josie, my wife, died a little over a year ago when a tornado took our house."

Recognition dawned in Gale's eyes. "The tornado in Rice County."

"That's the one." Mica lifted the box spring onto the bed frame. "Give me a hand with the mattress?"

"Oh, sure. I'm sorry about your wife." Gale slid her high heels off and unbuttoned her business jacket, letting it slide off her toned arms and land in a velvety pile on the carpet. A silky sleeveless shirt was tucked into a pencil skirt that hugged gentle curves. She was trying to get his attention, but he wasn't interested.

Mica looked away and heaved the mattress onto the box spring. "Never mind. I got it. Can you just put the bedding on for me? Thanks." Mica hurried out of the room, down the staircase, and out onto the porch. He drank in the crisp air. Finishing this house was becoming more difficult the further along it went. Even with Gale Wells by his side, helping to put things in order. Especially with Gale Wells. She made him miss Josie even more.

He sat on the porch swing and closed his eyes, letting his head clear. The front door creaked open and closed. He opened his eyes to see Gale, her jacket draped over an arm and her shoes dangling from her fingertips. "I guess I'll be going," she said softly.

Mica nodded, then closed his eyes again.

"Is it something I said? Something I did?" She shivered, hugging her arms to her chest.

He really didn't feel like consoling Gale's hurt feelings right now when he was overwhelmed by his own emotions. But he had not meant to make her feel bad. He stood and walked her to her car. "Thanks for stopping by and offering to help," he said when they approached her BMW. "Sorry to run out of the house like that. I just … I just miss Josie. It's hard moving in here without her. Please don't feel bad."

Gale smiled. She wrapped her arms around his neck, with a clunk of her shoes against the back of his head. "She was a lucky lady." She kissed his cheek.

As she drove off, Mica shuffled back to the porch. Gale Wells, try as she may, failed to turn his head. Since Josie, the only woman to come close to capturing his attention was Simone Clare. Despite her unpredictability—as Gale had called it—Simone possessed a genuine vulnerability—what you see is what you get.

Mica checked his watch. He had half an hour to complete the final touches before picking up Hannah from school. He cleared the kitchen countertop of tools, peeled painter's tape from the window frames, and unrolled a colorful rug in the entryway. The house had come together nicely over the week. Once he'd set his mind to finishing the house, he had worked with ardent passion. The home had morphed into the vision he and Josie had shared. Hannah would love it.

He climbed the stairs, excitement building with each step over revealing the house to his daughter. Her room needed to be perfect. *Gah!* The bed wasn't made. He ripped open the packaging for the new kitty-print bedding and stretched the fitted sheet over the mattress. Time was ticking away. He might be late to pick up Hannah, risking a tongue lashing from Simone. He draped the top sheet, not too neatly, over the bed, managed to stuff the pillow into its case, and topped it all off with a bright-pink downy comforter.

What was he forgetting? He'd missed something. Petunia's bed! Where was that thing anyway? He rifled through a couple of boxes stacked in Hannah's closet, coming up short. Forget it. Petunia could sleep in Hannah's bed tonight. Time to get to the school.

Hannah was dancing circles around the flagpole. The buses were long gone, so he decided to take a risk by parking along the curb. "Daddy!" She skipped over to the truck, flashing an enthusiastic smile. He helped her into the truck. "Are we having a Friday night barbeque tonight?"

"I have an even better surprise for you." He tapped her little button nose.

"Yay! Are Gigi and Sadie coming?"

"You bet." Adam, Brooke, and the girls would be bringing dinner to the house later. Moving into the lakeside house was cause for celebration.

Simone eased open the door to Pearl's hospital room. The aroma of freshly cut flowers filled the air. The windowsill resembled a florist shop. Vase in hand, Simone tiptoed across the room, situating her arrangement among the others.

"I'm awake."

"Oh!" Simone jumped, clapping a hand to her chest and nearly knocking over a vase of carnations and baby's breath in the process.

Pearl's eyes remained closed, but the slightest smile played at the corners of her lips. "I'm just resting my eyes, dear. Didn't mean to cause you a fright."

Simone took the only seat in the room—a vinyl-covered recliner sort-of-thing. "How are you feeling?" Pearl's skin appeared thin, almost paper white. Rather unnerving, considering the woman's African American heritage.

"That merciless therapist made me walk to the nurse's station today. Halfway there, I considered faking another heart attack so I could lie down. But I figured they'd just keep me here longer."

"You sound more like your old self today, Pearl."

"Thank you for the roses."

"You're welcome. Of course, they're not as beautiful as the roses from your garden, but I hoped they'd remind you of home." Simone chewed at her fingernails. "I sure have missed you. It's nice knowing Rose is over at your house. I feel less lonely that way."

Pearl coughed weakly. She grimaced, struggling to clear her lungs enough to draw an adequate breath.

"Are you okay?"

Pearl didn't answer. A monitor started beeping. Pearl continued to cough, choking on her own secretions. Her eyes widened as she struggled for air.

Simone jumped from her chair and pressed a red button on the side of the bed, setting off lights and more dinging noises. When there wasn't an immediate response, she ran to the hallway and flagged down a woman in scrubs. "Help!"

The nurse rushed in and suctioned mucus from the back of Pearl's throat. "Atta girl," the woman said. "Cough it up. That's right."

Simone exited the room out of earshot of the coughing and sucking noises. She stood at a bank of windows, holding her arms over her stomach to ease sudden queasiness. Seeing Pearl in this environment was distressing. Pearl had served as a pillar of strength in Simone's life. Now she was too weak to cough adequately or walk twenty feet on her own. Obviously, the nurse didn't know Pearl the way she did. Simone had wanted to scream at her to stop talking baby talk to her friend. Pearl was a grown woman, for goodness' sake.

Simone took her time regaining composure before returning to Pearl's room. The nurse was clicking away on a computer at the bedside. She peered at Simone over a pair of colorful reading glasses. "I'll bring in a dose of morphine. Your mom has had a big day, with all the walking. She's pretty sore." Simone's heart did a little happy dance every time she was addressed as Pearl's daughter. Pearl had signed the necessary paperwork assigning Simone and Rose as her powers of attorney. She was as good as family now.

Pearl had returned to a peaceful state—resting her eyes, as she called it. The morphine would relax her even more. Simone's stomach, however, remained unsettled. "Pearl, I need to grab a snack. I'll be back soon."

Pearl's eyes fluttered open. "That's fine, dear. I'm going to rest awhile."

Simone tucked the covers up under her friend's chin as Pearl had done for her after that regrettable night with Gale. Simone pushed all thoughts of Gale aside. There was only so much worry and heartache a person could cope with at a time.

After spotting Simone's little beater in the parking lot, Gale had thought twice about filling her prescription at the hospital pharmacy, but she'd already filled an Oxycodone prescription at the local drug store. This small town didn't lend itself to an addict's need for frequent opioid prescriptions. She would not allow a chance meeting with Simone to alter her plans. She had misplaced the last of her

Oxycodone and needed a refill to get through the weekend. The small-town doc had been easy enough to convince she had back pain from helping a friend move into a new home.

Gale spied Simone emerging from a patient room and lumbering down the hallway to the hospital café. The girl didn't appear to be much of a threat. Surely much too sullen to notice anything. Gale cracked a grin. Maybe Simone had gotten wind of Gale's coffee rendezvous with the hunky dad.

Gale slipped into the gift shop, peering at her long-lost sis from behind a bouquet of get-well balloons. What was Simone doing at the hospital anyway? She hadn't shown up at school on Monday, but it didn't appear Simone was the patient in this case. Must be a visitor.

Gale held her phone, giving the illusion of texting, as she eyed her faux sister. Simone ordered a pop and a bag of chips. She sat at a table inside the small café looking pathetic and depressed.

While Simone struggled momentarily to open her snack, Gale slinked out of the gift shop, retracing the steps back to the hospital room Simone had come from. She peeked into the room and saw a nurse push medication into an IV line. She recognized the patient right away—the tough old bird. Gale waited for the nurse to exit the room before she made her own entrance. The bird was sleeping. Perfect.

"How are you doing, friendly neighbor?" Gale asked, testing the lucidity of the patient.

No response.

"What are they giving you?" Gale read a white board hanging on the wall. "Hmm, looks like you just got a hit of morphine." Gale bent down and whispered into the patient's ear, "Be careful, old bird. Narcotics are addictive."

She spotted a pile of gift cards on the windowsill. Gale peeked out the door. All clear. The envelopes had already been torn open. Gale pulled the card from the first envelope and a twenty-dollar bill sailed to the floor. She picked it up and dropped it into her purse. "That'll do. Bye, bye, birdie. Get well soon."

She left the hospital.

Chapter Eleven

Ding dong!

"Sadie and Gigi are here," Hannah called. She swung the front door open. "Come see my new room." Mica stepped aside as three giggling girls nearly plowed him over on their way upstairs.

Mica welcomed Adam and Brooke, leading the way to the kitchen. The guests schlepped bags onto the kitchen counter. "Congratulations, Mica." Brooke hugged him. She stood back, admiring the newly finished space. "It's beautiful." Tears shone in her eyes.

"We're happy for you, man." Adam clapped him on the back.

Mica looked around the spacious room, proud of how the house had come together.

Brooke dangled a gift bag in front of Mica's face. "Brought you a housewarming gift."

Mica sifted through the tissue paper until his fingers met something rigid. He pulled out a small box, similar in size to the box that had held Josie's engagement ring. He lifted the lid, revealing a diamond-shaped crystal on a transparent string. Mica held the jewel up to his chest. "Thanks for the necklace?" he joked. Honestly, he didn't know what the gift was.

"What is that?" Adam asked Brooke. "I had nothing to do with the necklace. The food is my housewarming gift to you."

Brooke sighed dramatically. "Give that to me." She yanked the necklace-thing from Mica's hand, removed something from the little box, and walked to the window above the kitchen sink. She hung it from the window and gave the crystal a little twirl. "It's a prism, you idiots. When the morning sunlight shines through, you'll have pretty little rainbows dancing around the room."

"Ahh," the men said in unison.

"And," Brooke continued, "the crystal is the shape of a diamond. Like Lake Diamond."

"I get it," Mica said. "Josie loved rainbows. It's an incredibly thoughtful gift." A somber silence filled the air.

"Anyone hungry?" Adam removed boxes of rice, veggies, and what smelled like sweet-and-sour chicken from a bag. "We also brought egg rolls and cream cheese wontons." He pointed to a second bag situated in front of Brooke.

The girls came bounding down the steps. "Is it time to eat?" Hannah asked. "I smell wontons." She climbed up on a stool at the counter, already looking at home in this kitchen. Gigi and Sadie claimed stools on either side of their friend.

Brooke filled her girls' plates. "Gigi, are you chewing gum?"

Sadie pointed a finger in her sister's face. "I told you Mommy would yell at you."

"Where did you find gum?" Brooke held out her hand, prompting Gigi to spit it out.

Mica held up his arms. "I'm innocent."

"She found it on the floor in Hannah's room." Sadie took it upon herself to fill everyone in.

"It's cinnamon. Like Miss Wells's gum," Hannah said.

Mica rubbed his forehead. He had some explaining to do. The whole clan was looking at him, awaiting an explanation. "Okay, so I think I know what happened. Gale Wells was helping me get things ready today. It must've slipped out of her pocket when she took her jacket off in Hannah's room."

"Whoa," Adam said, shoving his hand out toward Mica. "Back up a minute here. Gale Wells, as in Senator Wells's daughter, was in your house?"

Brooke guffawed. "Cool down, Adam. She may be pretty, but from what I've seen in the media, that woman is trouble."

"Miss Wells stinks, and she's mean," Hannah said, pursing her lips and wrinkling her nose.

"Here's the thing," Mica said. "She's friends with Simone. The Wellses raised Simone as a foster child."

Adam nodded. "That family does a lot of great charity work. I voted for Senator Wells."

Brooke poked Adam's arm with a chopstick. "Good for you, Adam. Thank you for helping to make this world a better place."

Adam winked at Brooke. "My pleasure." He scooped sticky rice onto a paper plate. "So now you're dating Gale Wells? That stint with Miss Simone was short-lived."

Mica needed to set the record straight. "I'm not dating anybody."

Brooke moaned. "I like Simone. I vote for Miss Simone."

Hannah perked up. "I vote for Miss Simone too." She and Brooke high-fived each other.

"Look!" Sadie cupped her hand over her mouth, giggling. "Petunia is funny."

The tabby cat staggered into the living room like a drunken sailor. She attempted to leap onto the couch but flopped onto her back.

"Petunia!" Hannah shouted, running to her cat. Sitting cross-legged on the floor, Hannah lifted her kitty onto her lap. "Are you okay, Petunia?"

The adults rushed over and circled around Hannah and Petunia, studying the cat. "She's not breathing right." Mica watched the cat draw in slow, shallow breaths.

"Check out her pupils," Brooke said. "They're huge. Did she eat something outside or get into cleaner or something?"

Mica thought back through the day. "Not that I know of. She stays indoors. She's been napping in Hannah's closet most of the day."

Brooke began tapping on her phone. "You need to take her to a vet. I'm afraid they won't be open at this time on a Friday evening."

"There's an emergency vet in town," Adam said.

Hannah hugged Petunia. Mica hoped she wouldn't squeeze the life out of the cat. What little life remained. "Is she gonna die like Mommy?" Tears streamed down Hannah's cheeks. The cat hung limply in her arms.

The sadness of seeing his daughter so distraught broke Mica's heart into millions of pieces. This little girl couldn't lose her kitty so soon after losing her mommy. His vision blurred as tears formed in his eyes. He was too choked up to speak.

"Pray, Daddy. Pray that God will fix Petunia's difficult things."

Brooke stepped in, picking up the cat and helping Hannah to her feet. Hannah protested, saying she wanted to hold Petunia. But Brooke handed the cat to Adam. "I'll stay here with the girls. You guys go to the vet on Main Street. They're waiting for you. Go!"

Adam held the cat on his lap as Mica drove them to the vet just a few miles away. "Is she still breathing?"

"Barely," Adam answered. He examined the cat's face. "She better keep breathing because I'm not about to do mouth-to-mouth on a cat. Not even Hannah's cat."

"I'll give the animal CPR if that's what it takes to keep her alive. This cat cannot die on Hannah. I won't allow it." Mica stepped on the gas pedal, exceeding the speed limit.

He pulled up to the clinic. A woman in a white doctor's coat met them at the door and scooped the lifeless cat into her arms. "Hi. I'm Doctor Meredith. Come with me."

She led them past the front desk and through the waiting area to a room in the back of the clinic. It looked like a small operating room, with trays of surgical tools, high-tech-looking machines, and vials of medications neatly organized on open shelves. "So, tell me what happened." She examined the cat as she spoke, feeling its belly, looking at its legs and paws, and shining a light into the cat's eyes.

Mica scratched his chin. "I don't know. She was fine this morning when I brought her over to our new house. Then, just a little bit ago, the girls noticed she was stumbling around. We called you right away." Mica's stomach was in knots. He hadn't realized he could get so invested in a cat.

Dr. Meredith set the cat on the exam table, positioning an oxygen mask over its face. Then she drew medication into a syringe from a glass vial. By the way the doctor moved about the room, quickly yet efficiently, Mica guessed Petunia was as bad off as she appeared.

"Your cat has the classic symptoms of opioid poisoning." She injected medication into Petunia's thigh. "Dilated pupils, slowed respiratory and heart rate, drooling—"

"Opioid poisoning?" Mica mentally searched the lakeside house for any possible sources of narcotics. "It has to be something else. Maybe she ate some cleaner or something. I don't have any medications besides Ibuprofen and Children's Tylenol."

The veterinarian glanced at her watch. "The reversal agent takes effect within three to five minutes."

The three of them hovered over the cat, watching for a change. Mica's phone buzzed in his back pocket. He swiped to accept the call, not taking his eyes off the cat. "Stark Homes. Mica speaking."

"Mica, it's Brooke. I might know what's wrong with Petunia."

The wall clock showed one minute had passed since the reversal agent, and there was no sign of any change in the cat. "What is it, Brooke?" He rubbed his forehead.

"I found a little white tablet on Hannah's floor. The kids said it was the same spot they found the gum. I think you should call Gale and ask if she had any medications in her pocket."

"Um ... that will make for an awkward phone call." Calling Gale and asking her a personal question like what medications she takes felt like an invasion of privacy. "Maybe I'll just wait and see if the reversal agent works. We'll know in a couple more minutes."

"Are you sure Petunia can wait a couple more minutes? I mean, I hate to be pushy, but you need to call her."

Mica petted the cat's back. She still wasn't breathing normally. Hannah would be devastated if Petunia died because he wasn't man enough to make an awkward phone call. "You're right. Thanks, Brooke."

He hung up and dialed Gale. "Hey, there," she said, a flirty lilt in her voice. "Is your sweetie pie enjoying her new room?"

Mica stepped into the lobby where he'd have privacy. "She is, but that's not why I called."

"Is everything okay? You sound tense."

"Actually, we're having a bit of a crisis. Petunia is sick. We're at the clinic. I'm wondering ... I mean ... I just thought maybe you—"

"Petunia. Is that Simone's neighbor?"

"What? No." How would he know anything about Simone's neighbor? "Petunia is Hannah's cat."

"Hannah has a cat?"

Mica clenched his jaw. This phone call was only causing more frustration. "Yes, and the vet thinks the cat is suffering from opioid poisoning. Since I don't have any opioids, I was wondering if maybe you had dropped a couple—"

"Are you accusing me of poisoning your cat that I didn't even know existed?" The woman had flipped a switch from flirtation to hostility in a beat. Irked, he just wanted a straightforward answer to a straightforward question.

"Gale, I'm not accusing you of anything. It's just that the cat is sick, and there was a pill on Hannah's floor." He paced to the window. The sun had set, leaving a navy-blue sky in its wake. "Forget it. Maybe the pill belonged to the carpet installer or something. Sorry to bother you. I better go check on the cat."

Gale cleared her throat. "Good luck with everything."

Mica hung up and hurried back to the exam room. Adam grinned. "Look who's back," he said, pointing to Petunia. "The antidote is working."

Petunia tucked her head under Adam's hand, prodding him to pet her. Her green eyes had regained their sparkle. Mica sighed in relief. "Thank God." He kissed the cat on the head. "Petunia, you had us worried."

Adam patted Mica on the back. "I'm happy for you, man." He laughed. "But did you just kiss a cat?"

Mica gave Adam a playful shove. "I'm so happy right now I'd even kiss you." Mica lunged toward Adam.

Adam held up his hands in protest. "Save it for the cat. Or Gale Wells."

"Interesting," Dr. Meredith interjected.

Mica shot Adam a threatening look for mentioning Gale Wells. "It's a long story."

A surprising swell of disgust poured over Mica. He picked up Petunia, cuddling her in the crook of his neck. "I'm devoted to Petunia and the beautiful young Hannah."

"Back to Petunia," the doctor said as she typed on her computer. "Looks like she'll recover, but she'll need to stay in the clinic overnight. She may need a second dose of the reversal agent later. I'll keep a close eye on her, and I'll call you in the morning to let you know how she's doing."

Mica scratched the cat behind her ears. Petunia purred in response. "Do you think she can go home tomorrow?"

"That's my guess. In the meantime, I advise you to thoroughly search your home for any medications or poisonous materials she could've gotten into." She pulled a brochure from a rack on the wall. "Here's a list of substances that are harmful to cats. She got lucky this time. I'd hate for it to happen again."

Thank God Hannah hadn't been the one to eat the pill. He took the brochure, skimmed over it, and tucked it in his back pocket. "Thank you, Dr. Meredith. I'll talk to you in the morning."

Mica called Brooke on the drive home and explained the situation. He could hear Hannah's cheers at the news Petunia was better, followed by complaints the cat wouldn't come home until tomorrow. As relieved as Mica was about the cat's recovery, he was also bothered someone brought narcotics into his home and wasn't responsible with them. Even more unsettling was his conversation with Gale. She'd gotten defensive and snapped at him before he could even explain.

Admittedly, he'd been tense when he called her and was basically accusing her for the malady of his cat. He could've been more tactful. Especially with opioid addiction being all over the news these days. It was a sensitive subject. If he remembered correctly, Senator Wells was an advocate for the legalization of medical marijuana to abate the problem of opioid addiction. Mica made a mental note to apologize to Gale later. For now, he just wanted to get home to hug his daughter and celebrate their new house.

Early Saturday morning, Mica stepped in line at Lakeview Brew. He'd gotten word from Dr. Meredith that Petunia was in tip-top shape and ready to come home. The Calhouns had stayed the night. The girls had a slumber party in Hannah's room, and Mica had given up his bedroom to Brooke and Adam. He had crashed on the couch and was awakened at the crack of dawn by three giggly girls helping themselves to glasses of ice water from the fridge. A strong cup of joe was in order.

"Americano, please."

He took his coffee to a table tucked in the back corner of the shop, avoiding the blinding sunshine pouring through the ample windows. He had stayed up much too late with his friends, playing RummiKub and hashing out the bitter saga of the women in his life. Maybe after a hit of caffeine he'd appreciate the gorgeous weather.

He sipped the coffee, relaxing back in his chair, waiting for the caffeine to take effect. Typical Saturday morning patrons meandered into the café. Young moms occupied comfy chairs near a play area, their toddlers inspecting and drooling on the community toys. Men who looked to be approaching retirement age gathered around a high-top table, each sporting road bike spandex attire failing to contain their love handles. A few other customers were sprinkled around the shop, hunched over laptops, iPads, or smartphones. One elderly gentleman pored over a good old-fashioned newspaper.

And then he saw her, standing in line. Her silhouette backlit by sunlight pouring over her when someone opened the door. Simone.

Mica turned toward the wall and slipped his hoodie over his head, preferring to remain anonymous. He was still processing how he felt about Simone and wasn't ready for her to mess with his head again. The stuff Gale had said about her alcohol problem and drunk driving seemed far-fetched. Gale didn't come across as trustworthy. He respected her less with each encounter. He stole furtive glances at Simone. She balanced on her tiptoes, straining to read the menu items written on the chalkboard suspended behind the baristas. The tall gentleman in queue ahead of her was oblivious to the challenge he created for her. It was cute the way she strained her neck to see over the guy's shoulder, like a little kid at a parade trying to get a look at her favorite float from the back of the crowd.

Feeling a bit like a stalker, he shifted his gaze to the paintings by local artists hanging on the walls. But his attention remained on Simone, an uncontrollable magnetic force pulling his mind to her. If it were true she'd overcome a history of alcohol abuse, Simone was even more admirable. Not everyone could beat that problem.

As she inched forward in line, he got a better look at her. A stretchy headband held her dark hair off her forehead. Her face appeared free of makeup; her freckles more prominent than usual. She wore a half zipper athletic shirt and black leggings exposing her ankles. He didn't peg Simone as the athletic type, although her figure was perfect. The outfit was probably more for comfort. The sunlight shining on her skin revealed stubble on her ankles, as if she hadn't shaved in a day or two. He found the look sexy somehow. Natural. He felt like he might be getting a glimpse of what it would be like to wake up next to her in the morning. He rubbed his face. He could use a shave himself.

Okay, now he had crossed a line into the creep zone, comparing his stubble to hers. He needed a distraction, something to break the magnetic force tugging his thoughts to Simone. He opened the weather app on his phone. *High of 65 degrees, sunny, breezy.*

"Mica?"

Shoot. The magnetic force had pulled her right over to him. He looked up from his phone to see her striding toward his table, a to-go cup in one hand and a pastry bag in the other. He mustered a surprised look. "Oh, hey, Simone."

"You're looking a bit emo over here in the corner with your hood over your head. Is everything all right?"

As he feared, the conversation with Simone already had him puzzled. "Did you say 'emo'? I don't know what that is."

She smiled. "Never mind. How have you been?"

Mica thought back to where they'd left off. The last time he'd talked to her was after the barbeque at his apartment. They'd shared a nice hug, then suddenly she'd distanced herself. After that, he had learned Simone was possibly an alcoholic. He would stick to small talk from now on. "I closed on the house yesterday."

Her eyes lit up. "I'm so happy for you. Hannah must be so excited."

"She is. Gigi and Sadie had a slumber party in her room last night."

"I'm sure Hannah will tell me all about it on Monday." She looked around. "Where is Hannah?"

"She's at home with Adam and Brooke and the girls. We had a little ... incident last night." Mica drained the last of his coffee, then slid the cup and saucer aside.

"Oh no. What happened?" Simone sat in the chair opposite Mica, her eyes wide with concern.

"Hannah's cat got sick. We had to take her to the vet. She's better this morning. I'm on my way to pick her up now."

Simone relaxed her shoulders. "Poor Petunia. I'm glad she's okay."

Mica inwardly smiled at the fact Simone knew Hannah's cat was named Petunia.

"That must've been difficult for Hannah, sleeping in a new room without her kitty. I'm glad she had the girls to keep her company."

"How is it that you know her so well when you just met her a couple weeks ago?"

Simone shrugged, a smile lighting her eyes. "Hannah has been special to me since day one."

Mica laughed. "Let's not talk about day one. It wasn't my finest moment."

"I admit, you had to grow on me."

"Ouch." Mica placed a hand over his heart.

Simone looked over her shoulder at the door. "I should get going."

"You haven't touched your coffee. It's going to get cold. Feel free to stay and eat." What was he doing? He should not be spending any more time with this woman than necessary. She had a way of working her fingers around his heart, only to rip it right out of his chest.

"Are you sure?"

No. What happened to sticking to small talk? "Absolutely."

Accepting the invitation, she removed a chocolate croissant from the bag. "I'm famished." She took a bite of the pastry. "Mmm. So good." She licked a dollop of chocolate from her top lip. "You have to try this." She ripped a piece off and held it out to him. He opened his mouth, and she placed it on his tongue. She laughed. "I mean, I thought you would take it with your fingers, but that worked too."

Mica died a little inside of embarrassment, no longer tasting the buttery, chocolatey goodness. He felt like he was trying to swallow a cotton ball.

"Want some more?" She ripped off another piece.

Mica declined with a shake of his head.

She sipped her beverage—something sugary and topped with whipped cream according to the checked boxes on the side of the cup. She shifted in her seat. Mica sensed a sudden change in her demeanor. He'd expected nothing less. "Sorry about getting all weird after the picnic. I had such a nice time." She turned her gaze to a painting of Lake Diamond at sunset hanging on the wall. "Your friends are great, and I really appreciate you inviting me. Or, you know, letting me stay. I guess, technically, Hannah invited me." Fidgeting, she began ripping a napkin into pieces as she spoke.

"Don't worry about it." On second thought, he would appreciate a little more clarity on her behavior. "Actually, I'm perplexed by you."

She swept the shredded napkin pieces into a pile next to Mica's empty cup. "I'm guessing you don't mean that as a compliment."

Mica didn't want to say something hurtful. Her past had surely come with enough hurt as it was, but he needed to know how likely she was to break his and his daughter's hearts. He involuntarily released a frustrated sigh.

"I understand. I've been sending you mixed signals. Sorry for that." She gnawed at a fingernail. "I'm not perfect, and I never will be. Sometimes I question what qualifies me to act as a role model for little kids when my own childhood was so messed up. I mean, I did stay with some great families. I always hoped one of the nice families would adopt me. And when they didn't, I felt rejected all over again—like when my mom gave me up. It hurt. Kinda made me wonder what love looks like. Because just when I thought someone loved me, they would turn me away. I guess I'm a little afraid to be cared for, and a little afraid to let myself care too deeply for someone else." Her candor surprised him as much as it saddened him. On a happier note, if he read between the lines, she'd just admitted to caring for him.

"That makes sense. I'm sorry you had to go through all that." It broke his heart learning this amazing woman felt unloved. He would guard his feelings of attraction to her and be careful with her wounded heart.

"Sorry, I didn't mean to dump all that on you. I ... I wanted to explain." She finally looked into Mica's eyes again. "Despite my past, I vow to do my best for my students, though inadequate my best may be." She paused. "It worried me when you said you trust me. I mean, I can't even trust myself—that I'll always make the right decisions or say the right things. I can't promise I'll never drink too much again."

This was a lot to take in so early in the morning. But it seemed a necessary conversation that would feel unpleasant no matter the time of day. Mica remained quiet, allowing her to continue.

"That being said … there's something else I need to tell you." She paused to take a deep breath. "I'm afraid you've been misled. By someone from my past." She stared into Mica's eyes, her expression fierce and certain. Chills tickled the back of his neck. She leaned her forearms on the table. "I need you to see me for the person I present to you. Not the person Gale makes me out to be. I don't know what she told you, but I can almost guarantee that she is manipulating you."

Mica's defenses rose. He hoped he was smart enough to not be manipulated by anyone. Now both women had come to him, badmouthing the other. "Hold on a minute. I am not going to get in the middle of whatever is going on between the two of you." His mouth suddenly felt like the Sahara Desert. He tipped his cup to his lips knowing full well that it was dry. "I can think for myself. I don't need the two of you pitting each other against me like some episode of *The Bachelor*."

Simone wrinkled her nose. "Do you watch *The Bachelor*?"

"Josie used to force me to watch it with her, but that's beside the point."

Simone jumped to her feet, gathered her belongings, and raked the napkin scraps into her palm. "If you consider yourself to be America's most sought-after bachelor, and we desperate ladies are falling at your feet, vying for your attention, then you need to do some serious self-reflection."

Now he felt like a jerk. "No, I didn't mean it that way." So much for being gentle with her heart. "I meant that I need to sort things out for myself. I don't like it when people try to persuade me."

She marched to the door, pulled it open, paused, and returned to the table.

Mica braced himself for the next tongue-lashing, and he feared it may be deserved. He seemed to have let his male ego get in the way.

"Just hear me out on this. Keep Hannah away from Gale."

This is exactly why he'd pulled the hoodie over his head, trying to be invisible. Simone had a habit of complicating his already convoluted life. He groaned, watching her make a hasty exit.

In her absence, he could more clearly contemplate the words she thrust at him. *Keep Hannah away from Gale.* He had concluded on his own Gale could be trouble. She was a little too forward and not very considerate. Plus, Hannah didn't like her. But it wasn't Simone's business who he hung out with or exposed his daughter to. As a matter of fact, he was still trying to figure out if Simone was trustworthy. Just a couple of minutes ago, she confessed she didn't even trust herself.

Was Simone putting Hannah and him in the middle of her catfight with Gale? Mica wanted no part in their argument, or whatever this was. He wouldn't allow his daughter to be used as a pawn. From now on, it was better if Simone was strictly Hannah's teacher. Nothing more. She wouldn't be invading their family barbeques or traipsing through their home, telling him how to run his household. A woman who'd managed to make a disaster out of an impromptu chat in a coffee shop had no place in his or his daughter's life.

Simone threw open her closet door and grabbed the first articles of clothing within reach—a pair of worn jeans and a button-up shirt she'd been meaning to donate to the local thrift shop. She showered quickly, all the while muttering under her breath about what a pompous pig Mica was. Couldn't he see through Gale's act to the manipulative snake she was? He was probably so intoxicated by her beauty—as was the entire male species ever since she'd grown breasts, which wasn't until the tenth grade, by the way—he was blinded to her ugly, scheming lies and deceit.

Simone coated her right leg with shaving cream and managed to stave off her pity party long enough to move the razor in smooth, controlled strokes. A razor cut was the last thing she needed to deal with right now.

By the time her shower was finished, she had regained enough self-control to set aside thoughts of Mica and Gale to focus on preparing Pearl's home for her return. Rose had been keeping the house up during Pearl's hospital stay, deep-cleaning the kitchen and bathroom and dusting and vacuuming each room. There wasn't much work left to do. Simone spent the afternoon stocking the fridge with fresh fruits and vegetables, finishing the yardwork Pearl had started the day of her heart attack, laundering her bed linens, and taking out the garbage. Satisfied with her efforts, she returned to the hospital for what she hoped would be the last night of sleeping on a pull-out sofa. The doctors were optimistic Pearl could be discharged in the next day or two.

Pearl was sitting up in bed, bathed and wearing her own nightgown from home. She greeted Simone with a bright smile, her brown eyes shining. She was looking more like her old self every day. Simone relaxed into the recliner situated next to Pearl's bed.

She'd almost forgotten about the drama in her life until Pearl flipped on the local six o'clock news. A headshot of Wesley Wells filled a small box in the corner of the screen above the news anchor. Simone buried her face in her hands. "I can't escape that family. Pearl, Gale is infiltrating my life."

The room was swallowed in sudden silence. Simone looked up to see a blank screen. Pearl dropped the remote on her lap. "Let's just forget about the news."

"Gale is out to destroy me because I won't give her money. She's been talking to Mica and Hannah. That worries me."

"Now slow down a minute. No need to get all worked up."

"I'm not overreacting, Pearl. Not this time."

"The Lord your God is with you. The mighty warrior who saves." Pearl folded her hands in her lap.

"I can't let her do this." Simone stood, her mind reeling. She needed to find Gale and do whatever it would take to stop her from ruining her life. Even if it meant throwing money at her. She rummaged through her purse for her car keys. "If I don't make it back tonight, I promise to return first thing in the morning."

"Whatever you need to do, dear."

"Sorry to bail on you. Maybe we can break you outta here in the morning." She headed for the door.

"Dr. Carson seems to think I'm ready. Oh, before you go"—Pearl pointed toward the bathroom— "can you fetch my cosmetic bag?"

Simone was antsy to get going. On the other hand, she felt guilty for leaving Pearl to fend for herself. She found the bag and placed it on the bedside table. "If you need anything else, just push the call light and a nurse will come help you."

Pearl closed her eyes and rested her head on the pillow. "Is my red nail polish in there?"

A bit irritated, Simone gnawed on the inside of her cheek and drew back the zipper. She sifted through the contents. Buried under toiletries, there was makeup that looked to have been purchased in the 1970s. Red lipsticks, blue eyeshadows, false lashes in every imaginable length. Blue mascara? "Wow, Pearl. I didn't know you were a makeup artist."

"Oh, I shined up real nice back in the day. I used to buy magazines and study the close-ups of the models. Then I'd walk to the dime store and get myself rouge or press-on nails or whatever my budget allowed. Well, these days I don't wear that stuff around the house or when I'm working in the garden of course, but I still get dolled up for church and the like." Pearl sighed contentedly, her eyes still closed. "Charm is deceptive, and beauty is fleeting, but a woman who fears the Lord is to be praised."

"Here it is." Simone set the red nail polish on the bedside table and situated the tabletop directly over Pearl's lap. "Anything else before I go?" Dialogue played in Simone's mind of all the things she wanted to say to Gale. She couldn't wait to tell her off once and for all. She'd pay her to leave her alone; there was enough money in her savings account. Then she would promise to file a restraining order if she ever came back again.

Pearl lifted her head from the pillow and eyed the nail polish. "Unscrew the cap for me, dear. These arthritic hands struggle with those little bottles. Come to think of it, I'm shakier than I used to be. Can you just paint my nails for me?" She set her hands on the table, her fingers splayed.

Simone dropped her purse on the foot of the bed. "I see what you're up to. You're stalling me. You don't want me to chase down Gale, do you?"

Pearl grinned. "I'll need two coats. Then you can fix my hair."

Simone sat on the edge of the bed and began painting. "I should've known you were up to something. I've never seen nail polish on your fingers." Going after Gale probably wasn't the best idea, she had to admit. Besides, Pearl needed her. Not that she really needed her nails painted. She decided to focus on her elderly friend. Pearl was much more fun to think about than Gale. "I've been meaning to ask you about something you said to Gale."

"We're not talking about that girl." Pearl pressed her lips together in a straight line.

"I know. This isn't about her. It's about you."

"Oh?"

"You told her you danced at Juilliard. I didn't know that."

"Well, I did. I danced in the lobby with my friend Minnie. I was wearing a magenta taffeta dress and my first pair of high heels, dyed to match. Minnie and I had ridden the bus cross-country to watch our friend, Nikki, dance in the ballet. She was so graceful up on stage. Coulda sworn she was floating." Pearl had a dreamy look in her eyes. "I was inspired."

"Shame on you, Pearl. You lied." Simone dipped the brush in the bottle. The polish was dried out and difficult to work with.

"No, I did not. I danced. At Juilliard."

Simone raised an eyebrow. "You embellished the truth."

"Fair enough. But I did like to dance. Joined the cheer squad at my high school. That's the closest I could get to dancing. What I really wanted was to become a Rockette." Pearl's eyes lit up.

"Wow. I learn more about you every day." Simone realized how little she knew about Pearl's life, other than she contained a wealth of wisdom.

"I don't waste time rehashing the past. I prefer to enjoy the blessings of today. This is the day that the Lord has made. Let us rejoice and be glad in it."

Simone brushed paint onto the last nail. "We'll have to let that dry before the second coat."

Pearl examined Simone's work. "Looks like one of your students painted them."

"Excuse me? That was not nice." Simone looked at her friend's nails. They looked bad, all right. "In my defense, that polish is old and chunky. What did you expect?"

"Of course it's chunky. Haven't used the stuff in decades. I didn't even want my nails painted. Just wanted you to keep me company. Now, get this nasty stuff off me. Would a Rockette go around looking like this?"

Simone laughed. "I sure do love you, Pearl. I'll take it off. I'd do anything for you."

"In that case, I have one more request."

Simone tipped a bottle of ancient nail polish remover onto a cotton ball and began scrubbing Pearl's nails. "I'm listening."

"Go to my church in the morning. Tell Ethel and Hazel and Pastor I'm feeling better, and I'll be going home soon. The church is on the corner of Fifteenth Avenue and Jewel Street."

"You sly fox. You're just trying to set me up with that friend of yours."

Pearl winked. "You promised you'd do anything."

Chapter Twelve

"I can't believe I'm doing this. I haven't stepped foot in a church since I was eight years old." Simone took a selfie in front of the church and sent it to her Snapchat group. "Do I look all right?" She scoped out the flock of churchgoers. Some ladies wore dresses accessorized with scarves and jewelry, while others were in more casual attire. Some even wore jeans and T-shirts or sweatshirts. Simone's ensemble fell somewhere in the middle between formal and casual—a recently purchased sweater, black pants, and her favorite black boots. Comfy yet chic.

Rose side-glanced at her as she held open the door to the church for Simone. "For the second time, you look beautiful." Rose wore a conservative dress and flats.

An elderly gentleman, dressed in a brown plaid suit, dirty sneakers, and a blue-and-green polka-dot bow tie greeted Simone and Rose with a firm handshake as soon as they entered the building. A name tag stuck to his lapel read *Lyle* in purple ink. Next, they were offered a brochure from a preteen girl who, by the looks of it, had spent more time than anyone else in the building getting ready for today's service. A halo of bright red curls sprang out from an overworked bun that a half-dozen bobby pins failed to contain. And, from the looks of her makeup, it was suspect she'd gotten ahold of Pearl's cosmetic bag. Simone accepted the paper from the adorable girl, whose name tag displayed the name *Ginger*. The girl, distracted, looked over her shoulder at a pimple-faced boy who flashed her a flirtatious braces-laden smile. Simone could immediately picture Pearl feeling at home among this gathering of quirky Jesus-lovers.

Rose steered them through the crowd and chose seats toward the back of the worship center, as Rose referred to it. The church didn't bear the slightest resemblance to the cathedral Simone had visited with a foster family when she was young. That church had been a magnificent historic building with a tall steeple and stained-glass windows. The sanctuary had housed rows of benches, and at the front of the church there had been a pipe organ off to one side, with a grand piano on the other. Choir members, adorned in robes, were seated just beyond the piano. Up front, behind the priest, had hung a cross with a replica of Jesus nailed to it.

In contrast, this church building had previously been a warehouse. The modest exterior had been freshly painted, and beautiful flower arrangements filled oversized pots by the entrance. Inside, there were chairs as opposed to benches. Instead of an organ and piano, there were band instruments on the stage, complete with a drum set, electric guitar, and—wouldn't you know—a bass guitar. Simone thought back to the night Gale had met Pearl. Yep, Pearl knew all about the bass.

The brochure, Rose informed her, was called a worship folder, which turned out to be a churchy way of saying *program*. It listed the itinerary for the service, which started with music. The musicians were incredibly talented, and the lyrics to the songs brought tears to Simone's eyes. They spoke of forgiveness and love, and one song described God as a good father. How comforted these people must feel to think of God as their father. Simone had never experienced a father figure. Not in a positive way like these people spoke of God—a father who loved unconditionally.

The sermon was somewhat interesting, yet Simone's mind wandered. She couldn't help but wonder who the mystery guy was Pearl wanted her to meet. All the men her age seemed to be paired up with a wife. Most of the single men were either of Lyle's generation or had yet to graduate from high school.

"No way!" Simone whispered a little too loudly, judging by the questioning look from the preschooler in the row ahead.

"What's wrong?" Rose whispered back.

"I know why Pearl sent me here."

"To let her friends know she'll be discharged from the hospital. Ethel and Hazel—and normally Pearl—sit in the third row." Rose craned her neck, looking for the ladies through the crowd. "We'll have to catch up with them after the service."

"That was a cover-up. They have phones for that. She's really trying to set me up with a guy. And now I know who."

"Well, I'll be darned." Rose covered her mouth with her Bible to stifle a giggle. "That's just like Pearl."

The preschool kid turned all the way around in his chair and stared at Simone. She tried to ignore him, especially when he stuck his finger in his nose.

She pointed, as discreetly as possible, to the man she was sure Pearl had picked out for her. Ironically, she was already well acquainted with him.

Mica Stark.

Rose shook her head. "He doesn't look familiar. Must be visiting with the Calhouns. I don't think that's who Pearl had in mind."

Seeing as Mica was the only single man even close to her age, Simone was convinced he had to be the one. After the service, she tried to lay low, avoiding Mica. She updated the Bible study ladies on Pearl's progress and kindly asked them to relay the information to their pastor. Rose was mingling and doling out hugs. Simone prodded Rose to make an exit with a tilt of her head toward the door. She wanted to get out of there before bumping into Mica.

"Miss Simone?"

Simone turned around to see Hannah, Gigi, and Sadie standing in a row, smiling up at her. They were adorable, each wearing frilly dresses and patent-leather shoes and sporting matching French braids. Hannah stepped out of line and hugged Simone's waist. "Hi, girls. It's fun to see you here." Simone glanced around. No sign of Mica or the Calhouns.

Hannah stepped back in line. "I slept in my new room."

"Me too," Sadie piped in.

"Me too," Gigi echoed.

Hannah's eyes got big, and she inhaled a giant breath. Simone knew from experience a long story was to ensue. "Petunia got sick and went to the vet and stayed overnight, and now she's all better, and Daddy brought her home, but we can't find her bed, so she slept with me."

"I'm glad Petunia is better."

Rose joined the group. "Hi, Gigi. Hi, Sadie. My goodness you girls have grown."

Gigi and Sadie looked at each other. Apparently neither of the girls recognized Rose.

"Rose, this is Hannah Stark. She and her dad are friends with the Calhouns." She whispered in Rose's ear, "I pointed him out earlier."

"Ah, yes." Rose nodded.

"Miss Simone is the bestest teacher in the whole world." Hannah stretched her arms out to the sides.

Simone beamed with pride. "Thank you, Miss Stark. Hannah is a student in my class this year," she explained to Rose. "She is very smart."

Now Hannah beamed with pride. "I came to church with Sadie and Gigi. And I went to Sunday school. I got

Skittles and a Bible 'cause I'm a visitor." Hannah stacked the Bible and box of candy on top of her head, displaying her treasures.

Kids never ceased to crack Simone up. "That's exciting. I don't remember getting candy at church when I was growing up."

Brooke Calhoun appeared from the multitude of people milling about the lobby. "Nice to see you here, Simone. Are you visiting with Rose?"

"Yes. Her mother, Pearl, is my neighbor. Pearl is in the hospital, recovering from triple bypass surgery."

Brooke gasped, covering her mouth with her hand. "I'm so sorry. I hadn't heard. I'll keep her in my prayers." Brooke looked at the girls, who were bubbling over with energy. She removed the goodies from Hannah's head and flipped through the book, lingering momentarily on pages with illustrations. "Did you get your very own Bible at Sunday school?" Genuine interest shone from her eyes. Brooke knelt in front of Hannah. "Bibles are extra-special books, so you need to take extra-good care of it. Bibles contain God's words to us. You can even read words Jesus said to his friends."

"Wow." Hannah held the Bible reverently in her hands. Gigi and Sadie leaned in for a closer look. Then she furrowed her brow. "I can't read. Miss Simone, will you teach me to read?"

Simone nodded. "You're already learning, silly." She herself was registering the profoundness of Brooke's statement. The Bible contained words Jesus spoke. Pretty amazing. She'd never thought about the Bible in those terms.

"Teach me to read too," Sadie said.

"Me too," Gigi added.

Sadie shook her head at her little sister. "You're too little, Gigi. Three-year-olds can't read."

"Can too." Gigi made a face.

"I would love to teach both of you to read," Simone said. Time spent with these cute girls was always a treat.

"We'll see," Brooke said. "We better go find your daddies now. Hannah needs to show them her new Bible." Brooke hugged Simone and then Rose. "It's good to see you."

Simone was touched by the hug. Hannah, Gigi, and Sadie each hugged her in turn as well. Sadie's goodbye hug came with a statement that left Simone in a bit of a quandary. "I vote for you." Then the girl was whisked away by her mother.

"You dirty dog!" Mica ducked behind a pillar. "Is that why you brought me here?"

Adam contrived a look of confusion. "What are you talking about?"

Mica jutted a finger in the direction of his daughter, who was chatting it up with—of all people—Simone Clare. "That is what I'm talking about." Adam looked over at Hannah just in time to see Brooke hugging Simone. Then Adam's girls hugged her.

Adam squinted. "Hey, isn't that Simone?"

"Don't act so surprised."

Adam laughed. "She can't be that bad."

"She's evil."

"Evil people don't go to church."

"Sure they do. They come to find forgiveness."

"Well, you're a coward. A grown man hiding from a woman half your size."

He had a point. Mica crept out from behind the pillar, keeping a watchful eye on his nemesis. "I'll wait outside." Mica slipped out of the building. Fresh autumn air filled his lungs. The mid-morning sun peeked around puffy clouds, shining its golden light on the changing leaves. He wasn't afraid of Simone. She was just annoying as heck. Plus, he had a schedule to keep. He'd promised to take Hannah to the apple orchard for the afternoon.

He crossed the parking lot to his truck and pulled up in front of the church. Finally, Adam emerged from the church, shielding his eyes from the sun. He spotted Mica's truck and bounded over. "We have a change of plans. Found out a friend of ours is in the hospital. Had a heart attack. Happens to be Simone's neighbor. Small world, huh? Anyway, we're gonna pay her a visit before heading out to the orchard."

"That's fine. Swing by the orchard when you're finished at the hospital."

"Hannah wants to stay with the girls. She's planning to ask you if she can come to the hospital."

"I don't think she understands what a hospital is. I doubt she'd wanna go."

"Oh, she wants to go. She found out Simone will be there."

Mica groaned. "There's no escaping that teacher."

"Must be fate that keeps you two running into each other."

"Or maybe I need to move to a bigger town." Hannah and the Calhoun girls came running out of the church with Brooke trailing behind. The girls started in on pleading for Hannah to go to the hospital. "No, honey," Mica told Hannah. "We're going to pick apples." He licked his lips in an exaggerated motion and wiped his mouth on his sleeve.

Hannah reluctantly climbed in the truck.

Mica couldn't have asked for a more beautiful day to hang out at an apple orchard. Everybody else seemed to think so by the look of the jam-packed parking lot. Mica was ushered into a parking spot by a teenaged boy in a yellow vest, then he and Hannah joined the flock of people climbing a grassy hill that led to a big red barn. A painted sign above the barn doors announced, "Diamond Orchard." They passed a stake in the ground sporting arrows which directed people to the "Apples," "Pumpkins," "Hayrides," and "Petting Zoo."

"Apples," Hannah said, pointing to the sign. "I can read."

"That's right. Good job." Hannah seemed to have forgotten about the hospital. She had a skip in her step as they entered the barn and breathed in a delicious aroma reminding him of his grandma's kitchen. Growing up, Mica would help his grandpa pick barrels of apples from the overgrown trees in their backyard. Grandma would spend days in their farmhouse baking apple fritters, apple pies, and—Mica's favorite—apple donuts.

Families munching on baked goods and caramel apples sat at rows of picnic tables draped in red-and-white-checked tablecloths. The local Super Al's String Band, consisting of a banjo player, a fiddler, a mandolin player, an acoustic guitarist, and a bass player, serenaded the patrons with live bluegrass music. It was quite the shindig.

Mica held Hannah's hand. "Let's get two bags for apple-picking. One for you and one for me." They went to a table where they grabbed bags and got to sample the apples. They decided on their favorite varieties and joined the line of people waiting for the hayride that would bring them to their trees of choice.

A commotion off to the side drew Mica's attention. A group of people, many with dogs on leashes, were gathered around someone with a microphone. "Puppies," Hannah said, "Can we see the puppies?"

"Sure. We can see what's going on. But the hayride will be here soon."

Hannah pulled Mica over to the gathering. He stopped short. Hannah walked right up, kneeling in front of the dogs, oblivious to who was holding the microphone. Gale Wells. *Well, I'll be darned.*

Gale looked as though she'd stepped off the page of a fall fashion magazine, wearing a burnt orange shirt tucked into fashionable ripped jeans, a double-breasted jacket, and leather ankle boots. Her big jewelry seemed a bit over-the-top at an orchard but somehow worked with her outfit. Her blonde hair was in a windblown bun. She looked the part of a celebrity. Mica wondered why she was spending so much time in Diamond, especially when she and Simone were having a tiff.

Mica stood back and watched. He would let Hannah pet the dogs, and maybe they could get out of there without Gale noticing them. Gale, being a celebrity of sorts, had apparently been hired by the local no-kill shelter, or the radio station—however that worked—to host the event. She flattered the onlookers with flashy smiles and hearty laughter. She was a master of the limelight.

She managed to spot Mica and waved him over. The crowd parted as he walked over to her. She hugged him as if he were a long-lost friend. "My friend and fellow animal lover, Mica Stark, is joining me today to raise awareness and funds"—she winked— "for rescued cats and dogs."

"Mr. Stark, have you adopted a pet into your family?" Without warning, a microphone was thrust under his chin. Hannah stood next to him, looking up at him with bewildered blue eyes. She also seemed caught off guard.

"Uhh ..." He scanned the eager faces awaiting his response. "Yes. Petunia."

The onlookers clapped. "Petunia. What a pretty name. What breed is Petunia?"

What? Gale knew Hannah's cat was named Petunia. Was she really that oblivious? "Oh. She's a tabby cat. My daughter named her."

The audience oohed and ahhed.

"Are you planning to adopt a feline friend for Petunia today? Or perhaps a canine friend?" Nothing like being put on the spot.

The crowd cheered in encouragement. Gale grabbed Mica's hand and pumped it into the air in celebration.

"We'll check in with you later after you've reached a decision on that," Gale said. "There are dozens of pets in foster care their caregivers brought out today." Mica's mind snapped to Simone upon hearing the words *foster care*. He wondered if she'd be coming out to the orchard after the hospital visit. He wouldn't be surprised. He seemed to run into her everywhere.

"Mr. Stark?" Gale was waiting for an answer—to what, he had no idea. She repeated her question. "Do you have anything else you'd like to say?"

Mica cleared his throat, wishing he could clear away thoughts of Simone. "All foster kids deserve a good home." He put up his hand as a quick good-bye and backed out of the circle, bringing Hannah back to the line for the hayride. Simone was like an inescapable ghost, haunting him wherever he went—in thought if not in person.

He looked over his shoulder. Gale had the microphone held up to an older woman who looked pleased to be interviewed on the radio, living up her fifteen seconds of fame.

He and Hannah boarded the hayride. Under the open sky, his head cleared. In God's country, as they say. He surely did not feel at home surrounded by strangers and with a microphone shoved in his face. His gut told him Gale was bad news. He hated to pass judgment, and he sure had no interest in siding with Simone vs. Gale, but when he was around Gale, he got a niggling feeling she had ulterior motives, or she just didn't seem genuine. Maybe Simone was right to advise him not to bring Hannah around Gale.

It didn't take long to fill the apple bags to near capacity, and he got some great pictures of Hannah in the process.

They walked back to the barn, stopping to feed baby goats in a little petting zoo.

He spotted Gale outside the barn. She was kneeling in a bed of hay, letting a mangy dog lick her face. Mica cringed. But Gale was smiling and talking baby talk to the mutt. Children circled around her and the dog, their cheerful voices ringing through the air. Gale noticed him and tossed him a playful wink. He held up his wrist and pointed to his watch. She seemed to get the message he was leaving because she put her hand to her ear like a phone and mouthed, *Call me*. He never would.

Simone pulled her car up to the hospital entrance where Pearl, seated in a wheelchair, waited for her in the shade of an awning. The Calhoun family accompanied the patient, their arms weighted down with Pearl's luggage and an abundance of flowers. Sadie held a bouquet of balloons so plentiful Simone half expected the little girl to float up into the cerulean sky.

Simone opened the passenger door and assisted a hospital volunteer in positioning Pearl into the vehicle. "I'm not made of glass," Pearl said, shooing away the unsolicited help. "Don't anyone think of buckling my seat belt for me like I'm an invalid."

Simone laughed. "Oh, Pearl. I am so happy to see you healthy again." She stepped back and pretended not to notice when Pearl struggled momentarily with fastening her seat belt. The rest of the clan loaded the freight into the backseat. Simone stopped Sadie, who was eagerly bounding toward the car with the balloons. "Sadie, there is no way those balloons will fit in my little car."

Sadie twisted her face contemplatively, eyeing the balloons. "How will they get to Miss Pearl's house?"

"Why don't you ask Miss Pearl if she has any ideas?" Simone stepped aside and Sadie approached the vehicle. Simone couldn't hear the conversation the two shared, but it was obvious they'd found a solution to the balloon dilemma when Sadie skipped over to Gigi and divided up the balloons between them.

An enthusiastic send-off ensued as Simone pulled her Beetle away from the curb. The girls blew kisses as they ran down the sidewalk, keeping up with the car for as long as their petite legs allowed them, their colorful balloons bobbing over their heads. Adam and Brooke—and even the volunteer—were waving. Before turning the corner, Simone glanced one last time at the entourage in her rearview mirror. "What a small world. All this time you knew Mica Stark's best friend," she said to Pearl.

"I'd say it's a coincidence that both you and Mica attended my church this morning. But you know I don't believe in coincidences. I *do* believe in divine planning."

"I don't think it's a coincidence either."

Pearl's eyebrows lifted. "Really?"

"Nope. I think you knew all along. This is all just part of your matchmaking scheme."

Pearl laughed, then grimaced and swallowed her laughter long enough to hug a heart-shaped pillow to her chest before allowing her amusement to surface unrestrained. "You give me too much credit."

Simone steered the car onto the main road. "Are you trying to tell me you didn't know Mica Stark was going to be at your church this morning?"

"Trust me, dear. I had no idea. I've never met the man." The woman sounded convincing.

"Well, if Mica Stark isn't the mystery man, then the friend you wanted me to meet didn't show up at church this morning. The only single men I noticed were Mica Stark and an interesting fellow named Lyle. As nice as Lyle is, I doubt he's my type."

Pearl hugged the heart pillow again, her shoulders shaking with giggles. "No, Lyle isn't your type. He isn't my type either. Although, he is a gentleman. And the man can dance. At least he used to. He'd take me to the country-western club on Ruby Road, and we'd dance the two-step till we wore the soles right outta our boots."

"You dated Lyle?"

"Sure did. Never had that spark between us, though. We're better off as friends."

"You country-line dance?"

"Lyle taught me. It wasn't the Rockettes, but we had fun."

"I wish I could've seen that."

"By the way, my friend *was* at church this morning."

"Oh? He didn't introduce himself to me."

"Well, he noticed you were there."

"You talked to him about me?" Simone turned onto her street and parked in Pearl's driveway.

"Of course, I did. Honey, I've been talking to him about you since the day you moved in."

"That's weird and a little creepy. I'm not sure how I feel about that." Simone shifted uncomfortably in her seat. "I've been living in this small town for five years now. If it were meant to be, I think we would've run into each other by now." She turned off the ignition and dropped her keys into her purse. "Seeing that I haven't heard from him, he must not be interested."

"Oh, he's interested." Pearl looked her in the eye and smiled sweetly. "He says you're precious."

A warm, comforting sensation filled Simone's heart and spread through her—like sipping hot cocoa in front of an open fire after being out in the cold. "Precious," she repeated. She'd always seen herself as tough. But only because she needed to be, seeing as there was no one else in her corner, fighting for her. She'd never wanted to appear vulnerable. The word *precious* expressed vulnerability. But not necessarily in a bad way. This kind of vulnerability didn't make her feel weak, just worth fighting for.

She closed her eyes, soaking in the idea of being precious. Worthy of love. She glimpsed what it would be like having someone watching out for her, supporting her, caring for her. Not just meeting her physical needs like the foster families did but really loving her. Loving her enough to never let her go. Just imagining being loved lifted a heavy feeling off her chest she hadn't realized she'd been carrying. For once, she felt light and free. At peace.

Pearl's delicate hand rested on hers and gave Simone's fingers a gentle squeeze. Simone opened her eyes and looked at her friend. Tears welled in the sweet woman's eyes, and Simone noticed her own face was tearstained. Embarrassed, Simone laughed. "Your friend made me cry, and I haven't even met the guy."

Pearl took a rumpled tissue from her purse and blotted under her eyes. "Get used to it. He does that to people. He sees straight to the heart."

Simone wiped her tears with the sleeve of her sweater. She took a deep breath, regaining composure. "He sounds really sweet." Simone wasn't sure why she'd been so affected by simply hearing the dude had called her precious, but it had been just what she needed to hear. Maybe she should arrange to meet him after all.

"I told you." Pearl opened her door. Simone hurried out of the car to help her friend to her feet. She held Pearl's arm as they walked to the side door of Pearl's house.

"You know, maybe hanging out with this friend of yours will help get my mind off of Mica." Simone unlocked the door and helped Pearl take the two steps up into the house. She set Pearl's house keys on the kitchen counter and walked Pearl over to her recliner.

Pearl sat and put up her feet, sighing contentedly. "Home sweet home."

Simone poured a glass of water and set it on the side table next to the recliner. She gathered the phone, the remote, and Pearl's Bible, then set them on the table as well. "What else can I get you? Oh, how about a blanket?" She took an afghan from the sofa and covered her friend with it, chin to toe. "Let's get your shoes off. Where did I see your slippers? I think they're in the bedroom."

"Sit down a minute, dear." Pearl nodded in the direction of the sofa. Simone did as she was told. "Dr. Carson discharged me from the hospital because I'm well. You don't need to fuss." Her voice was patient, not accusing.

"I know, Pearl. I just care about you. You know that. Just because I'm taking care of you doesn't mean I think you're an invalid."

Pearl nodded, looking into Simone's eyes. "You deserve the same treatment as well."

Tears pricked at Simone's eyes.

"Don't get all weepy on me again," Pearl said. "I think we're both a little overtired and emotional from sleeping in that hospital room."

Simone reclined on Pearl's couch, propping her head on a throw pillow. "Fine. Get your own slippers." She was only half-joking. She closed her eyes, pondering the meaning of the word *precious*.

Soon Pearl was snoring softly, yet too loudly for Simone to fall asleep. Feeling a bit silly, she Googled the word *precious* on her phone. The Merriam-Webster dictionary defined it as "of great value" and "highly esteemed or cherished." She smiled from the inside out and continued the search, liking what she'd found so far. Oxford Dictionaries defined *precious* as "of great value; not to be treated carelessly." Tears clouded her vision as memories from a childhood of careless treatment resurfaced. A disproportionate number of chores in comparison with the biological kids. Spankings when chores were completed unsatisfactorily. Being left at home to tend to the dog while the family went on fun outings. Her eighth birthday with no party or presents or cake. At the time, she'd thought the harsh treatment was what she deserved. She'd believed her life was worthless. Now, she realized, more than ever before, the cruelty had been undeserved. She'd been an innocent child. Somehow, until this very moment, she'd let the term "foster child" define her. Not anymore.

Pearl had understood this long before Simone had. How many times had Pearl told her not to believe the lies people said about her? Mysteriously, it had taken a stranger, someone she had yet to meet, saying she was precious for her to see it for herself.

Chapter Thirteen

Time for a new approach. Since wooing Simone's obvious love interest was a failure thus far, Gale decided to compromise an even bigger love of Simone. Her career. That ought to make the woman sit up and pay attention. She needed to fork over the twelve grand, or Gale would make her life a living hell.

The lunch hour seemed like a good time for sneaking into a school. With students and staff traversing through the hallways and going outside for recess, it was easy enough to blend in with the crowd. She stood watch near the cafeteria until the kindergartners filed in. Perfect. Time to head to Simone's room. If anyone asked, she'd say she was meeting Miss Simone for lunch.

Which turned out to be unnecessary. Gale walked into the vacant kindergarten room and slipped two Oxycodone pills into Simone's bottle of iced tea. Just enough of the drug to make Simone a little dopey. She screwed the cap back on the bottle.

"Excuse me."

Gale whipped around to see a young guy with a patchy goatee wheeling one of those mop-in-a-bucket contraptions custodians use.

Play it cool, Gale. He's just a janitor. "Can I help you?" Sweat beaded up on her forehead.

"Is this the bathroom that needs to be cleaned? I heard a student vomited on the floor of one of the kindergarten bathrooms."

"Oh. I wasn't aware of that. Go ahead and check." When he walked by, she noticed the distinct stench of pot. Opportunity knocked.

The janitor looked in the restroom and came right back out. "All clear."

Gale approached him, studying his eyes. Bloodshot. Dilated pupils. "Have you been smoking marijuana on the job?" She folded her arms and looked down her nose at him.

"What? Me? No. No, ma'am." He averted his gaze. This guy was a terrible liar. "I swear. I don't—"

"Pity. Because I've got some pretty sweet joints burning a hole in my pocket. I was hoping you'd like to take them off my hands." She shrugged. "If you know anybody—"

"Yeah." He was flustered. "I know a guy. I mean ..." He scratched the scruff on his chin. "Meet me in the custodial closet after I clean the puke."

Gale smiled. "Lovely. It's a date."

Fifteen minutes later, she was ready to leave the building with extra cash in her pocket when a woman approached her. "Are you looking for the library?"

Gale bit her lower lip, considering her answer. Sure. Why not go with it? "Yes. Could you point me in the right direction?"

The woman smiled. "I'll walk you down. I was just on my way there. I'm Mrs. Whitfield, the librarian." She headed down the hall. "I didn't see a guest reader scheduled for today, but I was sure I had booked every day this month. I must've forgotten to pencil you in."

Being a guest reader should be easy enough. "No worries."

"Remind me. Are you a student's mom?"

A hideous thought. She was in no position to be raising a kid. "No. I'm Gale Wells. My father is Senator Wells. I was raised doing community service with him, and instilling a love of reading in children is so important for our future."

"Yes. It certainly is. Thank you for joining us today."

Gale produced a winsome smile. "My pleasure."

Mondays were typically the most dreaded day of the week, but Simone was happy to be back at school on this particular Monday. She could focus on her students, confident Pearl was being well taken care of by Rose. Her students were behaving and subsequently were rewarded an extra break to play outside. She watched girls take turns crossing the monkey bars. There was so much joy in observing kids just being kids. Each of the students in her class came from stable, happy homes—at least as far as she could tell. Their joy was infectious. Simone twirled happily, feeling like a kid again. *Oof.* She put a hand to her forehead to stop the dizziness. She couldn't twirl like she did as a little girl. Lucy and Jillian were watching her, giggling. They twirled a few times themselves.

She leaned against the brick exterior of the school. Despite sleeping the recommended eight hours last night, she felt as if she could take a cat nap out here on the playground. She supposed Pearl's health scare had sapped her energy.

Lazy clouds parted, exposing the sun's brilliant rays. She put on her sunglasses and pushed up her sleeves. The day was unseasonably warm, and she'd overdressed. As had most of the kids, by the look of the dozen or so sweatshirts and jackets haphazardly strewn about the playground. The lost-and-found bin would undoubtedly fill up today. Simone leaned her head back against the sun-drenched brick, closing her eyes. She breathed in deeply through her nose, enjoying the nostalgic scent of wood chips, blacktop, and freshly cut grass, taking her back to her own school days.

"Hello."

Simone opened her eyes to see Principal Norma Finch eyeing her suspiciously. "Are you okay?" Norma wasn't known for being friendly or for striking up casual conversation. The woman rarely ventured out of her office. Seeing her on the playground was almost startling.

"I'm great, thanks. It's been a good day. I thought the kids deserved some extra playtime." The girls, finished with the monkey bars, ran to a bin of jump ropes and began the formidable task of untangling them.

"I see." Norma crossed her arms. "I heard you've been making a habit of giving your students extra free time." An accusatory statement.

Simone smiled politely. "They're a good bunch. I lucked out with my classroom assignment this year. The rumor is true. I've definitely rewarded them for their good behavior."

The principal clucked her tongue. "We all enjoy fresh air and soaking up the sun, especially with winter lurking around the corner. But our priority is educating the students."

Simone bristled. Obviously, she was being accused of something more than excessive free time, and she didn't care for beating around the bush. "Principal Finch, is there a problem?"

The woman straightened her shoulders. "Come with me to my office. Larry's gym classes are finished for the day. He'll mind your students." Simone looked past Norma to see Larry joining a game of wall ball with some kids.

This was more serious than she thought. She'd be nervous if she thought she had done something wrong. But she couldn't think of anything. The women walked side by side to Norma's office, no words passing between them. Simone swayed a bit. Norma had rattled her so much she could hardly walk a straight line. She ran her fingers along the tiled wall to keep steady. There was nothing for Simone to be ashamed of, and she had nothing to hide. Her students' learning was right on schedule, if not ahead of where she'd expected for this week of school. These accusations, whatever they may be, had to originate from one source. Gale Wells.

Passing by the media center, Simone's suspicions were all but confirmed. She paused, falling behind Norma, and peered through the window of the media center door. Children were seated in a semicircle, their rapt attention on the guest reader. Anger rushed through Simone's body in a wave of heat that burned her face and neck. Propped on a stool in front of the students, Gale Wells turned the page of the book she was reading and looked up, meeting Simone's gaze. Gale waved, causing the heads of all the children to look in Simone's direction. "Why is Gale Wells here?" she asked a bit louder than intended.

Norma answered reluctantly, as if speaking to Simone was a bother. "She volunteered to read to the kids." Simone doubted Gale's sole intention for visiting Diamond Elementary was to read to the students.

In the principal's office, Simone took a seat in one of the two chairs positioned on the opposite side of the desk from Norma's. She resisted the urge to chew her nails. Instead, she gnawed at the inside of her cheek. The principal fixed herself a cup of coffee from a Keurig sitting atop a file cabinet, not bothering to offer a cup to Simone. Not that Simone would've accepted it. "I get the feeling I'm in big trouble, Principal Finch. Was I spotted running in the hallway, or is it because I forgot my gym shoes at home?" She wasn't being rude, just trying to lighten the mood ... unsuccessfully.

Norma sat, sipped her coffee, got up to add creamer, stirred it, sniffed it, tasted it, and finally sat back down.

"I'm afraid it's much more serious than that, Simone." She placed a packet of papers on the desk. "I'll be filing an official complaint against you with the chairperson of the board. This is your copy of the report."

Stunned, Simone grew dizzy. *What?* She glanced at the papers. The words were a bit fuzzy, but she could make out enough of them. "Disciplinary action?" she shrieked, jumping to her feet.

Norma set her mug on a coaster. She folded her hands and rested them on the desk. "Please sit." The principal nodded toward Simone's vacant seat.

Simone acquiesced. She took a calming breath before she spoke. "What are the allegations?"

"There have been complaints against you of unprofessional behavior and suspicion of"—she leaned forward and whispered—"drug use."

Simone's head began to spin. And it was not due to drug use! "Excuse me, did you say, 'drug use'?"

Norma relaxed back in her chair and took a swig of coffee. "I admit, you've been an excellent teacher the past however many years—"

"Five."

"Yes. Five years. Frankly, I'm disappointed. I don't want to lose you. Parents request your class each year, and your students excel, but I just can't have drugs brought into this school." The principal practically slammed down her cup. "You're lucky this didn't get splashed all over the news with that politician's daughter in the building. This is a fine district. We don't need our reputation dragged through the mud." She shook her head vigorously. "I don't even know what to say."

Simone fought an inward battle to keep her cool. "I assure you, Principal Finch, that I have never done drugs." She blinked, trying to focus on Norma's face.

"I'd like to believe you. Unfortunately—"

"What makes you believe I'm doing drugs?"

Norma looked over her shoulder, through the window that opened to the secretary's office. The secretary was immersed in a phone conversation. No one else was within earshot. "People are concerned about you. I've gone back and forth over filing this complaint, but after witnessing odd behavior myself, I need to follow up on these suspicions."

Simone would not back down. Squaring her shoulders, she stared into Norma Finch's flickering eyes. "Who tipped you off to my alleged drug use? How can I dispute the allegations when I don't know what they are? I'm quite sure you're under obligation to tell me." Her words were sluggish, but she managed to articulate them. Was she having a nightmare? She pinched her arm. *Ouch.* She needed a lawyer.

Norma sipped her coffee, stalling. "Mrs. Wilson reported your unusual behavior the other day. She said your class was causing such a ruckus she had to enter your classroom to see what the fuss was all about. When she couldn't find you, a student told her you were in the restroom. You came out with bloodshot eyes."

"You have got to be kidding me." Simone remembered the incident. She'd stepped into the restroom after finding out Gale had been interacting with the Stark family. "I didn't feel well. I wasn't doing drugs. That's absurd."

"I didn't think much about it. Mrs. Wilson can be ..." Norma gazed up at the ceiling, searching for an accurate yet professional description of the teacher who could best be described as a blabbermouth.

"So why are you disciplining me? It's a ridiculous assumption that I was doing drugs. I could've had hay fever, or dry eyes, or was crying over something personal."

"I'll get straight to the point." Finally. "I wanted to discuss Mrs. Wilson's concerns with you. So, I went to your room earlier, and I smelled weed."

"Weed?"

"I'm not naïve, Simone. I know the odor. The whole kindergarten pod reeked. A drug test is the only way to clear your name and put these suspicions to rest. There are just too many signs to ignore. Honestly, I wouldn't have expected this behavior from you." She sighed. "Later, the school nurse thought you seemed loopy when you were walking your students out to the playground today. She asked you if you were okay."

"Yes. I remember that. I told her I felt just wonderful."

"She told me your speech was slurred. I went outside to talk with you, and I saw you dancing. By yourself."

"Twirling," Simone corrected.

"The secretary arranged for you to take a drug test. A taxi service is waiting out front for you."

Shock slapped Simone in the face. "This is unbelievable." She bit down on the inside of her cheek so hard the metallic taste of blood seeped onto her tongue. *No. This couldn't be happening.* She concentrated on breathing, trying not to pass out. "I've done a really good job here at Diamond. You've admitted that yourself. Now after a few odd incidents, you're ready to sack me?" She was kicking and screaming inside.

"It does seem out of character. I hope the drug test comes back clean." Norma handed Simone a slip of paper detailing the testing process. "We'll be in contact with you." She slid her chair back from the desk and stood. "You are suspended until further notice."

Simone walked to the door, her body numb. If only she could wake up from this living nightmare.

Chapter Fourteen

Gale stepped onto Simone's kitschy porch and knocked on the front door, rattling a wooden door sign that read "Pumpkin Spice and Everything Nice." When there was no answer, she rang the doorbell. Still no answer. Either Simone was pretending not to be home—understandable since K9 dogs could be expected to sniff out the premises at any minute—or she really wasn't home, in which case Gale would wait for her arrival.

She jiggled the door handle. Locked.

She walked around the house and tried the side door. Also locked.

"Hey!"

Gale jumped. She snapped her hands to her sides and turned around to meet—wouldn't you know—the neighbor lady, head on. "Birdie!" She could deal with this old bitty. "How are you?"

"My name is Pearl. Simone isn't home. You best step away from that door before I call 9-1-1."

Gale backed away from the door. "No need to be dramatic, Birdie. It's not a crime to visit an old friend."

"No. But it is a crime to enter a residence uninvited."

True. Gale tapped her foot, contemplating her next move. "What time does Simone normally arrive home from school?"

Birdie crossed her spindly arms across her chest. She looked serious, with her lips pressed into a thin line, but she was hardly intimidating in her old-lady nighty and slippers. "I don't keep tabs on Simone. I suggest you call her to set up a meeting."

"I'll wait in my car." She headed for her BMW.

"Come on. You'll be more comfortable in my house."

Gale stopped dead in her tracks. "Excuse me?"

"I'll even feed you. People keep dropping off food. My counter is so full of goodies, it looks like someone died, I tell ya. You land in the hospital for a few days, and everybody acts like you're an invalid." She hobbled toward the house. "Don't just stand there. Do you want to talk to Simone or not?"

Gale, not normally indecisive, found herself at a loss for what to do. She would rather not go into the Bible lady's house, which probably smelled like an old folks' home inside. But maybe the old bird would supply some useful info on Simone. And with her cash supply dwindling, free food was hard to pass up. "Fine." She followed her.

The residence was surprisingly homey. Thankfully, it smelled more like apple pie than the musty, near-death odor she'd expected. Birdie hadn't exaggerated about the food. There were pies, cookies, and bars covering every surface of the kitchen. "You know you can freeze some of this stuff."

"The freezer and refrigerator are plum full of salads and hot dishes. Feel free to help yourself, dear." Birdie fell into a mauve recliner and struggled for a minute with the footrest until it finally flew up, flipping her tiny feet into the air. "Ah, there we go." She closed her eyes and folded her hands in her lap. How could the woman be so relaxed with a stranger in her house, who, admittedly, hadn't treated her very nicely? Must be senile.

Gale turned up the corners of lids on various bar pans until she discovered one with Seven Layer Bars. She dished one onto a napkin. "Do you have coffee?"

"Instant. In the cupboard to the left of the fridge."

Gale fixed herself a cup of coffee, keeping a watchful eye out for Simone's Beetle to pull into her driveway. She joined Birdie in the living room and placed her mug on the coffee table. She sank her teeth into the bar. Gooey chocolate and coconut melted on her tongue. "Wow. Have you tried this bar? It's to die for."

Birdie peeked one eye open. "Lyle brought those. It's his late wife's recipe. She owned *Adelia's Bakery* on Main Street. Their daughter owns the place now."

"My nanny used to make these for me." The taste instigated a flood of memories, back to when she was a little girl sitting at her child-size table, having tea parties with Nanny Bea. "She was my favorite nanny." She took another bite. "I wonder if Nanny Bea is still alive. She'd probably be about your age."

"You should look her up. I bet she'd appreciate hearing from you. If she's still alive, that is." Birdie smirked.

"Nah, she wouldn't remember me. I was probably just another kid, one of the dozens she raised while their parents focused on their careers." She relaxed into the couch, kicked off her shoes, and tucked her legs up underneath her. "At the time, I thought we had a special relationship, but then, one day, she left. Just gave me a hug and walked out the door for good. My mom told me Bea quit because I didn't need a nanny anymore. I was old enough to take care of myself. But I knew the truth. I'd overheard Nanny Bea telling my parents she'd found a higher paying job in California."

Birdie opened her eyes. "That must've hurt."

It had hurt. "Whatever." Gale set the remainder of her bar on the coffee table and wiped her fingers on a napkin. No one had ever acknowledged her feelings about Nanny Bea before. "After she left, I started following my parents around, whining that I was bored, so they decided I needed a playmate. That's where Simone came in. My parents fostered her."

"I see."

She put the coffee mug to her lips, blowing into the steaming liquid before taking a sip. "It was a smart move on their part. A foster kid was someone to keep me busy—plus it made them look good. You see, my parents are politicians, so community service beefs up their résumés."

"Did their plan work?"

"Sure. Everyone loved my parents. They were practically considered saints."

"So, fostering worked well for your parents. How about for you?"

Gale shrugged. She hated thinking about the time when Simone had butted into her life. The foster kid was showered with attention—trips to the Minnesota Zoo, pictures with Santa at the Mall of America, ice fishing on Lake Minnetonka, blah, blah, blah. And it was all captured on film and exploited in the media. All the while, Gale shrank into the background. Sure, Gale got to participate in the activities, but she was a tagalong. The family had never embarked on such adventures before Simone came along. Gale hadn't complained, not wanting to appear petty and immature. "Life was no longer boring. That's for sure."

Gale walked to the window. Still no sign of Simone. "I expected her to come home early today." Surely, she'd been suspended, if not fired. Spiking Simone's tea was intended to send a message she had better pay up. Gale needed the money, and Simone, being the responsible type, undoubtedly had a healthy savings account. Gale speculated Simone would rather dish out some money rather than have her little secret exposed.

She folded her arms to ward off the chill as goose bumps raised on her arms. Honestly, she would rather leave that night in the past too. She kicked herself for bringing it up to Mica.

Ever since speaking of it, the incident had been haunting her thoughts. She'd sworn she saw Arthur walking his dog outside of Willows B & B. Paranoid, she paced by the window around the same time the next day, waiting to see the man again. She did, and it wasn't Arthur. Flashbacks were the worst at night, filling her dreams with disturbing recollections, beginning with herself and Simone stealing the bottle of Amaretto from her parents' liquor cabinet. Her mom and dad coming home with guests for after-dinner dessert. Sneaking out and driving to the park in Simone's Toyota beater. Swinging. Laughing. Talking. Having fun with Simone.

Gale sighed. She wished the story stopped there. "Mind if I use your bathroom?" Her voice was shaking. She cleared her throat. "That coffee ran right through me."

Pearl nodded, pointing the direction to the bathroom.

She made her way on shaky legs and leaned over the sink. Looking into the mirror, she noticed sweat beaded on her upper lip. She rinsed her face, blotting it dry with a towel. Her hand trembled, and she found it difficult to refold the towel. She cursed. Then she noticed the sweet, little, amber-colored pill bottles. Of course, Pearl had been discharged from the hospital with pain medication. One by one, she turned each bottle in her hand to read the label. "There you are," she whispered. "You are a true friend. Always there when I need you most." She downed a couple of the Oxycodone pills and pocketed a few more. Soon she'd be relaxed, and the bad memories would fade.

Enough sitting in this house with an old lady. She went back out to the living room. Pearl had been snoozing but perked up when Gale walked by. "I'll talk to Simone another time." She put her shoes back on, threw away her napkin, and rinsed out her coffee mug.

"Take those bars with you."

"Thanks, Birdie. It's been nice hanging out with you. I'm really glad you invited me over."

Chapter Fifteen

Simone needed an attorney. An excellent attorney. Not having the funds to pay for one, there was only one thing she could do. She just hoped it wouldn't backfire.

After her meeting with Principal Finch and taking the drug test, she made the seventy-mile trip to Saint Paul. She'd forgotten how frustrating rush-hour traffic could be after living in small-town America for the last five years. Crossing the Mississippi River, she knew she was almost there. She turned onto the beautiful Summit Avenue. Historical mini-mansions lined the street. Lush trees littered the lawns with brilliant golden, orange, and magenta leaves. Turning into the driveway of the stately brick home recognized in the community for its manicured vines climbing up the side of the house, she mentally rehearsed the anticipated conversation.

Her stomach did a nervous twirl as she walked up the stamped concrete driveway. Everything was just as she remembered. The fountain centered in the flower garden, the neatly trimmed hedges lining the driveway, a seasonal arrangement of flowers in tall clay planters flanking the front door. It was almost like coming home.

She lifted the door knocker, took a deep breath, and knocked.

The massive door swung open, revealing a man with silver hair and eyes that crinkled at the corners when he smiled. He wore a polo shirt neatly tucked into a pair of khaki pants. Delight registered in his hazel eyes. "So good to see you, Simone."

"Hi, Wesley."

"Eleanor!" he called over his shoulder. "Look who's here."

His wife, a thin woman with white hair styled in a bob, emerged from what Simone knew to be the kitchen. An apron was tied at her waist. "Simone, it's been too long." Simone had kept in touch with the Wellses only through texts, emails, and the occasional phone call since graduating college. Eleanor Wells pulled her into a warm embrace. She smelled of makeup and expensive perfume. "Come in. I'm glad you could join us for dinner. I just took a pot roast out of the oven." She waved Simone into the house with a potholder in her hand.

Simone stepped inside, breathing in the aroma of a home-cooked meal. "It smells delicious. Thank you for letting me come over on such short notice." She felt nine years old again. The first time she'd entered this house, she'd been starving and in dire need of a bath. She remembered the expression on Eleanor's face when she'd first laid eyes on her. She looked sad. Red lipstick had colored the woman's lips, and Simone remembered how her mouth had turned down into a frown despite her obvious attempt to smile and make Simone feel at home. Today, Simone could swear she saw a hint of the same sad expression.

The three of them worked together setting the table and filling the water glasses. They chitchatted about what a beautiful autumn it had been so far. Simone talked about her favorite students and told them a little about visiting Pearl's church. They were interested in hearing more about the man Pearl wanted her to meet, but there wasn't much to tell. "I'll let you know if it leads to anything."

The meal tasted as delicious as it smelled. Eleanor and Wesley filled Simone in on their current endeavors. The couple continued to make time for service projects while maintaining successful political careers. They did so much good for the community. Unfortunately, they would be disappointed at what Simone had to say. She set her fork down and drained her water glass. "There's something I need to talk to you guys about."

Eleanor dabbed the corners of her mouth with a cloth napkin, then folded her hands in her lap. Wesley pushed his chair back from the table and crossed an ankle over his knee. "Do you need money?" he asked.

Simone shook her head. "No, I ... I need a lawyer."

Eleanor placed her hand on Simone's shoulder. "Honey, are you in trouble?"

"No. I mean, yes. But I'm innocent. My principal said my classroom reeked of marijuana, and a couple of the teachers reported I've been acting loopy and had bloodshot eyes. I was forced to take a drug test, and I'm suspended until further notice." Saying those words made her feel sick.

Admittedly, Simone had felt a little off this afternoon. A scary thought had taken residence in her mind. Was it possible Gale had slipped her a drug somehow? It was too coincidental she happened to be at the school when all of this went down. Gale probably volunteered to read to the kids so she could enter the school without suspicion. She probably smoked a joint in celebration of spiking Simone's lunch. "Someone must be setting me up."

Simone felt Eleanor's hand lift off her shoulder. The woman began clearing the table, and soon Wesley went to the sink and began rinsing dishes and stacking them in the dishwasher. Simone sat frozen in her chair while the couple busied themselves. She hadn't a clue what was going through their minds.

Fear cascaded down Simone's spine in a wave that practically made her black out. She couldn't speak. Couldn't move.

"I promise it's not true," she said quietly, her voice not quite cooperating. She licked her lips and tried again. "I would never bring drugs into my school. I have never done drugs in my entire life. I promise you." The Wellses would need to decide for themselves whether to believe her. Her history of trustworthiness had been sketchy.

Eleanor was scooping the leftovers from the pot into a storage container, rather sloppily, when she dropped the serving spoon into the pan. "Simone, please make yourself comfortable in the living room. Wesley, I'd like to speak with you privately."

Simone did as she was told, moving to the living room sofa. Her body was numb as she stared at a family portrait of the Wells family hanging above the fireplace. Simone remembered the day the photo was taken. She'd watched from the sidelines, pretending to read a book while secretly hoping they'd invite her to join them. They did take a couple of pictures of Gale and Simone together, but Simone had never seen those photos.

Eleanor and Wesley had tried to give Gale a semblance of a sibling by fostering Simone—a somewhat admirable move. But Gale had rejected Simone from the start. When it was clear Gale wouldn't accept Simone as a foster sister or even as a friend, Simone had wished Gale would simply ignore her. But that didn't seem to be enough for Gale. She tried to make Simone's life miserable. Maybe she'd thought if she were mean enough, Simone would leave the household. As if Simone had any say in the matter.

Down the hallway, a door creaked open, and Eleanor and Wesley came into the room. They shared the love seat. Eleanor perched on the edge of her seat, her back straight, her hands in her lap, her face straight and unreadable. Wesley, sitting closer to Simone, leaned forward and rested his elbows on his knees. "As you can imagine, we're experiencing a bit of shock and dismay."

"I understand. I am as well."

The two exchanged a look. "Simone, how do you explain these allegations?" Wesley asked.

"I have a hunch I was framed." Simone tucked her hands under her legs to keep from chewing at her nails. "I have no proof of any certain person—"

Eleanor cut in. "Are you insinuating that Gale set you up? She told us she was paying you a visit. I don't know why you girls could never get along."

Simone didn't answer. She didn't need to. They all knew Gale. Knew about her lies, her manipulative past, and her history with drug and alcohol abuse.

Eleanor walked over to the fireplace and looked at the picture Simone had been staring at moments earlier. "A little sibling rivalry is normal. But this is crossing a line."

So, Eleanor was seeing it her way. Simone went to Eleanor. "I wish it were different. I don't know why she's out to get me."

Eleanor turned to Simone, her lips pressed into a straight line. "I meant that *you* are crossing a line."

"Me?" She looked to Wesley. Surely, he understood. But his body language—the way his hands were clasped together so tightly his knuckles were white and the way he was shaking his head—conveyed his disgust with her. She desperately needed their help. She wouldn't give up this easily. "I didn't come here to accuse your daughter. I'm being falsely accused, and I can't afford to hire a lawyer, so I was wondering ..." Oh, how she hated asking for handouts. She closed her eyes and took a deep breath.

"You need to leave," Wesley said.

Simone felt herself breaking down inside, but she wouldn't shed a tear under this roof.

"Good grief. You girls are old enough to take care of yourselves and handle your disputes." Wesley sat back, resting an arm across the back of the love seat. His decision was clearly made. He wasn't going to help her. She would need to hire a lawyer on her own.

"I hope it isn't true," Eleanor said, her bottom lip quivering.

Simone didn't know what Eleanor hoped wasn't true. The accusations against Simone. Or Simone's accusation against Gale. She didn't care to ask.

She left the house. Before backing out of the driveway, she searched Google for an affordable lawyer.

Chapter Sixteen

Rain pelted the windshield, limiting the field of view despite the brisk tempo of the wipers. Mica switched on the hazard lights and crept along, following the yellow line at the edge of the road. At least Simone wouldn't be there to scold him for getting Hannah to school late.

Hannah flattened her palm against the window, rain streaming in rivulets on the other side of the glass. Lightning ignited the darkened distant sky, thunder cracking in its wake. Hannah withdrew her hand and ducked away from the window. "Is there a tornado, Daddy?"

"No, honey. It's just a rainstorm. We're safe in the truck." *God, keep us safe,* he prayed.

His prayer was soon answered when he delivered Hannah safely to school before the first bell even rang. She hurried into the building, the hood of her pink raincoat pulled over her head. Now he wished Simone would be there to witness his superb parenting skills. Her opinion shouldn't matter. He'd heard a rumor she had been suspended for bringing drugs into her classroom. The Simone he knew was smarter than that. He didn't believe the rumor, and he couldn't help but wonder if Gale had played a part.

His phone rang. It was Adam. He answered the call through his truck's Bluetooth system. "What's up?"

"A whole lotta rain. Supposed to continue all day. And with the lightning—we've got ourselves a day off."

"True. It's all outdoor projects we've got underway."

"So how about we catch a movie? There's one I've been wanting to see that Brooke refuses to go to. She says thrillers keep her up at night."

Going to a movie on a weekday just seemed strange. But he didn't have anything else going on. "Are you asking me on a date?"

"I'm not paying for your ticket or your large bucket of popcorn, if that's what you're wondering."

Mica laughed. "Okay. A movie sounds fun. Text me the time, and I'll see you there."

Mica took advantage of the free morning by running errands—paying bills, emailing clients, and buying a few days' worth of groceries—before meeting Adam at the theater. Adam and Brooke were waiting for him in the lobby. "Hey, Brooke." Mica tried not to sound too surprised she was there too.

She greeted him with a hug. "My hubby must've felt guilty for going to a movie when his wife thought he was at work." She winked at Adam. "Hope you don't mind that he asked me to come."

Mica shook his head. "Not at all."

Adam handed him a ticket. "I broke down and bought your ticket since I invited you. I brought my wife so you wouldn't get any ideas about this being a date."

"Instead, I'm a third wheel." Mica accepted the ticket. "Thanks, I guess." He looked the ticket over. It was a different movie than they'd discussed.

"Oh, we're not seeing the thriller. We're seeing the superhero movie instead." Adam tipped his head toward Brooke.

Brooke gave her husband the evil eye. "Don't blame your movie choice on me."

Adam whispered something in Brooke's ear. Whatever it was, what he said made Brooke smile and kiss Adam's stubbled cheek.

Mica looked at the seat assignment on his ticket. "I'm not sitting next to you lovebirds, am I? I don't wanna witness your PDA."

Brooke smiled. "I promise we'll just hold hands."

Mica bought a bag of popcorn and a pop. He felt like a kid playing hooky from school, sneaking off to the movies with his ill-behaved friends. Their seats were in the center of the theater, which was surprisingly full for a matinee. There was something cozy about watching a movie on a rainy afternoon. Josie had liked snuggling on the couch, watching classic movies, on gray days. She'd wear fuzzy socks—her feet were always freezing—and munch on a box of crackers.

Brooke led the way through the darkness as they found their row and shuffled to their seats. She stopped abruptly, causing Mica to bump into Adam and spill popcorn on the row in front of them.

"Hey, there," Brooke said.

"Hi." Simone's voice.

Mica gritted his teeth. He shoved his snacks into Adam's arms and hurried out of the theater. He paced the hallway, murmuring curse words aimed at Adam. Seeing Simone at church may have been a coincidence, but this was obviously a setup. His seat was right next to hers.

"Mica!" Adam strode toward him. "What is wrong with you? That was so rude."

Mica wanted to punch Adam squarely in the jaw. Somehow, he refrained. "That was not cute, Adam. You have no idea. I'm so irritated right now." He crammed his hands into his pockets to keep from smacking his so-called friend. He continued to pace, working out his anger.

"What's the big deal, man? Brooke invited her. So you wouldn't feel like a third wheel." He stepped in front of Mica, blocking his path. "Admit it. You like her. And she's a nice gal. So just sit next to her and stop blowing this out of proportion."

Mica leaned his back against the wall, crossing his arms over his chest. "Yes, I'm attracted to her. But haven't you heard?"

Adam's blank stare answered his question.

"She's suspended from teaching because she was high at school. Rumors are buzzing around town."

"Man, I had no idea." Adam slumped against the wall next to Mica.

"You need to stop meddling. I don't want to be set up with a woman. I just wanna be a good dad for Hannah. That's all I care about."

"Sorry." Adam put his hand on Mica's shoulder. Mica shrugged it off and resumed pacing. What was he supposed to do now? Admittedly, he had been rude and immature, running out of the theater. But the last thing he wanted to do was sit next to Simone for two hours. He needed distance from the lady.

"Let's go back in. It's just a movie." Adam stepped toward the theater. Villianesque music streamed out from behind the closed doors.

Mica considered swallowing his pride and returning to his seat. "I'll look like a fool." A mature human being wouldn't have run out of a theater because he was uncomfortable with the seating arrangement.

"You are a fool."

Mica laughed at the truth in his friend's statement. "You're right. What have I got to lose?" They retraced their steps back to their row. Brooke had taken the seat next to Simone. Adam sat next to his wife, and Mica shared an armrest with Adam.

He'd said hi to Simone as he stepped past her, right before shuffling his butt right in front of her face. As the movie played, Mica's thoughts remained on Simone. How ironic was this? She was the supposed criminal, yet he was flustered and felt the fool around her? Aside from the night at her house when she'd been tipsy—okay, downright drunk as a skunk—she'd been intelligent, professional, mature, and lovely. She didn't seem capable of putting her students in harm's way. She expected a lot of the parents. She seemed to take her job very seriously.

He tried to steal a glance at her through his peripheral vision, but he couldn't see past Adam chomping on his popcorn. He turned to catch a glimpse of her. Her chair was reclined, and a fleece blanket covered her legs. She was one of those people who brought blankets into a theater. What a weird trend. But she looked pretty darn cute all cuddled up. Her pale snow white skin stood out in contrast to her dark, shiny hair. Her beauty, in the dimly lit room, made him think how a black-and-white photograph's simplicity could be far more telling and exquisite than a color photograph. She whispered in Brooke's ear, and the two shared laughter. He could have been sitting in Brooke's chair, laughing with Simone. Indeed, he was a fool. Deep down, he didn't believe the rumors.

The movie gained his attention, and he eventually became absorbed in the action, forgetting about the formidable young woman down the row. Until the closing credits rolled. Adam clapped his hands, and the other moviegoers followed suit.

"Good movie, Adam. Sure beat going to work."

They filed out of the theater into the hallway. Mica decided to man up and talk to Simone. He stepped in stride with her. "Hey."

"Hey, stranger." She smiled sweetly, almost bashfully.

"So, you're into superhero movies?"

"Guilty." She unzipped her sweatshirt, revealing a Captain America T-shirt. He hadn't known a superhero T-shirt could look so attractive. "I've seen all the Marvel movies. I read the comics as a kid."

"You're full of surprises." Mica coughed, wanting to take back his words. "I mean, there's a lot I don't know about you." Open mouth. Insert foot. "Like what your hobbies are and stuff."

Simone shook her head, a half-smile playing at her lips. "I know what you mean."

Mica tossed his snack garbage in a trash can as they walked, and opened the door for her as they exited the building.

The rain had slowed to a drizzle, and the air had cooled considerably. They walked at a fast clip to her car, Simone holding her blanket over her head as a shield from the rain. Brooke and Adam waved good-bye from across the parking lot. Simone opened her car door, pausing before she got in. "Would you like to go somewhere to talk?"

Mica checked his watch. "Can't. School gets out in fifteen minutes." He hadn't wanted to mention school.

"Right. Of course. Funny how fast you can lose track of time." She chewed at her lower lip.

"But after that?" The words were tumbling from his lips before he had time to overthink them. "You can come over, and I'll light the fireplace." Did that sound too romantic? "It's freezing out here." He shivered for effect.

"Sure. I'll run home and check on Pearl. See you in about an hour?" She ducked into her car.

Mica nodded and closed her door. He jogged to his truck and turned on the heater. Giddy thoughts galloped through his head with the notion of Simone visiting. Maybe he shouldn't be inviting the teacher with the drug charges over to his house. But he decided to rest in the idea of *innocent until proven guilty*.

Simone remembered the last time she'd come to this house. She'd gotten full of herself and had lectured Mica on how to run his household. Today was a chance for redemption. She had no idea why Mica was taking a chance on her, inviting her to his home under the circumstances. But she appreciated it.

She stepped out of her car, skirting puddles as she made her way to the front door. The rain had ceased, but the sky remained overcast and the temperature chilly. Mica opened the door before she had a chance to knock. He looked relaxed, wearing jeans, a flannel shirt, and an easy smile. His short brown hair appeared damp and freshly combed. "Hi, Simone. Thank you for coming." He stepped aside, inviting her in. As she walked past him, she smelled his clean, soapy scent.

She left her shoes and car keys on a rug in the entryway.

"Make yourself at home." Mica gestured to the living room.

The home was much cozier now, with their furniture and belongings inside. A leather sofa faced a gas fireplace, which was blazing as Mica had promised. She made herself comfortable on the couch and breathed in the new house fragrances—leather, new carpet, fresh paint, and a hint of ... coffee. She turned to see Mica pouring coffee into two mugs.

"Do you take sugar and cream?"

She didn't have the heart to tell him she wasn't a coffee drinker. She'd hold the mug to warm her hands. Maybe something to cut the bitterness would make it palatable. "Creamer sounds good."

Mica brought her a steaming mug. The aroma was delightful. Cinnamon? She took a sip. Not bad.

Mica sat on the other end of the sofa, sideways, with a leg tucked under him and an arm stretched across the back of the couch so he could face her. "Does it taste okay? The creamer is some pumpkin spice thing Brooke left here."

"It's delicious." The creamer was good, anyway. She took another sip, then set her mug on the coffee table. "Brooke and Adam are great. You're really close, aren't you?"

"Like family." He blew on his coffee before taking a sip. "Adam and I went to high school together. We'd always planned to become entrepreneurs and business partners."

"Your dream came true."

Mica chuckled. "I set the bar low, didn't I? Dreaming of being business partners with Adam." She knew he was kidding. "We both graduated with degrees in business, working as carpenters to get through college. Then Brooke came along and tried to thwart our plans, right before we graduated. As soon as Adam put an engagement ring on her finger, she started telling him he had more to think about than just himself. She tried to persuade him to take some boring desk job that would give him a reliable paycheck and provide benefits."

Simone bit her tongue. She would've felt the same way if she were in Brooke's position. Security had been elusive much of Simone's life.

"Thank goodness our reputation preceded us, and we had a busy schedule that very first summer after graduation. We could hardly keep up with all the jobs."

Simone liked hearing his history. "How did you meet Josie?"

He seemed surprised by the question. He gave her a questioning look, as if confirming permission to tell the story. She nodded, encouraging him to talk. His blue eyes shimmered but not in a tearful way. It was as if thinking of Josie made his eyes sparkle. Simone wished she could have met his wife. Maybe they would've been friends.

Mica set his mug down and repositioned himself, crossing an ankle over his knee. He was more angled away from Simone now, his gaze focused on the flickering flames in the fireplace. "Brooke met her on a mission trip to Haiti. They were volunteering at an orphanage, and both had— let's just say—a difficult time adjusting to their new diet."

Mica laughed. "They had to fight over the bathroom. One time, Brooke took too long, Josie didn't make it on time."

"Gross!" Simone laughed along with Mica. "I can see how that was a bonding experience."

"It was. They became fast friends. So much so, Josie moved from Chicago to Minneapolis just to be close to Brooke. You can probably guess what happened next."

Simone tucked her knees up under her chin and leaned her back against the arm rest. She was thoroughly enjoying the story. "Brooke introduced Josie to you."

"Wrong." Mica laughed. "Brooke didn't think I was good enough for Josie, but she knew I'd find her attractive. Brooke wanted Josie to find someone adventurous who would travel the world with her. In Brooke's eyes, I was too boring and grounded." He shrugged. "She wasn't wrong. I mean, I didn't have the desire to travel, and I did want to find a nice community to settle down in. Build the business."

"So how did you end up together?"

"Brooke couldn't hide her from me forever. It was love at first sight. We had a short engagement, got married, and soon Hannah came along. None of that other stuff mattered anymore. We were just happy being together. No matter where we were or what we were doing." The sparkle in Mica's eyes dimmed a bit. He sighed, a heavy sad sound.

"Thank you for sharing that with me." Hearing him talk about Josie deepened her affection for him. He had shared a piece of his soul with her. Simone touched his hand resting on the back of the couch. His love story had ended in heartbreak. She wanted to extend him a bit of human comfort. For what it was worth.

He clasped her hand, giving it a squeeze. "Thank you for listening." His hand felt familiar, grasping hers. She remembered holding hands with him during the prayer at the picnic. His hand was calloused and strong from his work, yet gentle.

"By the way, where is Hannah? Is she up in her room?"

Mica released her hand. "She's spending the evening with the Calhouns."

Simone wondered if he had planned to be alone with her. Or if Hannah had asked to play at her friends' house. Or if Brooke and Adam had offered to take Hannah to allow Simone and Mica some alone time. Maybe he didn't trust her to be around Hannah. She didn't ask. But it was nice to have uninterrupted conversation. She wanted to assure Mica she wasn't using drugs. Having her name and reputation dragged through the mud made her sick to her stomach. The notion of Mica believing the lies was unbearable.

She took a swig of coffee, instantly regretting the bitter taste filling her mouth. "Sorry, can I bother you for a glass of water?"

"Sure thing." Mica poured her a glass of water and was seated again in a matter of seconds. She'd hoped it would take him longer while she gathered her thoughts.

"I'd like to say something." She gulped water, rinsing the coffee taste from her mouth and suddenly feeling parched. "I didn't do what they're accusing me of." She stared into his sky-blue eyes, willing him to believe her. "I have never taken drugs."

"Then why are you being accused of that? I heard you tested positive for drugs in your system." It was more of a question than a statement.

Wow, the town rumor mill was productive. Hearing Mica say those words made Simone want to jump out of her skin. She stood and walked to the window, staring out at the lake. She had a sudden urge to jump in the water and swim to the other side. To run away from all this nonsense. But her desire for Mica to believe her was stronger. She turned back around. "I don't know how I tested positive. Someone must have laced my food or drink. I'm being framed."

Mica let out a long breath, puffing out his cheeks. "I want to believe you, Simone. You don't seem like an addict or a liar. Hannah adores you ..." His words trailed off. He got up and refilled his coffee cup.

She followed him into the kitchen and sat on a stool at the island. "Do you remember what I said at the coffee shop?"

Mica thought for a beat. "That I was emo? I had to Google that. Learned a lot." He winked to show he was kidding. But the vibe between them remained serious.

"I asked you not to judge me based on what other people are saying about me. See me for the person I present to you. In other words, please believe me."

Mica leaned his elbows on the island, his face inches from hers. He locked eyes with her, his gaze penetrating her soul. Her heart started beating faster. Was he looking for the truth to emanate from her eyes? From her mouth? Or was he thinking of kissing her? She forced herself to blink.

Petunia leaped onto her lap. Startled, Simone gasped. "Oh, my goodness! Hello, Petunia."

"Petunia, get down." Mica shooed the cat away. "Sorry about that."

Simone regained her composure. "That's fine. She must be feeling better. What was wrong with her anyway?"

Mica sucked in a deep breath. "She ate something that made her sick. The vet thought it was opioid poisoning. Brooke found a pill on Hannah's floor. I figure a subcontractor must've dropped a couple of pills. I'm just glad Hannah or one of the other girls didn't find them and think they were candy."

This story had Gale written all over it. "Had Gale been in Hannah's room?"

Mica sighed. "Yes. She stopped by one day when she saw my truck out front. I asked her about it. Denied they were hers."

Simone hated the idea of Gale in Mica's house and Hannah's room. She wanted to protect Mica and Hannah from Gale's wickedness. Simone guessed Gale was using pills and had dropped them. Not on purpose, she hoped. The woman was even more malicious than she'd been in high school. "Like I said, keep Gale away from Hannah. She did drugs back when she was a teenager, and she was smoking pot at my house the other night. I have an inkling she dropped the pills in Hannah's room." *And in my tea.* She hadn't wanted to talk about Gale today. He'd already made it clear he didn't want to get in the middle of their rivalry. "I need to go." She put her shoes on.

Mica followed her to the door. "What's going on with all this drug stuff? Does Gale have something to do with your being suspended?"

Simone picked up her keys and turned the doorknob. "You said you don't want to get in the middle of it. Although, clearly, you already are."

Mica placed a hand on the door, preventing her from opening it. "Tell me what's going on." Desperation emanated from his eyes. "I want to hear your side of the story." He removed his hand from the door. "Sorry, you must think I'm a creep. You're free to leave." He backed away from the door. "But I'd like you to stay. Help me understand, Simone. Hannah really likes you. To be honest, I do too."

Her breath caught. She dropped her hand to her side. What did he mean by that? His resilient love for Josie was as apparent as the torrential downpour suddenly beating against the windows. On the other hand, it had seemed he wanted to kiss her a few minutes ago. There was also the possibility he just meant he liked her as his daughter's teacher.

Whatever the meaning behind his statement, she had come here to tell her side of the story. And as much as she hadn't wanted to talk about Gale, it seemed impossible not to. Gale's history was entangled with hers. In fact, it was imperative to discuss Gale. Mica had a right to know the facts, especially since Gale's actions had directly affected his family. "Okay."

Mica breathed a sigh of relief when Simone agreed to stay. Every conversation he'd had with this woman had ended in awkward discord. Yet he found her fascinating and adorable. He yearned to figure her out. The more he talked to her, the less he believed the rumors about her.

They made caramel corn as she talked. Well, she made caramel corn while he mentally took notes for making it someday with Hannah. He also took mental notes about Simone. She had a sweet tooth. She wasn't a coffee-drinker. She was considerate to a fault—choking down the coffee he'd made for her. She had a freckle that stood out among the others, under the outer corner of her left eye. After listening to a few minutes of her testimony, he learned how resilient she could be. Her mother had been homeless and had turned Simone over to the state when Simone was around four years old. There was no record of her father. Simone had been fostered by a whopping total of nine families, staying the longest in the Wellses' household.

Wesley and Eleanor Wells had been excellent providers. Even paid Simone's college tuition. But living with the affluent family had come at a cost that left her indebted to Gale. At least Gale seemed to think so.

"I'm sorry I ever doubted you." Mica hung his head.

Simone set down the wooden spoon she'd been using to stir the caramel corn. "Don't beat yourself up. You have Hannah to watch out for. As for Gale, she can be very convincing. She has a way of weaseling her way into your life, but then she turns around and stabs you in the back. Figuratively, of course."

Mica chuckled. "I certainly hope so."

Simone slid the pan back into the hot oven. The delicious aroma of melted butter and brown sugar swirled around the kitchen. "I don't get it," she said as she closed the oven and leaned a hip against the counter. "She has everything, but she wastes every opportunity. For some reason she won't be happy until everyone else around her is as miserable as she is." She shook her head. "I just don't get her."

Mica didn't have an answer to Simone's question. "Maybe she doesn't know what she wants."

"Hmm." Simone absently picked up a crumb of popcorn off the counter and licked it off her finger. "She's always seemed so sure of herself. But I guess you could be right."

"Well, she's good at deceiving people. Maybe her self-assurance is an act."

Simone shrugged, her body language telling him she was done with the topic. They sat in comfortable silence at the island while the caramel corn finished baking. Steady rain thrummed on the house, the white noise creating a cozy feel indoors. Mica hoped Hannah wasn't afraid of the storm. He guessed she was quizzing Brooke on the potential for a tornado.

Finally, Simone removed the delicious-smelling caramel corn from the oven. His mouth watered. "It has to cool for a few minutes," Simone said as she turned off the oven and returned to her seat.

"Oh, come on. You're torturing me. My stomach is growling." He looked at the stove clock. "It's almost dinnertime. I'll make a deal with you. We'll eat caramel corn in a few minutes—because I can't wait much longer—and then we'll order pizza for dinner."

"And how is that a deal?"

"It's a deal because you made the snack and I'll provide the pizza." He smirked. Of course, it didn't qualify as a deal at all. It was more of a way of inviting her to stay longer without trapping her inside the house—again—or asking her formally for a date. "By the way, how is Pearl doing?"

"She's as feisty as ever." Simone laughed. "She's trying to set me up with a guy." Her cheeks flushed.

His stomach tightened. He only wanted those captivating doe eyes looking at him. He hadn't realized how strong his feelings for her had become until he thought of her dating another man. "That's great." He smiled for proof. "Do you have a date set up?"

She grinned. "No."

Phew.

"I mean, I'm considering it. She's set me up in the past, and the men were always way older than me and ... not my type. But this guy sounds sweet. Still ... I'd rather meet Mr. Right naturally."

Mica pondered if the way she'd met him qualified as natural.

He heated apple cider in the microwave while Simone scooped gooey caramel corn into two bowls. He popped a piece of the treat into his mouth. It melted on his tongue. "Wow. So good. Hannah would love this."

Simone's phone rang. She took a drink of cider before pulling her phone from her back pocket. A shadow fell across her face as she read the caller ID. "It's Gale." She silenced the phone and set it facedown. "How dare she call me!" Simone tossed popcorn into her mouth, chewing rapidly. "Like I said. It's never enough for her. No matter how far she rises to the top or how far she kicks me to the bottom, she keeps coming back for more."

"Maybe you should see what she wants." Simone's phone signaled a message had been left. A voice mail could be used as evidence against her.

The phone rang again. Simone gritted her teeth and lifted the phone to her ear. "Hello? ... What?" She plugged her ear with her free hand and scrunched her face, concentrating. "Gale, slow down. I can't understand." She strained to listen. Terror radiated from her eyes, the fear as visible as the steam rising from his cup. "Gale, what did you do?" she screamed into the phone. She raced to the front door and crammed her feet into her shoes. "Did you call 9-1-1?"

Mica couldn't fathom what was happening on the other end of the phone. He feared Simone's safety would be compromised if she tried to handle the situation on her own. Mica stepped into work boots sitting out on the rug and grabbed his keys and wallet. Simone was in no shape to drive.

"Mica, call 9-1-1." Her hands were shaking so violently he thought she might lose grip on her phone. "It's Pearl. She's at home. She needs an ambulance. Have them send the cops too. I think Gale hurt Pearl."

Pearl. Simone's elderly neighbor. Friend of the Calhouns. His heart raced. He fumbled his own phone but managed to dial 9-1-1 and spoke to the dispatcher, relaying the scant information he had. As Mica drove to Pearl's house, Simone kept Gale on the phone. Most of her questions were probing and accusatory. Justifiably so. "Why are you in Pearl's house? What did you do to her? What room is she in? Is she conscious? Is she breathing?"

Mica silently prayed. He didn't know what kind of shape Pearl was in or exactly what to pray for. But God knew.

Simone shouted orders to Gale. "Put your face next to her mouth. Do you feel warm air? Give her breaths ... one or two ... I don't know ... just shut up and give her one."

Mica drove as fast as he safely could. "Simone, have her call 9-1-1. The dispatcher can guide her through CPR until the ambulance arrives."

Simone narrowed her eyes at him. She covered the speaker with the palm of her hand. "I'm not letting her hang up. Knowing Gale, she'd flee the scene."

Mica focused on driving, letting Simone deal with Gale until the medics showed up. Simone dropped her phone to her lap and her head flopped back, resting on the headrest. Her teeth were chattering. "I think Pearl is having a heart attack. What was Gale doing there? She better not have hurt her." By the time Mica turned onto Pearl's street, two squad cars and an ambulance were parked in front of Pearl's house, illuminating the small rambler in flashing blue and red lights. Simone jumped out of the truck and ran up the driveway, past Gale's BMW.

Before she reached the house, first responders rolled a gurney out the door. "Pearl!" she shouted. The medics were moving swiftly. "We're rushing her to the hospital, ma'am," one of the men said. From the truck, Mica watched Simone look back and forth from the ambulance to the house. He guessed she was torn between going to the hospital with Pearl and making sure Gale wasn't responsible for the crisis. Sure, Gale had a hankering for causing trouble, but it was likely a ninety-year-old would have complications following heart surgery. He said another prayer for Pearl.

Simone shouted at the police officers inside the house. Then she strode toward the truck. "Mica, take me to the hospital."

How could this be happening again? How many times would she have to see sweet little Pearl whisked away in an ambulance? Simone couldn't bear the thought of losing this woman who cared for her and championed her and acted as a mother figure to her. Logically, the old woman's days were numbered. Even so, Simone wasn't ready to say good-bye. There was comfort in having her next door. When Simone had stopped by this afternoon to check on her, she'd looked fine—settled in her recliner with a novel and a cup of tea. Pearl said she'd planned to read a bit and then rest her eyes awhile before a guest dropped by this evening.

Wait! Was Gale the guest? Had Pearl been anticipating Gale's visit? Simone shook her head, dismissing the thought. There was no way. Gale must've busted into Pearl's home uninvited. She probably laced Pearl's tea with drugs. Simone had told the cops as much.

Simone covered her face with her hands. This was all her fault. Pearl would be perfectly fine and healthy, resting comfortably in her chair right now, if it weren't for Simone introducing Gale into her life. Her eyes stung with tears. She was helpless to contain the heartache, the guilt. She sobbed shoulder-shaking, moaning, snot-producing tears, leaving her weak and almost numb by the time Mica pulled into the hospital parking lot. Gale was far more dangerous than Simone had realized. She'd never imagined the girl she'd shared a home with was this ruthless. Capable of attempted murder. The whole Wells family was shady. Were Wesley and Eleanor behind this? Simone would be sure anyone who hurt Pearl would be held responsible. For now, she wouldn't waste energy thinking about the Wellses. She would focus on Pearl's well-being.

At the hospital, Simone was ushered into the all too familiar stuffy waiting room with the fake flowers. Mica stayed with her. He asked if she would like him to hold her hand. She said *yes*. He poured her a cup of water she only sipped from when he insisted. He sat quietly, knowing she wasn't in the mood for conversation. He distracted her with words only when he somehow sensed the thoughts inside her head could make her implode.

He stayed even after Rose showed up. He allowed her space to cry with Pearl's daughter. He showed Rose the same courtesies—bringing her water and a box of tissues. After what felt like an eternity, Mica went to the front desk to inquire about Pearl's status. Simone was grateful for his presence. He took care of particulars so she could focus on Pearl.

Mica returned, accompanied by a doctor—a man who looked too young to have completed medical school—yet she knew he must be at least her age. Simone and Rose took seats at the small round table. They knew the drill. The doctor would tell them she was getting tests. Someone would let them know when she was settled and ready for visitors. Family only. Which wouldn't be a problem this time around now since she and Rose were listed as next of kin. They would progress to the roomier, more accommodating waiting room, and they would be scared yet relieved Pearl was going to recover. Simone just wished the doctor would get going with his spiel and move things along, so they could begin working toward getting Pearl better and bringing her home. Maybe this time wouldn't involve surgery and the extended hospital stay. Maybe they would give her some medicine and just send her home. Simone should have thought to pack a bag for Pearl back at her house, just in case. Rose scooted closer to Simone and held her hand. Simone leaned into her for support, both emotional and physical.

"I'm Doctor Harris." He sat in the third chair, rested his elbows on the table, and folded his hands.

Simone reminded herself to breathe. She looked at Mica. He leaned against a wall, his arms crossed, his gaze angled to the floor. He sniffed. She guessed he was crying. Disconcerting.

The young doctor cleared his throat. He looked at Rose, and then Simone. He shook his head. "I'm sorry."

Chapter Seventeen

Gale vacuumed the last step of the staircase and shut off the machine. This grunt work was not what she had signed up for when she'd offered to work for the B & B. She'd seen herself designing their website while lounging on a chaise and sipping a glass of wine. Instead, she'd been earning her keep by scrubbing floors, washing dishes, and raking leaves.

The doorbell rang. *Great.* She looked like a sweat ball. She wiped her hands on her shirt, smoothed down her hair, and pasted on a smile. "Welcome to Willows—" Ugh. It was the school janitor. She dropped the smiling act. "What do you want now, Gage? I don't have any more stuff for you." She was lucky no one was at the inn except for her. "You need to get out of here. You can't come here like this."

"Meeting at the school didn't work out so hot either."

"No kidding. I got roped into being a guest reader for the day."

"You think that's bad. The stuff fell outta my sweatshirt pocket when I was folding tables in the cafeteria. The principal practically stepped right over it, but she didn't pay any attention." He laughed as if it were funny.

"Don't be such an idiot. You could get in serious trouble for having weed on school grounds." She was done making deals with this moron.

"Whatever. I'll make this quick. I got this back injury playing college football—"

"Dude, I'm not a pharmacist. Go to a doctor."

"I did. Doctors, physical therapists, chiropractors, you name it. They won't give me any more painkillers. I heard you have—" His voice dwindled in volume, and his gaze focused beyond her.

Gale turned around to see a wide-eyed Frankie. *Crap.*

"Whoa," the girl said to Gale. "Looks like you're running a small business on the side, huh? First me, and now Gage. Hey, Gage. Your brother is in my Algebra class. Don't worry, I won't tell him about this meeting. We don't talk much. You know, since we run in different circles. Him being a football jock and me being … me." She quirked a smile.

Gale groaned. "This town is too small."

"Wait a minute," Gage said, smirking at Gale. "You gave me grief for having weed in a school when you're selling the stuff to a minor?"

Hearing the truth spoken out loud sounded bad, even to Gale. "I didn't sell to Frankie." *Just handed it over.* She had sunk to a new low. She'd never planned on selling drugs when she came to Diamond. She'd only needed a place to stay. But when Simone wouldn't let her bunk at her place … well, desperate times called for desperate measures. "Guys, I hardly had any of the stuff. It's not like I grow it or anything. And as for painkillers, they're prescribed to me." Things were getting messy real fast. "How about what happens at Willows, stays at Willows? Deal?"

Frankie laughed. "Paint that slogan on the sign out front. Alice will love it. Bet we'd get some new customers."

Gale looked at the purple-haired teenager and the twenty-something-year-old janitor. How on earth had she gotten to this place in life? She'd had college tuition and an upstanding family reputation handed to her on a platter, and she'd ditched it all for this? For a temporary job cleaning a small-town inn and selling drugs for measly pennies? It was time to take back a smidgen of control in her life. "Forget it, Gage. Do yoga or something. Don't talk to me again." She shoved him out the door.

Gale leaned against the closed door. She could use a chat with Birdie. Gale would talk, Birdie would listen—and doze off—and eventually Birdie would read to her from the Bible and force Gale to memorize verses. The words had seemed foreign at first, and Gale had trouble making sense of the mumbo jumbo. But as she mulled over the words, eventually they began to make sense. And she even found encouragement from them. *Trust in the Lord with all—*

"Gale?" Frankie was staring at her.

"Skedaddle," Gale said, shooing her away. "Pretend none of this ever happened."

Frankie backed away. "A couple of my friends want—"

"No. Never speak of it again." Gale began winding up the vacuum cord.

Frankie scoffed. "I thought you were cool."

"Yeah, well, I'd like to stay out of jail. I'm guessing you would too."

"Whatever, loser." Frankie went into the kitchen.

Gale decided she'd need to put in more effort at the inn so she could ask for a permanent position. She was lucky to have stumbled across this place that provided her housing and meals. Without this job, she would be homeless. And if it hadn't been for Birdie yammering in her ear about Jesus, she would've lacked the wisdom to turn Gage and Frankie away from her so-called small business.

Simone had dealt with heartache. Far more than was typical by this stage of life. Yet nothing could have prepared her for the feeling of loss she suffered following Pearl's death. The world had been a better place with Pearl in it. The world was gloomy and hollow without her. Pearl had been a mother to Simone, for too short a time.

A steady stream of friends went through Pearl's house—cleaning and sorting her belongings as they reminisced about how she'd touched their lives. Simone helped on occasion, when she felt restless. When being alone with her thoughts was enough to drive her crazy. She hadn't seen MJ or Jade much lately. When they did get together, it felt as if there was an elephant in the room. Both friends said they believed her about the accusations being false, but whether it was Simone's imagination or for real, she felt as if they weren't one hundred percent sure.

At times, she wondered if she was being punished by God or the universe for the crime she committed against Arthur Briggs. Would happiness elude her as long as she concealed this sin? Would the people she loved suffer as well?

These questions kept her awake the night before Pearl's funeral. She read a chapter of a novel but couldn't concentrate on the story. Not even a boring Netflix documentary could dull her thoughts. She pictured Pearl dancing when she listened to music—which made her smile for a moment, but eventually brought her back to questioning whether Pearl's death was an atonement for Simone's sin. Since escaping the thoughts proved impossible, she lay on her back, staring at shadows on the ceiling, and faced them head on.

More than anything, she wished to go back to that night and do things differently. Granted the opportunity for a do-over, she and Gale would put the Amaretto back in the cabinet the moment they heard Eleanor and Wesley return home. Or at least they would walk to the park instead of drive.

That night was such a blur, bits and pieces lost to the alcohol. She remembered goofing around at the park. Climbing up the slides. Crawling across the top of the monkey bars. Swinging on the swings and seeing who could jump the farthest. Eventually, she became nauseous and threw up under a tree. That's where her memory drew a blank.

The next thing she remembered was Gale shaking her awake. Warm liquid was running from her nose onto her lips. Blood. She'd pried her eyes open and found herself in the car, behind the wheel. Gale was screaming at her that she had hit a man. Gale's eyes were wild with fear, and tears streamed down her face. Her voice was high-pitched and screeching.

Simone had tried to unbuckle but realized the belt wasn't fastened. She'd been in a car crash with no seat belt. She could've been ejected from the car and killed. Then adrenaline had shot through her veins as she was struck with the realization she'd hit a guy, and he might be dead.

Simone went to the man, collapsing on all fours beside him. He was facedown. His silvery hair and partially bald head glowed in the moonlight. Visions of a wife or family filled her imagination. Someone would be waiting for this man to return home from his walk. How long until they noticed he was gone?

Gale was yelling for Simone to get in the car, or she'd go to jail. Simone didn't want to go to jail. But she couldn't just leave the man. She placed an ear to his back and listened for any sign of life. She heard breathing. He was alive.

"Let's go. Let's go," Gale shouted. To this day, Gale's pleading echoed in her mind. She couldn't think straight with Gale hollering.

Simone found a cell phone in the man's pocket and dialed the last number he had called. She was careful not to leave fingerprints. "Hello? Hello? Arthur, are you there?" His name was Arthur.

"Let's go."

Panicked, Simone set the phone on the road next to the man's head. She ran to the car and drove back home.

Ten years later, Simone continued to question whether she'd made the right decision. Turning herself in would've meant risking time behind bars. Driving away as she did, granted her freedom. She did live a good life, and

Arthur recovered from a concussion and underwent a knee replacement, according to the news report. Yet she remained captive to the secret.

She pulled the blanket up under her chin and closed her eyes, conjuring happy thoughts of puppies and ice cream sundaes and fields of daisies. Joyful thoughts to oust the dreadful memories. She even allowed a picture of Mica to fill her mind. Finally, a sliver of delight pierced the darkness.

The morning of the funeral, remnants of frost speckled the grass, glittering in the sunlight. Simone walked the few blocks from her house to the church despite the crisp temperature, hugging her arms to her waist to keep warm. Leaves crunched under her boots and swirled around her legs in the breeze sweeping across the sidewalk. She had never been to a funeral, never having been close to anyone who'd passed away. She'd never been as transparent with anyone the way she'd been with Pearl. Pearl knew of mistakes Simone had made yet hadn't judged. She hadn't pushed her away or shamed her when she was in the midst of making those mistakes. Instead, she had pulled her closer, as Simone imagined a mother would.

The worship center overflowed with people who'd been touched by Pearl's graciousness. The smell of freshly cut flowers filled the building. Wherever Pearl was, there were sure to be flowers. Rose had told Simone to meet her in a back room. The two women embraced, comforting each other yet knowing nothing could take away the pain or replace the loss of their adoptive mother.

A few distant relatives of Pearl's were sprinkled throughout the church. Simone and Rose had front row seats for the service since they were considered family. A woman sang a hymn. Simone recognized the tune from

Pearl's Bible studies. She had never made it to a Bible study, but the song would drift from Pearl's open windows into Simone's. *I'm sorry, Pearl.* Fresh hot tears streamed down Simone's cheeks. She was self-conscious about her public display of tears until she heard sniffles from around the room. Of course, she wasn't the only one missing this cherished friend.

After the song, Rose walked to the microphone. "Good morning." Her voice cracked. She cleared her throat before continuing. Her eyes were red and swollen, and she clutched a tissue in her hand. "Pearl was my mom." She beamed, her happiness shining through the anguish. "I couldn't be prouder to call her my mom. See, when I met Pearl, I didn't have a mom. My mother left my dad and me when I was a baby. So, when I met Pearl, I was fifteen years old and in desperate need of a mother figure. She was about thirty years older than me. The perfect age to be my mom. She said she'd always wanted to be a mother." Rose blotted her nose with the tissue. "She had that maternal gift." A collective voice of agreement scattered around the room. "She was nurturing, patient, loving, forgiving. She spoke words of wisdom. Modeled her life after Jesus."

"Uh-huh," a man mumbled.

"Amen," a woman shouted.

Rose continued. "Most of you know Mom was hospitalized recently from a heart attack. Well, one day when I was visiting her in the hospital, she handed me something." Rose held up an envelope. Simone recognized Pearl's writing on it but wasn't close enough to read it. "She'd written a note she asked me to read at her funeral. Maybe she knew God would be calling her home soon. Or maybe she was just being prepared." Rose shook her head. "I couldn't bring myself to read it until last night. Just so you know, she gives me way too much credit." Rose laughed lightly. "Typical Pearl, right?" The audience murmured agreement.

Rose opened the envelope and slid the contents out. She set the paper on the podium, smoothing out the wrinkles. She took a deep breath, exhaling audibly through the sound system. Her eyes met Simone's.

Simone smiled, encouraging Rose, although her heart was splintering into a million pieces. Rose winked at her in response. Then she read the letter.

> Dear friends,
> I must be dead. Oh well. I guess it was inevitable. That was supposed to make you laugh, by the way. I'm afraid you will gather together, cry, and tell sappy stories about me. I bet Rose has already been doing that.

Rose looked at the audience guiltily, dabbing a tissue under her nose. There was a murmur of laughter.

> Don't be sad. I'm in a better place. That statement can come across as insincere when people say it at funerals, but I'm hoping it's acceptable coming from the dead woman. It's true. I know I'm in a better place because I'm with Jesus. I'm at home with my creator.
>
> I'm writing this letter because I want today to be about Jesus. Not about me. You see, I wouldn't be who I am (or was) without Jesus. Few people know about my life before I met my savior. I don't talk about it because it was in the past, and my past doesn't define me. We are not the sum of our mistakes. For as high as the heavens are above the earth, so great is his love for those who fear him; as far as the east is from the west, so far has he removed our transgressions from us.
>
> I want to share my testimony now so you may hear of God's saving grace and know he can transform your life the way he transformed mine.
> When I was a young girl, I loved to dance. Oh, how I loved to dance! Ballet, tap, swing, ballroom. You

name it, I tried it. In my bedroom, that is. I put on my hand-me-down patent leather shoes and danced away on the wooden floor of my bedroom. My parents didn't have money to send me to dance lessons. See, I was the youngest of eight children. It's not that they didn't care about my dream to become a professional dancer; they simply didn't have the time or money to invest in this dream. But that wouldn't stop me.

I was determined to make it on my own. I wanted to be the first black woman to dance with the Rockettes. After graduating high school—a feat in itself—a friend and I packed up and moved to New York City. We worked as waitresses, saving up money—me, for dance lessons; my friend, to buy a place of her own.

On a late shift at the diner, a handsome, well-dressed man was seated in my assigned section. He was sophisticated and distinguished-looking, smoking his cigar and reading his newspaper. He ordered blueberry pie and decaf coffee, black. I felt his eyes follow me around the room as I served other customers and refilled water glasses. He made me feel pretty and desirable. A man like that had never paid attention to me before.

You can imagine my reaction when he told me I looked like a dancer. Maybe he had connections. That's partly why I moved to New York, after all. To make connections. I told him of my dream to dance for the Rockettes. He told me he could fulfill my dreams.

Friends, you probably have an icky feeling in your stomach right about now. I, however, was naïve and blinded by my youthful passions. That's what I believed about myself two years later when that man was my boss, and I was dancing at a club in the wrong part of town. Now, I know the truth.

I'd been an innocent young girl with hopes and dreams, trusting that an older man would care for a young woman and make good on his promise.

I realize this doesn't sound like funeral material. Friends, just because we're—I mean you're—in a church, doesn't mean we pretend we're all holy and lead perfect, happy lives. Rather, church is a place for people to gather, to share how God overcomes the difficulties in our lives. We can't talk about Jesus being our Savior without talking about what he saved us from.

Let's get to the good part. Many years later, I got off the bus one stop early, delaying my arrival at the club. I dreaded going to work every day. But I still treasured the idea I could get noticed and one day dance for the Rockettes. I believed what that smooth-talking, smartly dressed man had told me. Every Rockette had to start somewhere. Had to pay their dues. On this day—it was cold and there was a slick dusting of snow on the sidewalk—I debated not going to the club. No, I'd go to the club. I'd just get off the bus early and fool myself into thinking I was walking somewhere else. To a different job. A respectable job.

I believe God made me get off that bus one stop early. It was part of his plan.

A young woman with red curls that spiraled down from underneath her hand-knit red stocking hat offered me a cup of hot chocolate. Anyone would've been a fool not to accept a warm beverage on such a frigid day. I accepted. The young woman, whose name was Rose, walked with me. "Can I keep you company?" she asked. Again, I obliged. I told her I was on my way to work. I told her I hated my job. To make a long story short, Rose told me she had a friend who could help me. Naturally, I bristled. I'd had enough help from men. She insisted I meet him. "He is loving, kind, gentle, and good." Truth shone from Rose's eyes. She looked so sure of herself. She seemed to be at peace with the world. And anyway, this friend of hers couldn't be worse than the man from the diner. I had nothing to lose. I abandoned my job, risking the only source of income and the only path to my dreams of dancing, to follow this young woman. I wanted whatever it was that made her eyes shine. To me, it was worth risking everything for.

That day, in a McDonald's restaurant, Rose introduced me to Jesus.

A sound that was half laugh and half cry flew from Simone's mouth. The mystery man Pearl wanted her to meet was Jesus. Rose, pausing from reading the letter, winked at her again.

I abandoned my life for him. But you know what, friends? He gave me a better life. I never looked back. John 10:10: I have come that they may have life and have it to the full.

Since meeting Jesus, my life has been rich. I never danced with the Rockettes, but that didn't matter after befriending Jesus. Instead, I danced like David danced. I danced for Jesus. And now, in heaven, I'm dancing with Jesus.

Simone choked back sobs as best she could. She closed her eyes, envisioning little old Pearl in the arms of Jesus, swaying to the old hymns that Pearl loved so much. What a beautiful scene.

Chapter Eighteen

Pearl Jones was obviously a special lady. Her funeral was touching and sad to Mica even though he hadn't met her. But celebratory fireworks were exploding in his heart. He knew Pearl, looking down from heaven, wouldn't be offended. The so-called man Pearl wanted Simone to meet was Jesus. He didn't need to worry about her dating some other dude. He'd nudged Adam during the funeral and tried to convey the revelation to him, but Adam was too lost in his sorrow to make the connection. Now the funeral was over and loved ones were filing out of the sanctuary and heading to the cafeteria for refreshments.

"Why are you smiling like a sixteen-year-old who just scored his first kiss?" Adam asked, looking perplexed.

Brooke, overhearing her husband's ridiculous comment, had to see for herself. "You *are* smiling like a boy who's been kissed. What's up, Mica?"

Mica motioned for them to hang back while the other people left the sanctuary. Then he explained.

Adam and Brooke were blissfully pleased. Adam clapped a congratulatory hand on Mica's back. "I'm happy for you."

Brooke hugged him.

Mica held up his hands. "Slow down. I haven't won her heart yet. Besides, I don't even know if she wants her heart to be won. She's grieving her friend. And she's suspended from her job. And—"

"Mica"—Brooke put a hand on his shoulder— "we got a little ahead of ourselves. Sorry about that. I just have a good feeling about you two. I really like Simone. I don't believe any of that rubbish she's accused of. Doesn't seem like the Simone I know."

"Go talk to her." Adam pushed Mica toward the exit.

"Now?" Mica's heart galloped at the idea.

"Don't ask her out or anything," Adam clarified. "Just talk to her."

"Right. I knew that."

Mica spotted Simone sitting at a table with some jovial silver-haired ladies. She looked as though she needed someone to talk to. Someone closer to her age, maybe. "Is this seat taken?" he asked, pointing to the vacant chair next to Simone.

Simone looked up at him, her golden-brown eyes sweeping over his face. "Mica. What are you doing here?" Her words came out slowly, as if each syllable took effort. A plate of food sat in front of her, untouched, although she held a fork in her hand.

"I came with the Calhouns."

She looked past him to Adam and Brooke, who were balancing paper plates in their hands and wearing dorky grins. She waved to them, and they waved back. "They look … happy." She poked her fork at a grape halfheartedly and unsuccessfully. She looked anything but happy.

He claimed the empty seat. "It's easier if you use your fingers."

She looked at him quizzically. "Huh?"

"The grapes. They're finger food." He picked one up off her plate and popped it into his mouth. Then he picked up another and held it to her lips. She smiled and opened her mouth to accept the grape.

"I like grapes," an elderly woman sitting across from Simone chimed in, batting her eyelashes.

"I do too," the woman next to her said, leaning her plump arms on the table and making googly eyes at Mica.

Finally, Simone cracked a smile. "Mica, this is Ethel and Hazel, Pearl's Bible study friends." She divvied her remaining grapes between the two women's plates. "Enjoy, ladies."

Ethel frowned at the grapes and pushed her plate aside while Hazel shrugged and popped one in her mouth. Those two were a hoot. "Nice to meet you," Mica said.

"Speaking of Bible study," Ethel said to Simone, "we will continue to meet every Saturday night. We'll be at my house this week, and we'd love for you to come." She dug a pen out from her purse and scribbled her address and phone number on a napkin. "You don't need to bring treats. I'll make a fresh apple pie. My grandkids keep bringing me crates of apples. My freezer is already plum full of apple pies and apple fritters."

Simone gnawed at her bottom lip. "I'll think about it."

"Just bring your Bible," Hazel said. "We'll take care of the rest."

"Oh," Simone said. "I ... don't own a Bible."

Of course she didn't. Pearl had wanted her to meet Jesus. It was obvious she was uncomfortable with this conversation on an already trying day. "You can download a Bible app or order one off Amazon. Or you can borrow one of mine," Mica said, hoping to ease her discomfort.

Ethel scooted her chair back and stood with a hefty grunt. "Nonsense. I'll get you a Bible right now." She disappeared down the hall and, in a few moments, reappeared clutching a Bible identical to the one Hannah had brought home from Sunday school. "Now you have your very own Bible." Ethel plopped back into her chair, opened the cover of the Bible, and wrote Simone's name inside. She slid the gift across the table to Simone.

Simone seemed at a loss for words, for once. She ran her hand over the cover, touching the colorful picture of Jesus with a flock of sheep. "Thank you, Ethel." She smiled, looking genuinely touched by the gift. "I guess I'll see you Saturday."

The two old ladies clapped giddily and hugged each other. Mica surmised they'd been hounding Simone to attend one of their studies for some time.

Simone glanced at her watch and then looked toward the exit. Mica could tell she was ready to bolt. "Would you like a ride home?" he asked. He guessed she'd walked the few blocks to the church since he hadn't seen her car in the lot. He'd been hyper-aware of Simone lately. A day didn't go by without him thinking of her, and he missed her when their paths didn't cross.

She nodded.

On their way out, Mica let Adam know he was taking Simone home. Adam didn't congratulate him as Mica had expected. "Are you coming back?" Adam asked. "You're our ride home too."

Mica shrugged. "Not sure. You can always call an Uber."

"Thanks, man," Adam said sarcastically. "Thanks a lot."

"I knew you'd understand."

Mica waited for Simone in the foyer while she went to a back room to get her coat. He peeked in on Hannah, playing with her friends in a supervised classroom. Brooke had promised to watch her after the funeral. He heard a commotion in the sanctuary. People were raising their voices, almost yelling. Curiosity getting the best of him, he peeked through the small windows of the double doors leading into the worship center.

It was Simone. "What the—" She was yelling at a woman who was sitting in the front row of the church. A man and woman had pulled out chairs from the front row to sit facing Simone's target. The lady suffering Simone's wrath stood and shouted back.

Mica stepped inside, and their faces turned toward him. His stomach clenched, and so did his fists. Mica understood the source of Simone's anger as it became his own. "Gale, what are you doing here?"

The man, who turned out to be the pastor, accompanied by his wife, stood and tried to deescalate the situation. "It's okay."

"It's not okay," Simone cried. "She has no right to be here."

The pastor's wife spoke in a calm voice. "The doors are open to anyone who wishes to celebrate Pearl's life and grieve in company."

Simone, shaking, hugged her arms to her chest. "She needs to get out of here. Don't trust anything she says." Simone faced Gale. "How dare you show up after what you did to Pearl!" Mica worried Simone would go ballistic on her. Deserved or undeserved, he couldn't let that happen. Simone looked ready to explode. On the contrary, Gale appeared composed, self-assured. He wouldn't allow her to affect him the way she'd rattled Simone. Gale was probably loving every minute of this.

Mica stepped between Simone and Gale. He spoke to the pastor and his wife. "I can vouch for Simone. This woman, Gale Wells, needs to leave."

The pastor and his wife looked at each other, clearly bewildered.

Mica felt Gale's gaze bore into the back of his head. He turned and locked eyes with her. She frowned, her eyes pleading. He looked away, shaking his head.

He took a minute to assess the situation. It was true, Gale had every right to attend Pearl's funeral. No matter Gale's intentions for entering the church, a discussion with the pastor could be a stepping-stone for her to turn her life around. He turned to Simone. "I'll take you home," he said softly.

Simone didn't move, her anger discernible by the vein that protruded from her neck.

Mica held out his hand, hoping with all his might Simone would place her hand in his and go with him. The pastor was capable of discerning Gale's intentions and handling the situation.

At last, Simone rested her shaking hand in his. He curled his fingers around hers, wanting to lift her hand to his lips and promise to take care of her. Promise her he wouldn't let Gale harm her or anyone else she loved. But it wasn't a promise he could keep.

Chapter Nineteen

"Have you seen anything more beautiful?" From atop her trail horse, a palomino named Butterscotch, Simone absorbed the view as they plodded along the ridge overlooking the Mississippi River. The water sparkled in the sunlight as it flowed at a leisurely pace. Scarce golden-brown leaves clung to branches, reluctant to join the blanket of foliage swishing and crunching under the horses' hooves. Simone filled her lungs with the cool, invigorating air. It was easy to forget her troubles, surrounded by all this beauty.

"I never saw anything more beautiful than Rufus. He's the beautifullest horse in the whole world." Hannah patted her horse's neck. "Good boy, Rufus. Daddy, can I keep Rufus?"

"No." Mica held up the back of the caravan with his horse, Snickers. "The view isn't as spectacular from back here. Rufus's breakfast isn't agreeing with him. It's disgusting."

Simone laughed, grateful for her place in line behind the trail guide. The beautiful outdoors was helping to soothe the ache of missing Pearl. The last week had been incredibly lonely, her bereavement magnified by the temporary loss of her job. Mica had been checking in with her almost every day. Sending a random sweet text or a funny GIF, occasionally calling to talk. He also seemed to know when she needed time to herself. Time to grieve. Time to learn how to get back in the swing of life absent of the only person she'd considered family. It was sweet of Mica to invite her along on this trail ride.

After much consideration, she decided to open up to Mica about the night she'd hit Arthur. The incident was constantly on her mind these days and Mica, being so caring, seemed a safe person to trust with her deepest regret. Keeping it to herself was no longer an option. Her conscience could no longer bear carrying the full weight of it. And being blackmailed by Gale was exhausting. She hoped he would respond with the same comfort and compassion he'd shown regarding Pearl's death.

She looked back at him, craning her neck to see past Hannah and Rufus. The man was a sight for sore eyes. He'd purchased a cowboy hat just for this day, and he looked mighty fine. He'd failed to shave due to the early reservation for their trail ride, his five o'clock shadow enhancing the ruggedly handsome look. He smiled and winked at her, tipping his hat. She smiled in return while her heart did a little cartwheel.

After riding, they stopped for soup and sandwiches at a café, then polished off the meal with made-from-scratch chocolate chunk cookies. Delectable.

Hannah had taken one bite of her cookie and then wrapped it in a napkin to finish later. She busied herself, coloring on a paper placemat with cheap waxy crayons the restaurant had provided. Her blonde hair hung like a curtain over her face. Simone swept the locks behind the girl's ear. "I wish I could tell Pearl about this day," Simone said.

Mica swallowed a bite of cookie. "What would you tell her?" He grinned, probably waiting to hear what a prince he'd been.

"For starters, I'd tell her that Hannah had the beautifullest horse." Hannah looked up briefly, then went back to her creation.

"And?"

"And I'd tell her the river was magnificent. Serene." Simone closed her eyes, recapturing the beauty in her mind before the memory faded.

"And?" Mica cleared his throat, no doubt suggesting she mention him.

"I'd tell Pearl that a handsome cowboy lassoed my heart."

Mica grinned in satisfaction.

But Simone wasn't done. She pursed her lips, feigning deep thought. "What was that handsome trail guide's name again?"

"Not funny!" Mica tossed his napkin at Simone.

"What?" Simone said, laughing. "Bert. That's it. Bert was a good-looking gentleman."

"Sure, if you're into men three times your age."

Simone was fairly certain Mica was aware of her developing feelings for him. But she wasn't ready to turn over her heart just yet. Not that she doubted her feelings for Mica or even his feelings for her. She had wrinkles to iron out in her life. Furthermore, Pearl had wanted Simone to meet her friend Jesus. She couldn't properly contemplate welcoming Jesus into her life with Mica taking up all her thought space.

After two Bible studies, Simone remained open to the idea of Jesus in her life, but she couldn't say that she'd *met* him. How does one meet Jesus anyhow—without being dead, that is?

They spent the afternoon at Mica's house, watching the *Heartland* series on Netflix upon Hannah's insistence. Hannah watched the show with rapt interest—lying on her tummy, her chin resting on her hands. Simone was grateful both Hannah and Mica had opened their home to her. Surely they felt Josie's absence here. She knew from experience loss is something one carries throughout a lifetime. Opening your heart again can be equally freeing and painful.

Simone and Mica shared the couch, sitting close enough to bump elbows and knees—sometimes by mistake and most times not. She was allowing her heart to open up to this man. A scary realization. Each person she had loved, she'd lost. For now, she would set her fears aside and enjoy the moment. She whispered in Mica's ear, "I bet someone will have a horse on her Christmas list this year."

Mica chuckled and shook his head. "It's not happening." He looked into her eyes, his face inches from hers. She touched his cheek lightly with the back of her hand, the stubble tickling her fingers. He closed his eyes, leaning into her touch. Her hand slid to the back of his neck, and she leaned in, kissing his cheek. His neck. And then laying her head on his shoulder. He sighed and clasped her hand in his.

Encouraged by Mica's affection, Simone worked up the courage to tell him about Arthur. "I need to tell you something."

Mica's posture stiffened. "I don't like the sound of that."

"Don't worry. It's not about you." She kept her head on his shoulder to avoid looking him in the eye. "I have this huge regret that I never talk about with anyone. I need to get it off my chest."

"I'm listening."

She took a deep breath. "I was seventeen. Gale and I were hanging out at home, drinking and actually getting along. Her parents came home, so we snuck out and drove to a park. It was stupid. I don't know why I drove."

"Daddy, look at the horse," Hannah said.

"I see it, honey." Mica nudged Simone. "Go on."

"We had fun at the park. Drank way too much. So much that I don't remember getting back in the car. I ... I ..." Mica remained quiet. "I hit a man." Now it was her turn to sit quietly while Mica formed his words and contemplated if he still wanted a person like her in his life and around his daughter.

After a minute, he cleared his throat. "Did you try to run him over?"

"What?" The question took her by surprise. She looked up at his face. He knew her better than that. "Of course not. I would never do something like that."

"Do you still drink and drive?" He gave her a look suggesting he knew her answer.

She shook her head. "Never."

"Then maybe it's time to forgive yourself."

"He didn't die." Saying so emphasized his point.

"Even if he had, you can't carry that burden the rest of your life."

"Whoa. I could never forgive myself if I killed someone."

"You learned from your mistakes. We all make mistakes. It's how we respond to them that matters most."

She couldn't have hoped for a better response. Tears welled in her eyes. "Thank you." Here in Mica's arms, curled into his side, it seemed as if the two of them fit together like pieces of a puzzle. His fingers stroked the back of her hand. He pressed his lips to her knuckles one by one, his tenderness softening the jagged edges of her damaged soul. She contemplated his words. How had she responded to her mistakes? Sure, she backed off on drinking and never again drove under the influence. But she'd fled the scene and never fessed up. He'd made it sound like she was a hero of her life story when really, she was a criminal on the run. She wouldn't have peace until she told the whole story. "Mica, there's—"

"Daddy, can we go horseback riding again?" The credits were rolling on the screen and Hannah jumped up and stood in front of Mica. "Please, Daddy. Can we go tomorrow?"

"Honey, we'll go again someday, but not tomorrow."

"Can we bring Gigi and Sadie?" Hannah hopped on the couch next to her dad.

"Hannah, we'll see. Right now, I'm talking to Simone. Go on up to your room for a few minutes."

"Why? I wanna be with you and Simone."

"Hannah—"

"It's okay, Mica." Simone didn't want Hannah getting in trouble only for her to increase tension in the home by telling Mica she was guilty of a hit and run. "We can talk another time."

"Are you sure?"

"Yes."

She untangled her fingers from his and wiped her damp palm on her jeans. He did the same, and she couldn't help but feel a pinch in her heart seeing the metal band that encircled his fourth finger. Maybe it was better if she didn't bear her soul to a man whose heart still belonged to another. She didn't fault him for loving his late wife. Rather she admired his devotion to her. Josie hadn't died all that long ago. At the same time, she also wasn't going to expose herself to hurt by falling in love with him when he didn't love her back.

"Thank you for today. I should get going."

Mica looked confused. "You don't have to go."

"I had a really nice time."

Hannah wrapped her arms around Simone's waist. "Bye, Simone."

Mica stood and hugged her as well. "I had a nice time too." He kissed her cheek. "Thank you for trusting me. For being candid."

She needed to finish telling the story soon.

Chapter Twenty

Simone ordered a pumpkin scone and the largest chai tea latte Lakeview Brew offered. Sugar and caffeine would be crucial today when she would make the last walk through on Pearl's house, preparing it for market.

When Simone entered Pearl's home, she was welcomed by the comforting smell of apple cinnamon tea. Despite the hordes of people who'd come through the last few weeks, the place still felt warm and comforting. The house had been emptied all but for a few pieces of furniture left for staging. After the sale of the house, the furniture would be donated.

Simone got to work before she started getting all nostalgic and melting into a puddle of tears on the freshly scrubbed kitchen floor. She started in the kitchen, setting out a bottle of liquid soap beside the sink, rolling out a new rug, and hanging up pretty towels on the oven door handle. Next, she moved on to the bathroom, repeating what she'd done with the kitchen.

She saved Pearl's bedroom for last.

Here, in the room where Pearl had slept and prayed, her presence was almost palpable. Or maybe it was the memory of her.

Her scent.

Her voice.

Her tenderness.

Her sass.

Simone sat on the edge of the bed, giving in to the tsunami of emotion. Eventually, she had to grab a roll of toilet paper from the bathroom to mop her face. She remembered Pearl blotting her tears with napkins or whatever absorbent material she could find in her purse on too many occasions. Whose shoulder would Simone cry on now? Who would tell her just the words she needed to hear to snap her out of her pity parties?

She curled up on Pearl's bed, snuggling into the cozy pillows. The bed linens had been changed—they were too trendy for Pearl's taste. Someone younger must have bought them and made the bed. Simone supposed it was a good idea to appeal to a younger generation. There weren't likely to be ninety-year-olds house hunting. The buyers would most likely be a young family. Simone tried to talk herself into being happy about acquiring new neighbors, potential new friends to fill the void Pearl had left behind. But it didn't work.

When her tears finally ran dry, she pulled herself together and straightened out the bedding. She checked to make sure the closet and dresser drawers had been emptied, then she opened the bedside table drawer. A package, wrapped in rose-patterned paper, had been left behind. She picked it up and read the envelope taped to the front.

To: Simone

For me? With shaking fingers and a racing heart, Simone opened the envelope and read the enclosed letter. It was dated the day before Pearl's death.

Dearest Simone,

This gift isn't for you. Well, it is. But in a roundabout way. Let me explain.

Gale has been visiting with me. Now, don't get mad. I didn't tell you earlier, because I didn't want you to worry and fret about me. I'm a big girl. I can take care of myself. She needs a friend to talk to, and I've got the time to listen. That woman can talk a blue streak. Once in a while, I nod off during her monologues, but mostly I rest my eyes and let her prattle on. She even visited me in the hospital while I was resting my eyes. She doesn't know I'm even sneakier than she is. (More on that in my diary, if need be.)

I've come to enjoy Gale's visits. She reveals her inner thoughts to me while she believes I'm snoozing. It's true—she lets evil get the better of her, yet she is as deserving of love as the rest of us. I haven't been feeling well lately. I'm afraid I'm not strong enough to overcome this ailment. Forgive me for not troubling you with this information. Hopefully, I will recover. But in case I don't, please do me this favor. Please give this package to Gale. It contains my Bible. Rose gave it to me when she introduced me to Jesus so many years ago. It's the Bible I've read through and through. I scribbled notes in the margins and highlighted verses I worked to memorize. I'd like you to deliver it to Gale personally. You will know when the time is right.

Please understand why I'm not giving this special gift to you. It's just that I trust Ethel and Hazel will take care of you, while I fear Gale may get lost in the shuffle. If it feels like we're scheming to win you over to Jesus, you're correct. Don't be creeped out (as you kids say these days). He won't enter your heart without your permission.

I love you,
Mom

Pearl had trusted Gale. Simone paced the room, her blood coursing hot through her veins. "Pearl, why didn't you tell me about Gale?" Even if a natural cause took Pearl's life, Gale probably brought it on by bugging her with disturbing stories all the time and not letting her rest.

Simone read the letter again, this time pausing on the part about Pearl's diary. "More on that in my diary, if need be," Pearl had written. Simone needed all the info she could obtain on Gale. She would read the diary cover to cover if need be. Surely Gale hadn't been paying an old woman visits out of the kindness of her heart. She was probably stealing from her or plotting to hurt her as a threat to Simone.

Pearl was a smart woman. Maybe she was on to Gale all along but offered her friendship in hopes she'd have a change of heart. Simone only hoped there was evidence of Gale's misconduct logged in Pearl's diary.

She combed through the house again, searching for the diary. When she came up short, she called Rose. "Do you have Mom's diary?"

"Hi, Simone," Rose was taken off guard by her abruptness. "Um, yes. It's right here. In a box. I haven't unpacked her things yet. I just don't have the energy."

"I'm coming to get it." Simone ran out the door.

"Are you sure you should be driving? You sound awfully upset."

"I'm fine. See you soon." Simone hung up, shutting down Rose's protests.

Rush hour had begun. Simone had to work at cooling her temper so she wouldn't ram her car into anyone's bumper. Her eyes ached from all the crying. She slipped on her sunglasses. Traffic crept along on Interstate 35. The delay was torture. Simone needed to read that diary. It would hold the key to Simone's freedom if Pearl repeated Gale's rantings in it. Maybe Gale had confessed to Pearl she'd been setting Simone up with drugs.

The possibilities swirled through her imagination. She turned on classical music to quiet her mind.

A text came in. After briefly contemplating the hazards of texting and driving, she gave in and read the text.

MJ: Gale Wells was arrested for selling drugs!

No way! Gale actually got busted for once? It was about time. Simone pulled off the road at the first chance she got. Her heart was pounding. She wasn't sure if she was happy Gale got what was coming to her or was horrified Gale was selling drugs or was just plain freaking out about the whole situation. Fear intruded her celebratory thoughts when she realized Gale might have mentioned the Arthur Briggs incident to the authorities.

She called MJ and got the 4-1-1. The whole town was talking about it. Cops arrested Gale while she was working at Willows B & B. Apparently, she'd sold weed to a janitor on campus at Diamond Elementary. Selling drugs on school grounds is a felony. She was in possession of Oxycodone and was suspected of selling it too. As great as Gale's arrest was, these facts didn't help Simone's case. In fact, Simone probably looked worse since she had a connection to this drug dealer.

"MJ, you believe me that I don't have anything to do with this, right?"

There was too long of a pause for Simone's comfort. Then MJ answered, "I believe you, Simone. You wouldn't even drink a glass of champagne at the New Year's Eve party last year."

Simone felt her shoulders relax. "Thank you, MJ. That means so much to me."

"Of course. When are you coming back to school?"

"Good question. My drug test was positive, and the school board doesn't believe me that it's either a false positive or I ate or drank something spiked. Can't blame them. I've been asking to repeat the test."

"Gale was at the school, reading to kids that day."

Simone sighed. "I have no doubt that Gale is responsible."

"There's an explanation for the pot stench in your classroom."

"Really?" Simone was anxious for any bit of good news. "The janitor?"

"Yes. That young custodian named Gage. He was fired for smoking weed on campus."

Simone chewed at her nail. "I guess that's good. For me, anyway."

"Do you have a lawyer?"

"Yes. Some guy I Googled."

"Branson and I are praying for you."

"That's sweet. Thank you."

Young voices murmured in the background. "My third-graders are coming in. Gotta go."

Simone continued on her way to Rose's.

Monday night football at the Calhoun's house was no small affair. The dining room table displayed a buffet of chicken wings, hot dogs, baked beans, potato chips, baby carrots (because Brooke insisted on at least one item from the vegetable group), and frosted sugar cookies shaped like footballs. The Minnesota Vikings played tonight, making the game even more exciting. Their next-door neighbors and a family from church showed up as well, decked out in purple and gold.

Mica had texted Simone just before kickoff, inviting her to the party. He hadn't heard from her since she'd run out on him in typical Simone fashion. Shouldn't have surprised him. Silly how he'd thought they'd become closer since she'd cuddled up to him on his living room couch after a romantic morning of horseback riding. He sighed and tucked his phone in his back pocket, resolving to be patient with her in consideration of her circumstances.

"You better eat more wings than that." Brooke eyed Mica's plate. "Adam made me deep-fry ten pounds. Don't be shy."

"I'm just getting started. Don't you worry." He pointed to Hannah over at the kitchen nook, her plate heaping with chicken and a generous side of chips. "Hannah's doing her part too." Barbeque sauce dripped from her chin and was smeared across her face, ear to ear. He snapped a picture with his phone. "Is she cute or what?" He turned the screen to show Brooke.

She took the phone to get a closer look. "Simone texted you. Check this out."

Mica read her text.

SIMONE: Thanks, but I'm busy.

Mica couldn't help but worry about her. She'd been too quiet lately, and her last brief text didn't put his mind at ease. He texted her back, asking if she was okay.

Cheers exploded from the other room. Hannah ran to see what the commotion was about. She returned to the kitchen with her arms extended above her head. "Touchdown!" she exclaimed, although he doubted she understood what that meant.

He mimicked her, gesturing a touchdown. Then they did their celebratory dance, swinging their hips, spinning in a circle, and finishing by bumping hips—which required him to squat down to her level, sending her into a fit of giggles every time. Then he steered her back to the table before she dripped barbeque sauce on the floor. Normally he wouldn't miss a single play of the Vikings game in the first half, but the lure to discover what was happening with Simone was stronger. Only two other women in his life had trumped football.

"No way," Brooke said, her eyes fixed on her phone. "The story is all over the Diamond Facebook page. Gale Wells was arrested for selling drugs at Diamond Elementary School." Mica peered over Brooke's shoulder. The post chronicled Gale's illegal sale of recreational marijuana to a custodian. She was also under suspicion for selling Oxycodone since she possessed multiple bottles of the drug, prescribed by different doctors. Anger roiled in Mica's gut. He'd had a feeling Gale was who'd dropped those pills in Hannah's room. "That woman was in my house. Around my daughter." Mica looked at Hannah, nibbling innocently at her chicken, her little legs swinging under the table. Hannah had never liked Gale. She'd been a good judge of character.

Adam wandered over, munching on a handful of chips. "You guys are missing out on a good game." He did a double take. "Whoa. Why so serious?" They caught him up on the breaking news. "Oh, man." He shook his head, speechless for a moment. "I was planning to vote for Wesley Wells, but now I'm not so sure. I'll have to do more research. Maybe he's as crooked as his daughter."

The election was the furthest thing from Mica's mind. He was concerned for Simone's safety. His phone buzzed. A message from Simone.

SIMONE: I'm going to talk to Gale.

He texted her back, begging her not to go near Gale. To let the authorities handle it. Gale Wells was off-her-rocker psycho. Mica cared too much about Simone to stand by and allow Gale to mess with her life any more than she already had.

But Simone didn't respond to his text.

Chapter Twenty-One

Only a table separated Simone from Gale. If it weren't for the table and the law enforcement loitering about, Simone would rip Gale's hair out. "I don't know what you're up to, Gale, but you are not going to take me down." She thought of Pearl's diary out in her car. She hadn't found incriminating evidence in the entries she'd read so far, but Pearl had hinted there was some in there.

"I'm not up to anything." Gale's innocent act infused Simone's anger. How could Gale sit there looking all upright and proper in her expensive suit and think she could get away with corruption?

"So, you're not fessing up?"

"I am." Gale glanced at the one-way mirror. Then she lifted her chin in an air of confidence. "I've always treated you like crap. I'm sorry." Her tone lacked remorse.

"That's it? You're sorry?"

"Truly. Please forgive me."

"Never." Simone clenched her jaw.

"What are you doing here, Simone? I already pled guilty."

"Why were you at Pearl's house the night she died?" Her chest was heaving. Never in all her life had she experienced so much rage. Not when an angry drunk foster father broke a plate on her foot because she hadn't dried it thoroughly enough. Not when a foster mom stole Simone's bracelet she'd bought with her own money. Not when a family refused her simply because she didn't blend well with their children. She hadn't even experienced this much rage when Gale blamed her for stealing her mom's handbag.

Gale did her fake frown, turning out her bottom lip and making sad puppy-dog eyes. Her chin even quivered. "I didn't do anything to hurt Pearl, if that's what you're insinuating. I miss her too."

"Liar!" Simone sprang up, her chair thundering to the tiled floor.

Gale stood too. She leaned her hands on the table. Tears ran down her face, leaving tracks of mascara in their wake. "It's true. I ... I loved Birdie. She changed my life."

"Birdie? What—?" Simone covered her face with her hands. What was happening here? "Her name is Pearl. You didn't even know her. She was like a mother to me." A torrent of tears dampened her own face and impaired her vision. She wiped her eyes, hating that she was crying in front of Gale.

Gale sat down and motioned for Simone to do the same. "I want to tell you something."

Simone remained standing and crossed her arms. She would not bend to Gale's will.

"Fine," Gale said. She closed her eyes and folded her hands in her lap, not moving for a good thirty seconds.

"Hello?" Simone interrupted Gale's meditation. "I thought you were going to tell me something."

Gale looked up. Her demeanor had softened. "I'm forgiven."

"Says who? I certainly do not forgive you for anything." Gale couldn't just steal forgiveness. Hatred filled Simone's heart, pumping throughout every inch of her body.

Gale, on the other hand, lacked even a hint of a fight. "I understand if you won't forgive me." She looked down at her hands. "I was awful to you." She met Simone's gaze.

"Don't you get it?" She laughed lightly. "I was jealous of you."

"Me?" No. Simone did not get it.

"Yes, you. My parents have adored you since the first day you walked into our house. They chose you over me."

"That's not true." Simone sat, her knees feeling weak.

"My parents cut me off. They're actually on the fence about helping me out with these drug charges. What loving parents turn their backs on their own flesh and blood?"

So, they'd basically shunned both Gale and her. "Maybe they cut you off because you're a drug dealer."

Gale shrugged. "I'm not a drug dealer, exactly. Besides, that's all in the past. Today is a new beginning."

Now Simone looked to the one-way mirror. She hoped someone was recording this conversation. Gale was starting to creep her out.

"This is going to sound crazy. I can't believe it myself." Gale smiled, heightening the creep factor. "I talked with Birdie a few times. I liked her. She was a good listener. As it turns out, she and I have a lot in common. Did you know she was addicted to heroin when she was about my age?"

"No."

"Well, she was. Anyway, she told me about a friend of hers she wanted me to meet."

Pearl had used the same line on Gale? It felt like a betrayal at first, but after giving it some thought … it was typical of Pearl not to discriminate. She was kind to everyone she met. "Let me guess. She wanted you to meet Jesus."

Gale perked up. A smile lit her face. "You know him?"

"What does that even mean? Everybody knows who Jesus is."

"But do you know him personally?" Gale was leaning forward, sincerity shining in her eyes. It was a look Simone had never seen from Gale before.

"Um … no. Are you telling me you know Jesus personally?"

"I know, it sounds crazy, but Jesus changed my life. Just like that." She snapped her fingers. "He forgave me. For everything."

Yep. Certifiably crazy. Must be the pills talking. "That's great, Gale. I'm happy for you, but I don't forgive you. I'm leaving now." The less time she spent with this psychopath, the better. Simone walked out the door.

Hannah was tucked into bed, sound asleep. Mica lay in his bed, wide awake. Concern for Simone blanketed his thoughts. She hadn't texted him back after he'd pleaded with her not to hunt down Gale.

Since sleep eluded him, he rolled out of bed. He padded down the hallway and peeked through the partially open door at his sleeping little princess. Her golden hair was splayed across her pink pillow, her arms were flopped over her head, and her mouth hung wide open. Not quite angelic but still adorable.

He moved down the hallway to the room he rarely entered despite it being his favorite. The scrapbook room, as Hannah called it. Mica flicked on a table lamp which provided ample light for him to see yet didn't hamper the view of the moon reflecting off the lake, visible through the large window. This room was meant to have been a surprise for Josie. She'd seen the blueprints and knew the architecture of the space, but she didn't know he'd saved a snapshot she'd sent him from an upscale design of a similar room with a stone fireplace flanked by bookshelves. He'd copied the design down to the pattern of the stones and the repurposed solid pine mantle. The bookshelves would have been extra special, as they would have housed her dozens of novels and—more importantly—her loads of scrapbooks previously piled up on the dining room floor of their cramped rental house.

Mica removed an album from the shelf and reclined in a leather chair. He opened the cover to see a beautiful young Josie smiling at him from the page. Her hair was held off her face with a bandana. The picture was a selfie, a close-up that allowed him to see the way her two front teeth just barely overlapped. According to the caption she'd handwritten, she was riding an elephant in Cambodia. He turned the page to see Josie surrounded by children. All eyes were fixed on her. Mica guessed she was telling a story or singing a song. Knowing Josie, she'd probably picked up enough of the language to communicate with the locals.

He reshelved the book and picked up another. Their wedding scrapbook. Oh boy. His heart ached, and he hadn't even peeked inside yet. He took a deep breath, then began the journey down memory lane. The journey they had shared. She was breathtaking that spring day, wearing her mother's wedding dress. A few alterations, and the gown looked brand-new. As if it had been made for Josie. Her mom had died when Josie was in her teen years. Josie said the dress made her feel as if her mom were there, accompanying her down the aisle.

Mica had recommended a small wedding, but Josie didn't want anyone to feel left out. Typical Josie, always thinking of others. It turned out to be a huge gathering and a day to remember. One of the best days of Mica's life.

As happened with most milestone events, the day went by way too fast. The final photograph was captured during the closing song of the dance. It featured Mica, Josie, Adam, and Brooke. They were sweaty, their hair disheveled, and their fancy clothes rumpled. They exuded sheer bliss. The caption Josie wrote under this photo was "Don't cry because it's over. Smile because it happened."

Mica wanted to heed his wife's advice today, but his sadness was unquenchable. Tears rained down his face. "Josie, I miss you." Their life together had been wonderful, but he wasn't ready for it to be a memory. He wanted the life they shared to be his present, his future. Josie's absence had left a gaping hole in his heart. "Josie, I will never stop loving you." He hoped she could hear him and feel his lasting love for her, without sensing his pain. He didn't want her to feel bad for leaving him. He'd heard some survivors experience anger toward their deceased loved one for leaving them alone to travel through life in solitude. But Mica felt differently. His anger was directed toward himself for not protecting her. And he felt bad she would miss out on watching Hannah grow up. There had been so many times when Hannah said something cute or funny, and he'd longed to call Josie and tell her about it.

He slid his wedding ring off, remembering how foreign it had felt on his finger those first weeks of marriage. Now his finger felt naked without it.

"Daddy?" Hannah was standing in the doorway, rubbing her eyes with one hand and holding her tummy with the other. "I don't feel good."

Mica dried his eyes with the sleeve of his shirt. He grabbed the wastebasket from the corner of the room. "Are you gonna throw up?"

She shrugged.

"Will cuddles help you feel better?"

She came to him and climbed up on his lap.

He kept the garbage can close by. "Too many chicken wings?"

She nodded, then rested her head against his chest. "Daddy?"

"Yes, honey?" He kissed her head.

"When you marry Miss Simone, will you wear two wedding rings?"

He laughed a guttural sound, her candor catching him off guard.

Hannah looked up into his eyes, waiting for an answer.

"No, honey. I'd only wear one ring."

"Mommy's ring or Simone's ring?"

Mica's emotions were warring between laughing and crying. He did his best to give her a straight answer. "When I was married to Mommy, I wore her wedding ring." His voice cracked. "I still love Mommy." He cleared his throat. Took a moment before he was able to continue.

Hannah waited patiently, listening intently. She touched his cheek, wetting her dainty fingertips with his tears. "Are you sad, Daddy?"

"Yes, honey." He swallowed around the lump in his throat.

"Does Miss Simone make you happy?"

He didn't need to think long before he answered. "Yes. She does."

"She makes me happy too. She says I'm important."

Mica hugged his baby girl. "Oh, Miss Stark. You sure are important."

Chapter Twenty-Two

On her way home from the police station, Simone bought a box of donuts from the convenience store. She snuggled into bed with the donuts, a cup of chamomile tea, and Pearl's diary. Never mind it was after midnight. She had to read more of the diary.

Where to begin? Flipping through the pages, she settled on the month she'd moved in next door to Pearl. Upon further digging, she found the exact day.

Dear Diary,

The first rose of the season opened on this beautiful summer day. It was the first thing I saw this morning when I looked out my kitchen window. When I saw that pretty little thing, I just knew this was going to be a special day.

It was. A new tenant finally moved into the run-down rental next door. She's quite young. She's going to be the new kindergarten teacher at Diamond Elementary, and I think she will fill Mr. Nichols's shoes quite nicely. She has a firm handshake, and that says a lot about a person. I know I'm going to like her. I invited her for tea tomorrow. Her name is Simone Clare.

I have no doubt that the Lord brought Simone to Diamond, Minnesota. My prayers have preceded her.

The Lord brought her here? It was amazing to think God paid any attention to Simone's whereabouts. But how could Pearl have prayed for Simone before she even met her? Simone flipped back several pages. Sure enough, Pearl had listed prayer requests with each entry, and daily she'd prayed for the new tenant of the vacant house.

Pearl had been praying for *her*.

Awe overwhelmed her. Pearl's prayers had brought Simone to this house. *If you believed that kind of thing.* She set the diary down and pondered the possibility. Moving to Diamond had seemed a bit miraculous. She had been ready to accept a position in another school district, teaching the fourth grade. She'd all but given up on landing a kindergarten job when the opening at Diamond Elementary popped up. Her interview was the best she'd had. Everything about the job just felt right. And then, when she saw this little rental she could actually afford, she knew Diamond was where she was meant to be.

She dunked a donut in her tea and took a bite—gross. Soggy. She tossed the donut back into the box and set down the tea. Back to the diary.

She skimmed through the entries, spending more time reading, when she glimpsed her name. It was interesting to read about her life from Pearl's perspective. The woman seemed to have known Simone almost better than Simone knew herself.

Then she noticed Gale's name written in an entry. Pearl noted how troubled Simone had been by Gale's note. Simone remembered that day. She had been troubled, to say the least. For good reason. But what Pearl wrote next surprised her.

> I believe God brought Gale back into Simone's life for a reason. I gather the girls have deeply hurt each other. I pray they will find forgiveness so they

will be able to move on from whatever has been holding them back from a life of peace, joy, and friendship.

Disgusted, Simone tossed the book aside. She'd given up on friendship with Gale a long time ago.

The next morning, she woke to find the lamp had been on all night, and she'd apparently rolled over on the donuts. There were crumbs in the bedding, smooshed in her hair, and plastered to her clothes. Nice.

She showered and then brought Pearl's diary to Lakeview Brew, where she sipped on a pumpkin chai latte and peered into the window of Pearl's uncensored thoughts. Simone could hear Pearl's voice saying the words. She could see her facial expressions—her stern glare when something upset her, her spunky smile when she was joking. She could feel the love and peace Pearl received from her faith as she closed her entries in prayer. Bible verses were scattered throughout the pages—scrawled in the margins, boldly printed across the tops of pages, embedded in the body of the entries.

Pearl had constantly been quoting Bible verses. Scripture was as much a part of her language as cussing was to a sailor. The words had blown over Simone like a soft breeze. Refreshing yet fleeting. Occasionally annoying. At times, the quoting of verses had seemed preachy or pretentious. Simone hadn't realized just how meaningful the verses had been to Pearl. Until now.

Now Simone understood. Pearl drew strength from the verses, and they had naturally infused her language, her thoughts, her identity.

"Is this seat taken?"

She looked up. Mica Stark was dressed in a fluorescent jacket and carpenter pants. His handsome face was a welcome surprise. "I get the feeling you're stalking me." She motioned for him to join her. "Or would you like to order your coffee first?"

He sat in the plush chair facing hers. "I had coffee at home. I saw your car out front, so I stopped in to see how you're doing."

"So, you admit to stalking me?" she asked playfully.

He grinned. "Guilty."

"Sorry I didn't text you back last night. There's been a lot on my mind." Simone made eye contact with Jade, who was clearing dishes from a nearby table. Jade placed a hand over her heart, like she was seeing the most adorable thing ever. Simone grinned and trained her attention on Mica.

"I was worried about you. That's all."

Jade came over to say hi to Mica and offer him a cup of coffee, which he politely declined. She returned to her work.

"You didn't need to worry. I met with Gale at the police station." She recalled Gale's odd, completely out-of-character remarks. "I don't know if that woman should be locked up in a jail or an insane asylum. She was saying she met Jesus." After reading Pearl's diary, it did seem more plausible Pearl had won Gale over to Jesus. "Psycho, right?"

"Huh." Mica looked contemplative.

"She said Pearl introduced her to Jesus, and he changed her life." Simone rolled her eyes. "Am I really supposed to believe that?" Mica was a churchgoer. Maybe he could help her understand. "Do you think Jesus can really turn someone's life around in the blink of an eye?"

Mica took a minute before answering. He leaned forward, propping his elbows on his knees and intertwining his fingers. The morning sunlight shone on Mica's back and cascaded over his shoulders. The fine hairs on his hands glinted in the light. Something was missing. Something that would catch the light. *Oh.* He wasn't wearing his wedding ring. "I do."

"What?" Simone couldn't remember what question he was answering. What had they been talking about?

"I know it seems farfetched. It's not that I'm taking her side. But I've seen people completely turn their lives around after accepting Jesus as their savior."

Oh yeah, they were talking about Gale. "You sound like Pearl."

"Thanks." He smiled, his eyes strikingly gorgeous. "By the way, Gale texted me this morning."

"What did she say?"

He took his phone from his jacket pocket and read the text aloud. "Sorry for what happened to your cat. It was probably my fault. Please forgive me."

"What did you say?"

"I told her Petunia is fine and that I forgive her."

Simone's eyes grew wide. "You forgave her just like that? What if she was lying?"

"Maybe she is. Maybe she isn't." He shrugged. "Doesn't matter. I still forgive her."

That was admirable of Mica. Simone did not forgive quite so easily. Gale deserved to be locked up.

She couldn't help but stare at the indentation around Mica's ring finger, wondering why he'd taken the wedding ring off. Feeling like an insecure preteen, she asked, "Are you seeing someone?"

He cocked his head to the side, rubbed his chin, and cleared his throat. "Why? Do you have someone in mind for me?" His crooked smile told her he was giving her a hard time.

A bashful smile betrayed her affection for him. "Yes. She's kind of a handful."

Mica laughed. "That doesn't intimidate me. My only requirement is for Hannah to love her as well." He was flirting.

Simone blushed. "I adore Hannah."

"Hannah adores you." He touched the back of her hand, and her skin tingled in response. "What do you have there?"

He pointed to Pearl's diary. She was grateful for the change in subject because she was ready to start making out with him right here in the coffee shop.

"This," she said, tapping on the book, "may hold some of the answers we're looking for." She fanned through the pages. "It's Pearl's diary."

"Are you sure you should be reading that? Isn't that one of those forbidden things like digging through a woman's purse, only worse?"

"She gave me permission." It was sweet of Mica to consider Pearl's privacy. "She kinda recommended it in a letter she left for me. She also told me to give Gale her Bible."

"Why does she want *you* to give it to Gale?"

"She thinks it will help us to make amends somehow."

"Did you give it to her last night?"

Simone shuddered. "No. She doesn't deserve it. Pearl treasured that Bible. Anyway, let's get back to the diary. I'll see if she wrote about her new BFF, Gale Wells."

He sighed, a look of irritation sweeping over his face. Maybe her obsession with destroying Gale was getting to him. He probably thought she should forgive Gale like he did.

"I'll let you read. I need to get back to work. I was on my way to the hardware store." He put his phone back into his jacket pocket. "I'm glad you're okay. I was so worried I could hardly sleep last night."

"Really?" He was more invested in her than she had realized.

"Really. I can't tell you how relieved I was to spot your car out there." He pointed toward the parking lot. He stood. "Well, see you around."

"Wait. I didn't tell you the whole story." He needed to know exactly the kind of person she was.

He sat back down. "What story?"

"The one I was telling you after horseback riding. We left him there." She spit it out before having a chance to change her mind. "We just drove away."

Mica stared at the floor.

"Say something." His silence was worse than being berated.

"Did you ever admit to it?"

She shook her head. "I know I should have. But I wanted to make a life for myself. I didn't want to go to jail. Plus, he lived. It's not like I killed him."

Mica made a guttural sound. "You can't tell me something like this and ... what do you expect me to do?"

"Like you said, I'm different now. I've learned from my mistakes."

"It's called a hit and run. That could be charged as a felony." He looked at her with disdain, crushing a piece of her soul. "You need to figure it out. And I need some time to think." Then he got up and walked away.

After perusing the last few months recorded in Pearl's journal, Simone rubbed her eyes and set the book aside. The entries hadn't been as incriminating against Gale as Simone had hoped. In fact, the only nefarious thing Gale did was steal twenty dollars from a get-well card. That tidbit wasn't surprising. It was typical behavior for Gale.

Simone was relieved Gale had been good to Pearl. Or not bad anyway. Pearl seemed to get a kick out of Gale's blatant narcissism. And she looked beyond it to Gale's heart, which Simone hadn't ever considered doing. She had assumed a black hole would exist where Gale's heart should be.

The biggest thing she'd learned from reading Pearl's diary was how much Gale felt unloved by her parents. That was crazy. Eleanor and Wesley gave their girl everything. But apparently, they didn't give her enough time and affection. The whole scenario was pitiful. There were two young girls feeling lonely and unloved when they could've been best friends instead of competing with and hating each other.

But Simone couldn't feel guilty about any of it. She'd tried to befriend Gale, and the girl was nothing but nasty to her. Simone hated to think Pearl was right—she and Gale needed to see past their differences. Gale wasn't a threat anymore since she was facing felony charges. What a hefty price to pay, and with probable lengthy jail time. An ounce of compassion tugged at her heart.

Simone could face felony charges of her own if Gale blabbed about the hit and run. Even worse, thinking Mica might never speak to her again depressed her. She hoped he'd understand why she'd made the decision to flee the scene. He was a forgiving man.

After sitting in the café for a couple hours, she stood and stretched. A trip to the ladies' room was in order. She gathered her belongings and headed to the bathroom, noticing the turnover of patrons since she'd last looked around. Jade was standing by a table, talking to a rather handsome man in a three-piece suit. By the way Jade was all smiles and extra giggly, it made Simone believe Jade found him handsome as well.

After freshening up, she stopped by Jade, who was still flirting with the cute guy, to say goodbye. She touched Jade's arm to get her attention. Jade spun around. Her face was flushed. "Oh, hey, Simone."

Simone would have felt embarrassed for Jade's unabashed flirting if the man's giddy grin didn't match her friend's. "Sorry to interrupt. I was just on my way out and wanted to say goodbye."

"Okay, I'll see you later." Jade hugged her. "Let me introduce you to Drake Partington. His friends have a cabin in the area. He's on his way to see them."

Simone shook his hand. "Nice to meet you." He had a young face, yet his dark hair was graying at the temples. Very distinguished looking. She whispered to Jade, "Call me later. I want all the details."

Simone's phone rang. She left the two to "fall in love at first sight" while she took the call near the front door to the shop. She didn't recognize the number. These days, random phone calls gave her anxiety. *Please be good news.* "Hello?"

"May I speak with Simone Clare, please?" the male voice said.

"This is Simone Clare." She bit her nail, ripping a hangnail. *Ouch.*

"Simone, this is Superintendent Ross Thorpe. How are you today?"

"Um, okay, I guess." *I'm not on drugs, if that's what you're asking. But I am a felon.*

"Well, your day is about to get better. You're no longer under investigation, and I'd like to be the first to extend an apology. I'm sure this must have been a difficult time for you, and I hear from Norma Finch that you are an excellent teacher."

Simone was tongue-tied. "I ... thank you."

"A woman confessed to lacing your iced tea with Oxycodone." The turn of events was shocking and wonderful and sickening all at once. Her legs carried her over to Jade on their own accord. Jade paused her conversation and turned to Simone. "Honey, are you okay?" When Simone didn't answer, Jade guided her into a chair.

"Miss? Are you still there?"

"Yes. I'm processing. Um, so when can I resume working?" She looked up at Jade, who jumped up and down in celebration upon hearing Simone's question.

"We'd love to see you back in class tomorrow morning. I understand if you need more time."

Tears of joy welled in her eyes. "I'll be back tomorrow." She would cherish every day in her classroom, because she needed to consider turning herself in—if Gale didn't beat her to it—and that could result in the end of her teaching days.

Chapter Twenty-Three

Simone clapped the pattern her students had been trained to repeat. The idea was for it to capture their attention and require them to free their busy little hands. Apparently, they'd forgotten the routine in her absence. She blinked the lights off and on, then tried clapping again. Slowly but surely, they responded.

"Students, sit on the circle rug." They reluctantly obeyed. "Were you well-behaved for your substitute teachers?"

The children looked at one another, no one wanting to be the first to admit their disobedience. One by one, heads began to shake.

"You had an opportunity to show other teachers how smart and kind you are. More importantly, you had an opportunity to make someone feel good and happy."

"Who?" Tommy asked, sitting crossed-legged, his knees bopping up and down.

"Your teachers. Adults have feelings, just like each of you. We have good days and bad days."

Kenzie raised her hand. "You had bad days. My mom saw you in the newspaper."

"That's true, but today is a good day because I'm here at school with you." Enough on that subject. "Stand for the Pledge of Allegiance."

She was happy to be back with her students. Although getting them back into their usual routine and steering clear of her personal issues would take effort. After school, she would be meeting with Gale to give her the Bible. The package had been staring her in the face from the kitchen counter for more than a week. The last thing she wanted to do was waste any more of her life interacting with Gale. She still didn't want to give Gale Pearl's most prized possession. But Pearl wanted Gale to have it. She'd do it for Pearl.

At four thirty, Simone was sifting through a rack of men's suit coats at Vintage Treasures, shopping for pilgrim costumes for a school play. The bell above the door jingled and Gale walked in, wearing a cardigan sweater over a tight-fitting shirt, snug jeans, and high-heeled boots. Casual for Gale, yet she looked overdressed for this small-town store. Maybe it was less the outfit and more the way Gale carried herself that made her stand out. "Hello, Simone. I was happy to hear from you. How have you been?"

"Fine." Simone wasn't about to pretend this meeting was for shooting the breeze. "I have something for you." She pulled the wrapped package from her purse, her fingers lingering over the rose-clad paper. "It's from Pearl. She wanted you to have it."

Gale touched the package tentatively as if it were fragile or forbidden. She traced a finger over a rose, turned the gift over in her hands, and peeled back the paper. She gasped. "Her Bible." She tore off the remaining wrappings and leafed through the book. "Wow." Tears gathered in her eyes.

"Pearl cherished that Bible." Gale needed to understand how precious this gift was.

"I know. Believe me, I know. She forced me to memorize a verse. After hearing her recite it a million times, I couldn't forget it even if I wanted to." She flipped through the pages. "Here it is."

Simone leaned in, looking at the spot on a page where Gale pointed. The passage was highlighted in yellow. Simone took the Bible, positioning it so Gale couldn't read the words. "What does it say?"

Gale closed her eyes. "Trust in the Lord with all your heart and lean not on your own understanding; in all your ways acknowledge him, and he will make your paths straight." She opened her eyes and grabbed the Bible. "Am I right?"

"Word for word." Astounding. Simone looked on as Gale flipped through the Bible, pointing out highlighted and underlined verses Pearl had quoted to her. Gale seemed familiar with several of the markings. Admittedly, this gift was more meaningful to Gale than it would have been to Simone.

"Can I help you ladies find something?" the store clerk, a middle-aged woman wearing an orange knit poncho and a necklace with an acorn pendant, asked.

Simone shook her head. "So far, so good."

The clerk eyed the wrapping paper. "Are we celebrating something special today?"

Simone really wished the woman would stop asking questions. Interacting with Gale put her on edge. She didn't have the energy for small talk.

Gale looked up from the Bible and smiled. "My friend gave me a ... going away gift."

Sadness washed over Simone at the thought of Pearl not coming back. Gale made it sound as though Pearl just went on vacation.

"How nice. You gals enjoy your time together. My name is Esme. Let me know if there's anything I can help you with."

Simone and Gale thanked Esme, and the lady moved on to a different customer.

Simone was starting to believe that Gale was serious about this Jesus stuff. "How did learning some verses change you? You really seem different."

"It wasn't just the verses. Pearl prayed with me."

"What did she say?" Simone wanted to hear the words that had changed Gale from dismal to virtuous in an instant, even to the point of admitting she'd framed Simone for drug use. Maybe she would say the prayer herself.

"She had me close my eyes. Well, you don't have to, but Pearl said it helps to cut out distractions. Then she told me to say something like, 'Hey, Jesus. I'm a major screw-up. Please forgive me and teach me how to be like you.'"

"And then what?"

"And then ... I mean, there weren't any lightning bolts raining from the sky. Nothing happened. Except now I feel ... free."

"That's ironic considering you could get locked up in jail."

"True."

From across the room, Simone felt someone watching her. She looked over in time to make eye contact with a man. He immediately looked down at his iPhone, pretending he hadn't been ogling. His stare was unnerving. It didn't feel flirty; it felt intrusive. Simone moved behind a tall shelf, hidden from the guy's direct line of vision. She motioned for Gale to follow her.

"I'm glad you had the decency to acknowledge you drugged me." In her mind, she'd rehearsed quite a different monologue for Gale, but decided she'd rather keep this meeting brief than turn it into a cat fight. Gale would pay her dues in prison. "So, what's happening with your arrest?"

"My court date is tomorrow already." A look of shame passed over her face. She lightly shook her head, took a deep breath, sighed, and smiled. "I still feel freer than I've ever been."

Strange. "Good for you. How are things with your parents?" Maybe her parents were willing to bail her out. That would explain her optimism.

Gale half-smiled. "They're helping me out, even though I'm a distraction from Dad's campaign. He said most people already had their minds made up about who they would vote for, so this stuff with me shouldn't sway the election."

"That's nice of him." Simone really did wish for Gale to have a healthy relationship with her parents.

"By the way, I talked to Arthur."

"You what?" Simone's most dreaded fear was coming true. Her entire body went numb.

Gale looked around. "Let's go outside."

Simone's legs felt as though they were wading through water as she followed Gale out to the sidewalk. "I need to sit down." She walked to a café table outside Adelia's Bakery. She shivered from the cold. Gale sat across the table from her. Simone wanted to strangle her, but at the moment, her limbs felt like rubber.

"I went to his house. I just couldn't live with the secret any longer. And he had a right to know what happened."

"No." Her teeth chattered, making it difficult to speak. "You ratted me out because I wouldn't hand you thousands of dollars. You're going to jail for your drug shenanigans, so you're making sure I go as well. Misery loves company."

Gale shook her head emphatically. "Simone, I was driving."

She squeezed her eyes shut. "What did you just say?"

"It's true. I was driving. You were passed out. You had no idea." Gale sniffed.

"You're trying to tell me that you actually hit him, but you made me believe I did it?" No wonder she didn't remember the accident.

"I'm sorry."

Heat flushed through Simone's body in a flash of anger. She fought for composure. Patrons of the bakery smiled politely as they passed by. "I need to walk."

Gale stepped in stride. "We got back in the car after you barfed. Remember? I helped you into the passenger seat.

We listened to music. Well, I listened to music, and you begged me to turn it off because it hurt your head. You were such a lightweight."

Simone didn't recall any of that. Her pace quickened.

"You passed out. I thought I was fine to drive." Gale grabbed Simone's arm. "Stop walking."

"Don't touch me." Simone pushed her, knocking her into the brick building. Simone crossed her arms. She no longer cared if she drew an audience. "How am I supposed to believe anything you say? You're a liar. You only care about yourself."

"I'm sorry, Simone." Gale was crying. Her perfect makeup was running. She leaned a shoulder against the building—a posture of defeat.

Simone thought back to that night, considering Gale's claim to have been the driver. "But I was in the driver's seat with a bloody nose."

"I was freaking out after I hit him. I panicked. I dragged you over into the driver's seat." She crossed her arms, hugging them tightly to her chest. "I was scared."

Simone paced. Her legs were no longer rubbery. Her body was ready to fight.

"I went to Arthur's house. I told him everything. His wife looked like she wanted to kill me."

Simone knew the feeling.

"Arthur isn't mad."

"Why not?"

"He said he wasted too many years being angry. He was recently diagnosed with pancreatic cancer, and he wants to enjoy the rest of his time on earth. He's not pressing charges. He made me promise never to drink and drive again."

Simone slowed her steps. "Did you tell him about me?"

"I told him a friend was passed out in the car at the time of the accident. I told him I shook you awake, and you didn't want to leave him, but I persuaded you to. I told him you dialed his phone."

The anguish of the moment flooded back. "Was it his wife?"

"His sister."

Simone leaned against the building next to Gale. What did this mean for Simone? Was she innocent? Was she pardoned? Should she sock Gale in the stomach for all the misery she'd caused or thank her for telling the truth?

"Oh, and he said he'd rather not see me again." Again, Simone could relate. "He said if I—or my friend—felt morally obligated to turn myself in, he wouldn't stand in my way. But he'd rather not have all of this dredged up again. His wife agreed. Said they'd been through enough. She's still angry. But she doesn't want this resurfacing in the media. With me being the senator's daughter, that would be sure to happen."

"It's unbelievable they'd let us off the hook like that."

"Well, I don't think they could press charges since it happened ten years ago. The statute of limitations is two to three years for a hit and run."

So, she really could put this behind her. "This is a lot to process."

"It's good news."

Simone was cautiously optimistic. Arthur might not be pressing any charges, but his kindness didn't help her feel any less guilty. Even if she hadn't been driving, she'd still left him there on the road. She still had to live with her guilty conscience. "I guess it's good you talked to him."

Gale nodded. "I don't know about you, but I'm freezing." They'd reached a truce of sorts. There wasn't much more to say.

"Me too." She began the walk back to her car, Gale walking alongside her.

"Thanks for the Bible."

"Of course."

The creepy guy from the store was standing outside Vintage Treasures. "Looks like we've got a reporter on our trail." A reporter. That explained it. "Don't say anything. Don't make eye contact." Gale took off in the opposite direction.

"Excuse me," he said, striding toward Simone.

She gripped the pepper spray clipped to her key chain.

"What is your relationship with Gale Wells?"

Ignoring him, she got in her car. Before she closed the door, he asked, "Are you involved in dealing drugs in Diamond?"

She slammed the door and drove off.

Simone mixed up a batch of chocolate chip cookie dough and ate at least a third of it. Just one more spoonful, she would tell herself before each scoop. When her stomach felt like it would explode, she covered the bowl and put it in the fridge. Usually baking was a stress reliever, but tonight she didn't have the patience for it.

The conversation she'd had with Gale earlier in the afternoon repeated on an endless loop in her mind. Since Arthur hadn't wanted to see Gale again, she wondered if he would be opposed to meeting her. She wanted to apologize, but also wanted to respect his privacy. Instead, she wrote him a letter and texted Gale for his address. Then she drove to the post office and dropped it in the box. Amazing how a simple act made her feel so much lighter.

Back at home, she cleaned her kitchen, dusted and vacuumed the living room, and then scrubbed the bathroom, processing her thoughts as she worked. Gale had really made a mess of things when she came to Diamond, but Pearl was right. Simone and Gale needed to find forgiveness and move on from what was holding them back from living a life of peace. The forgiveness they'd received from Arthur meant the world to Simone.

She really was sorry for hurting him and putting others in danger as well. She hadn't been driving at the time of the accident, but she had driven under the influence that night. In her eyes, she was just as guilty as Gale. Both women were suffering regret. Gale had apologized to Simone. Now Simone needed to offer apologies as well. She texted Gale and told her so. Like Arthur, she wanted to move forward with her life and stop dwelling on the past.

She scrubbed the bathroom floor, tears dripping onto the tile, releasing the resentment and guilt she'd bottled up the last ten years. Enslavement to her misdeed and to Gale was in the past. No more pretending she led a perfect life, afraid her fraudulency would be exposed. She could simply be.

The bathroom shone like a new penny. Simone tossed the rag in the bucket and went to the kitchen for a drink of water. Although it was midnight, she was just beginning to feel tired. There was one more person she needed to contact before she would be able to rest easy. He was probably sleeping, but she at least wanted to start the conversation. She texted Mica.

SIMONE: Sorry.

Her phone dinged an immediate response, taking her by surprise.

MICA: What for?

SIMONE: What are you doing awake at this hour?

MICA: Thinking about you. About your situation.

SIMONE: Sorry for not being up front with you. Sorry for my past. Gale and I are on good terms now.

She admitted she was the one who hit the man. I was passed out. She contacted him to apologize. He wants to put it behind him. Doesn't want to press charges.

MICA: Glad you are finding closure.

SIMONE: Me too. Please forgive me.

MICA: I forgive you. Call me?

Simone curled up on the couch and called Mica. She relayed her conversation with Gale in detail, and they talked about everything from Simone's abandonment by her mother to the various foster homes she stayed in, to her experience at the Wellses', and finally her adulthood of chasing perfection. He thanked her for being transparent and promised to pray for her. With only a few hours until her alarm would ring, she said goodnight.

Friday evening, Simone hung out with the Calhouns and the Starks. Mica ordered pizza at his place, and they all lounged around. It was exactly the kind of low-key night Simone needed. By the time Brooke and Adam were rounding up their girls, getting ready to say good-bye, Simone felt as though she'd known the Calhouns her entire life.

Mica waved to his friends through the window as they drove off. "All right, Hannah, time for your shower. Get upstairs and pick out jammies and undies."

"Already?" Hannah whined.

Mica pointed up the stairs. His stern look scared her into action. He turned to Simone. "Make yourself comfortable. I'll be back soon. You can make some tea or watch TV."

"I'll be fine." She reclined on the couch, enjoying the glimpse into everyday life at the Stark household. Petunia kept her company, settling into her lap. The shower turned on and off, and soon the scampering of little feet crossed the hallway upstairs.

Mica came down the steps, his shirt spotted with water droplets. "Hannah wants *you* to tuck her in tonight."

"Aww, I'd love to." She carried Petunia up to Hannah's room.

Hannah was sitting in her bed, paging through a picture book. Her face lit up when she saw the cat. She dropped the book onto her nightstand and held out her arms. Petunia snuggled in.

Hannah's damp hair left rings of moisture on the shoulders of her pajamas. "You know," Simone said, "if you braid your hair when it's wet, it will be wavy the next day."

"Really?" Hannah crawled to the end of her bed where she was able to look in her dresser mirror. She stared into the glass with a dreamy look on her face. "Will you braid my hair?"

"Of course."

Hannah was a little chatterbox as Simone twisted her hair into two French braids. "Mommy braided my hair but not when it was wet. Daddy does braids, but he's not good at it. Sometimes Brooke braids my hair and Gigi's hair and Sadie's hair. She's really good at it. And now you braid my hair." Hannah bounced on the bed, challenging Simone's dexterity.

A framed photograph of a young woman was propped on Hannah's dresser. "Is that your mommy in that picture?"

"Yep. Sometimes I forget what she looks like, so Daddy gave me a picture just for my room." Hannah's words came out matter-of-factly, but it was among the saddest proclamations Simone had ever heard. Josie would want to be remembered by Hannah, but Simone guessed Josie's biggest desire would be for her daughter to be happy. Hannah sure seemed to be a cheerful, well-adjusted little girl.

"You know, I lost my mom too."

"You did?" Hannah turned around to look at Simone's face, causing strands of hair to slip from her fingers.

"I did. She'll always have a special place in my heart even though I don't remember what she looked like or the sound of her voice." She wrapped an elastic band at the end of the second braid. "There you go, Miss Stark. Tomorrow you'll have gorgeous wavy locks."

"Yay." Hannah checked her hair in the mirror, running her fingers down the braids. Then she hopped to the head of the bed and slid between the covers.

Simone knelt by the side of the bed and tucked the blanket up under Hannah's chin. "Are you cozy?"

Hannah nodded. "Pray with me."

Simone's stomach clenched. "I don't know how to pray. I'll listen to you."

"Fold your hands like this and close your eyes."

Simone followed Hannah's instructions, except she peeked at Hannah. Her eyes were squeezed shut, her blonde eyelashes almost glowing in the dim light. Too cute. Then Simone closed her eyes and listened.

"Now I lay me down to sleep. I pray the Lord my soul to keep. The angels watch me through the night and wake me with the morning light. In Jesus's name, amen."

It was the same prayer Pearl had recited when she'd tucked Simone into bed in a similar way. A lump formed in her throat, and soon tears trickled down her cheeks.

"You can open your eyes now," Hannah said, tapping Simone's shoulder.

Simone looked at Hannah, loving her more than she could even put into words. "That was beautiful. Thank you for teaching me how to pray."

Hannah giggled. "It's easy."

Simone wiped her face with her sleeves. "Can I give you a hug?"

Hannah opened her arms wide. Simone hugged her and kissed her cheek.

"I love you, Miss Simone."

Simone thought her heart might explode with joy.

"I love you too, Miss Stark."

"Good night." She rolled onto her side and closed her eyes.

Downstairs, Simone sat next to Mica on the couch. He noticed her tear-stained face. "Whoa, was it that rough?" he joked. "She can be a stinker at bedtime, but she doesn't normally drive me to tears."

Simone laughed. "Hannah was perfect. She taught me to pray. She said the same prayer Pearl said with me once. It's like a poem."

"Now I lay me?"

"Yes. That's it." At that moment, Simone wanted more than anything to belong to a world where prayers were spoken each night before bed. To gain strength from memorizing Bible verses. To know Jesus. If Jesus could change Gale Wells's life, then he truly was a miracle worker. "Mica, how do you ...?" She didn't have the vocabulary to express what she was trying to say. "How do I get to know Jesus? Like, where do I start?"

Mica's mouth dropped open. Clearly, he was surprised by the question. Then he smiled. "Just talk to him like you're talking to me right now. It's easy."

"That's what Hannah said."

That night, in front of a blazing fireplace in Mica's living room, Simone prayed for the first time—clumsy, stilted words.

"Jesus, I haven't talked to you before, but I want to change that. I'd like to get to know you." She looked at Mica. His eyes were closed. After an awkward silence, he peeked an eye open. She held out her arms, palms up, asking what she should do now. Mica encouraged her with a smile and closed his eyes again. She didn't really have anything else to say. "Um ... Love, Simone."

"Amen," Mica said.

Simone opened her eyes, processing what had just happened. She felt vulnerable in front of Mica. But in a good way. More like ... transparent. As if she didn't need to hide the tender spots of her past—or present—with this man. His eyes were misty. He leaned over and hugged her. "You're welcome to come with Hannah and me to our church sometime. We go to a different church than Pearl and the Calhouns. It's similar, but a few more people our age attend my church. In fact, Jade Powers, the owner of Lakeview Brew goes there. You're friends with her, right?"

"Yeah. We hang out with MJ Oliver a lot. I know MJ's family goes to church with Jade." How shocked would her friends be to see her walk in on a Sunday morning? "I'm willing to give it a try." She felt a surprise spark of excitement about the prospect.

Mica gazed at her with a sappy grin on his face. He laid a sweet kiss on her cheek, and her face flushed. "You're an amazing woman." Mica stood and extended his hand to Simone. "Come with me."

Simone cocked an eyebrow. "What exactly do you have in mind?"

"Don't get too excited," he said, chuckling. "I just want to show you something."

Simone held his hand as he led her upstairs. They peeked in on Hannah, who was sleeping like an old man with her mouth agape. They shared a quiet laugh and then continued down the hall to the scrapbook room.

"Wow," Simone said, looking around. A lamp was all that lit the room. Through the large window, she could see millions of stars twinkling over the still lake water. Under the window was a round table with three chairs encircling it. A puzzle was centered on the table, just as she'd suggested to Mica the first time she saw the room. "I can't believe you remembered." By the fireplace, a cushy rug was rolled out, and throw pillows were stacked along the edges. Mica and Hannah could lounge on the rug, reading to each other from the collection of books stored on the shelves. On the mantle was the placemat Hannah had colored at the restaurant after horse riding.

Simone stepped up to get a closer look. What she saw touched her heart in a way nothing ever had. On the back of the placemat, Hannah had drawn her dad, Hannah, and Simone riding horses. They all had smiles on their faces, including the horses. There was a hairy sun that, likewise, sported a grin. And perched on a cloud was Hannah's smiling mommy. "Oh, Mica. She wrapped her arms around his waist, snuggling her face into his chest.

"It's a room that will bring the family together." He kissed her forehead.

Simone tilted her head back and looked up into his beautiful blue eyes. "Thank you for this."

He ran his fingers through her hair and cradled the back of her head in his hand. She closed her eyes, sinking into his embrace. He softly pressed his lips to her forehead, her cheek, her earlobe, and finally her mouth. His lips were gentle and giving. He nestled his face into her neck and pulled her to him in a tender embrace. "I love you, Simone." His fingers traveled down her arms and laced with hers.

She rested her face against his chest and closed her eyes, listening to his heartbeat, inhaling his masculine scent, tasting his kiss lingering on her tongue. Here, in Mica's arms, she felt at home. "I love you too."

Epilogue

At Christmastime, Diamond transformed into a land suitable for a backdrop to a Norman Rockwell painting. Twinkle lights wound around the trees along Lakeview Drive. A dusting of fresh white snow glittered on branches and rooftops and crunched under Simone's boots as she and Mica walked from his house to Lakeview Brew for the shop's first ever Saturday night event. And hopefully, the last karaoke night.

"You're quiet," Mica said, his breath visible in the cold air.

Simone linked her arm through his, and he pulled her into his side to keep her warm. "Just thinking."

"About?" Mica could always tell when something was on her mind. She wasn't about to tell him she was having anxiety about singing karaoke after not singing in front of people for over a decade. He would remind her it's just for fun. The same thing she'd been telling herself.

"About how much I love you." She looked up at him. His cheeks and the tip of his nose were rosy. A black beanie hat covered his head and the red scarf she'd bought him for Christmas was wrapped around his neck and tucked into his double-breasted wool coat. Incredibly handsome.

He chuckled. "Is that all?"

"And how much I love Diamond." It was true. Diamond had enticed her with its small-town charm, but it had become so much more. Here, she had made genuine friendships, started a rewarding career, and fallen in love with a man who cared for her enough to open his heart and home to her. To welcome her into the life he shared with his sweet daughter, and to teach her about his faith that became her own more each day.

Mica stopped walking and pulled Simone into an embrace. "I love you, Simone. And I love Diamond because you are in it."

She drew back and gazed at his gorgeous face. He was looking back at her with adoration. "That was cheesy. But thank you." Her heart swelled as she kissed him.

A car full of teenagers driving by honked and whooped at them. Simone and Mica shared a laugh and kept walking.

Lakeview Brew's front patio exhibited a festive atmosphere with patrons gathered around a gas firepit, their gloved hands holding steaming beverages. Potted evergreens were lit with colored lights.

Indoors, there was standing room only. Jade had set up extra tables, now occupied by families and groups of friends. Currently, a trio of girls held center stage, singing "Tomorrow" from the *Annie* musical. Simone recognized the young voices before laying eyes on the girls. Gigi, Sadie, and Hannah. Simone snapped a picture.

Brooke and Adam were at a table near the front counter, waving Mica and Simone over. Simone signaled they would be right there, but MJ, balancing a toddler on her hip, and Jade stopped them before they had a chance to take two steps. They looked like two giddy little girls, so excited they were bouncing on their toes. "I'm so glad you came," Jade said, pulling her into a hug. "Hi, Mica. Did you guys walk over? It's kinda chilly out, but I noticed people are hanging out by the firepit." Jade's excitement bubbled over in a stream of words, preventing anyone from getting a word in edgewise.

The crowded café was plenty warm, and Simone shrugged out of her coat. "What a great turnout." She really was happy for Jade, despite not wanting to sing. "Hi, Ivy," Simone said to the little towhead, MJ's youngest child. Ivy attempted a wave with a twirling motion of her chubby hand. "Oh, you're adorable." Someday, Simone would love to have a child of her own.

Branson stepped up beside MJ, looking dapper in his plaid button-down shirt and Mr. Rogers-type zipper sweater—except for the wet spot on his shoulder that was likely from the three-year-old with the runny nose he juggled in his arms. "Nice to see you two finally made it," Branson said with a smile. "These ladies have been as impatient as kids waiting for Christmas morning." To Mica, he said, "They picked out a song for us guys to sing. Me, you, Adam, and Drake."

Mica threw his head back in laughter. "Sounds like I don't have a choice in the matter."

Branson shook his head. "No sir. We'll be singing Johnny Cash. 'Ring of Fire.'"

That was sure to be entertaining.

MJ added, "And we're singing 'Stop in the Name of Love' by the Supremes."

Simone's stomach clenched. She needed to be a good sport. It's not like she couldn't sing, and nobody would be judging her. She could sing backup. "Okay. You take the lead."

"Yay." MJ turned to Jade. "I told you she'd do it." The two friends hugged. Oh, boy. She was committed now.

The little girls' song ended, and Simone and Mica joined the Calhouns to congratulate the kids on their fine performance. Gigi and Sadie glowed under the praise and then listed off the Christmas gifts they'd received while the owner of Willows B & B stepped into the limelight. The intro to a Karen Carpenter song began to play. The atmosphere was sensory overload, but in a fabulous way. Simone's nerves relaxed about singing. The joy in this place was contagious.

Brooke stood and offered Simone her seat. "I insist," Brooke said. "I need to catch up with a friend from church real quick." She pointed into the crowd and took off.

Mica set a bowl of popcorn and a cup of hot cocoa, topped with whipped cream and candy cane sprinkles, on the table in front of Simone. When the Carpenter song ended, Mica kissed Simone's forehead and walked up to the mic. Brooke, MJ, and Jade rushed to her table. "What is he doing?" she asked her hyper friends. They shook their heads and shrugged, but the starry-eyed looks on their faces told a different story. Simone's palms broke into a sweat. Mica was up to something.

Guitar music began to play. She didn't recognize the song yet. Mica gripped the microphone and closed his eyes. He rolled his shoulders as if to work out nervous energy. Simone wiped her sweaty palms on her jeans. Mica opened his eyes, looking straight at her, and began to sing.

A love song. *Aw, he's so sweet.* She still couldn't place the song. She looked at her friends. They were busy glancing back and forth between Mica and Simone dreamily—MJ oblivious to her child sucking on her necklace.

As Mica's rather impressive voice filled the café, he knelt on one knee and flipped open a small white box he held in the palm of his hand.

Simone gasped. The cacophony of the café grew dim, her focus solely on Mica, as if they were the only two people in the room. He continued to sing, his voice strong and sure, love radiating to her through his eyes. The song was "Marry Me" by Train.

He set the microphone down on the floor and placed his hand over his heart. A spray of color glinted off the diamond he held with his other hand. Jade nudged her to go to Mica. Simone looked around the café. People were clapping and cheering, oohing and ahhing, and several had their phones angled at her, capturing the moment on video.

The moment felt surreal as Simone stood on wobbly legs and took one step at a time toward Mica. Her future husband. With the song still playing in the background, Mica took her hand in his. "Miss Simone Clare, will you be my bride?"

Simone guided him to stand, unwilling to wait another second to smother him with affection. She kissed him and wrapped him in a hug, relishing the feel of him in her arms. "Yes. A million times yes." Eternity wouldn't be enough time to spend with this man.

He slid the ring onto her shaking finger. She placed her left hand on the side of his handsome face and kissed him again. A child's arms seized hold of her waist. Little Hannah. She included the sweet girl in the hug. "Mica Stark," she said to her fiancé, "because of you, I know what love looks like."

Mica shifted her left hand to his lips, then clasped it to his heart. His eyes scanned the room filled with friends before finding their way back to her. "This is love."

Adelia's Seven-Layer Bars

Ingredients:
1 stick butter
1 cup graham cracker crumbs
1 cup coconut
6 ounces chocolate chips
6 ounces butterscotch chips
1 can sweetened condensed milk
1 ½ cups chopped nuts

Directions:
Melt butter in a 9 x 13-inch pan. Layer graham cracker crumbs, coconut, chocolate chips, and butterscotch chips. Drizzle condensed milk over layers. Top with nuts. Bake at 350 degrees for 30 minutes. Cool, and cut into squares.

Discussion Questions

1. Is there someone in your life who you look to for wisdom as Simone looked to Pearl?

2. Which character do you relate to? What is it about this character that you connect with?

3. Pearl didn't tell Simone about her regrettable history of dancing at the club and addiction to heroin. Do you feel it is imperative to tell your close friends about your past? Is it dishonest to withhold such information?

4. Scripture was infused in Pearl's language. What Bible verses do you draw strength from daily?

5. Simone had a soft spot in her heart for Hannah from the beginning and took her under her wing. Is there a teacher who positively impacted you?

6. The taste of Seven Layer Bars brought Gale back to her childhood. Is there a food that is nostalgic for you?

7. Do you feel that Simone has a moral obligation to confess the hit and run to the authorities despite the victim not pressing charges?

8. Is there a relationship in your life, like Simone's and Gale's, needing healing and forgiveness?

9. Did the book change your perspective about anything?

10. At what point in the story did you realize the mystery man Pearl wanted Simone to meet was Jesus?

11. Why do you think Pearl wanted Simone to hand deliver the Bible to Gale?

12. Simone has a secret talent of singing. Share with the group a gift/interest/hobby that brings you joy.

13. How did you feel about the ending?

14. If *What Love Looks Like* were adapted into a movie, what actors do you envision playing certain characters?

15. What do you think is the theme of the story? What message do you feel the author wants to convey?

About the Author

When not dreaming up stories, Stacy enjoys running in peaceful solitude, kayaking with her friends and high school sweetheart-turned-husband, or reading on her front porch with a cup of steaming coffee sprinkled with cinnamon—a retreat from the beautiful noise of her daughter, three sons, and Labradoodle.

A graduate of Bethel University in Saint Paul, Minnesota, Stacy Boatman is a pediatric nurse. She believes every soul is deserving of love; and what better way to demonstrate love than through a heartrending romance novel.

Visit Stacy at Facebook: Stacy Boatman; Instagram: stacyboatmanbooks; YouTube: Stacy Boatman. Drop in at stacyboatman.com for an opportunity to subscribe to Stacy's newsletter and receive an exclusive short story.

Also by Stacy Boatman

- "Snapshot"—A Lake Diamond Christmas Romance in *Christmas From the Heart: A Collection of Christmas Romances*
- "Sewing a Legacy" in *Chicken Soup for the Soul: Miracles & Divine Intervention: 101 Stories of Faith and Hope*

Made in the USA
Monee, IL
23 August 2021